anvils & avatars

A Cozy Fantasy

Tales from the Broken Claw
Book Two

don jones

praise for anvils & avatars

"*Anvils & Avatars* is a charming and heartfelt fantasy that reminds us that true magic isn't in a sword, but in a community. With a cast of lovable characters and a story that balances small-town charm with real stakes, this book is a must-read for anyone who's ever wondered what happens after the quest is over." —TheList

"A cozy fantasy delight! The tale of an ogre blacksmith and a magical town, this book feels like a wam meal and a heart laugh with old friends. The world-building is rich and original, the characters are wonderfully human (and non-human), and the story's central question —what do we do when the magic is gone?—is handled with warmth and grace. A genuine pleasure from start to finish." —Fantasy Insider

"At a time when the world feels more chaotic than ever, *Anvils & Avatars* offers a beautiful, poignant reminder of what really matters. Warren is a character for the ages, a gentle giant with a loving family and a fierce dedication to his home. This is a powerful story of community, kindness, and finding purpose in the most ordinary of tasks. It's a book that stays with you long after the final page is turned." —Readers Review Magazine

also by don jones

Find more at DonJones.com, including a free fantasy trilogy, a free superhero duology, two collections of short stories, and even more short stories and flash fiction. You can even listen to free music inspired by the books!

contents

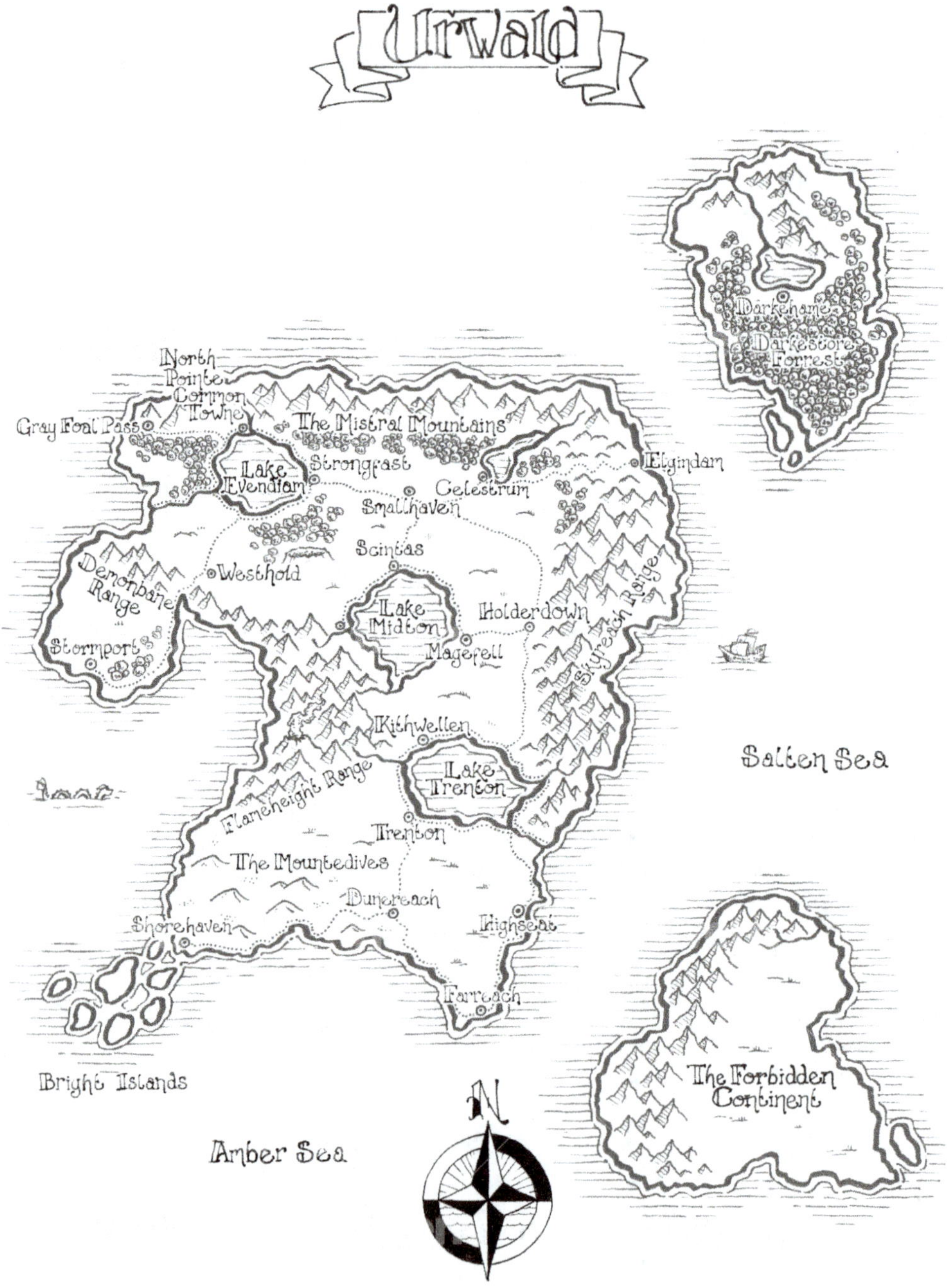

Urwald

North Pointe Common Towne
Gray Foal Pass
The Mistral Mountains
Lake Evendim
Strongfast
Celestrum
Smallhaven
Scintas
Elgindar
Demonbane Range
Westhold
Lake Midton
Holderdown
Skyreach Range
Stormport
Magefell
Kithwellen
Lake Trenton
Salten Sea
Flameheight Range
Trenton
The Mountedives
Dunereach
Highseat
Shorehaven
Farreach
Darkehome
Darkestone Forrest
Bright Islands
Amber Sea
N
The Forbidden Continent

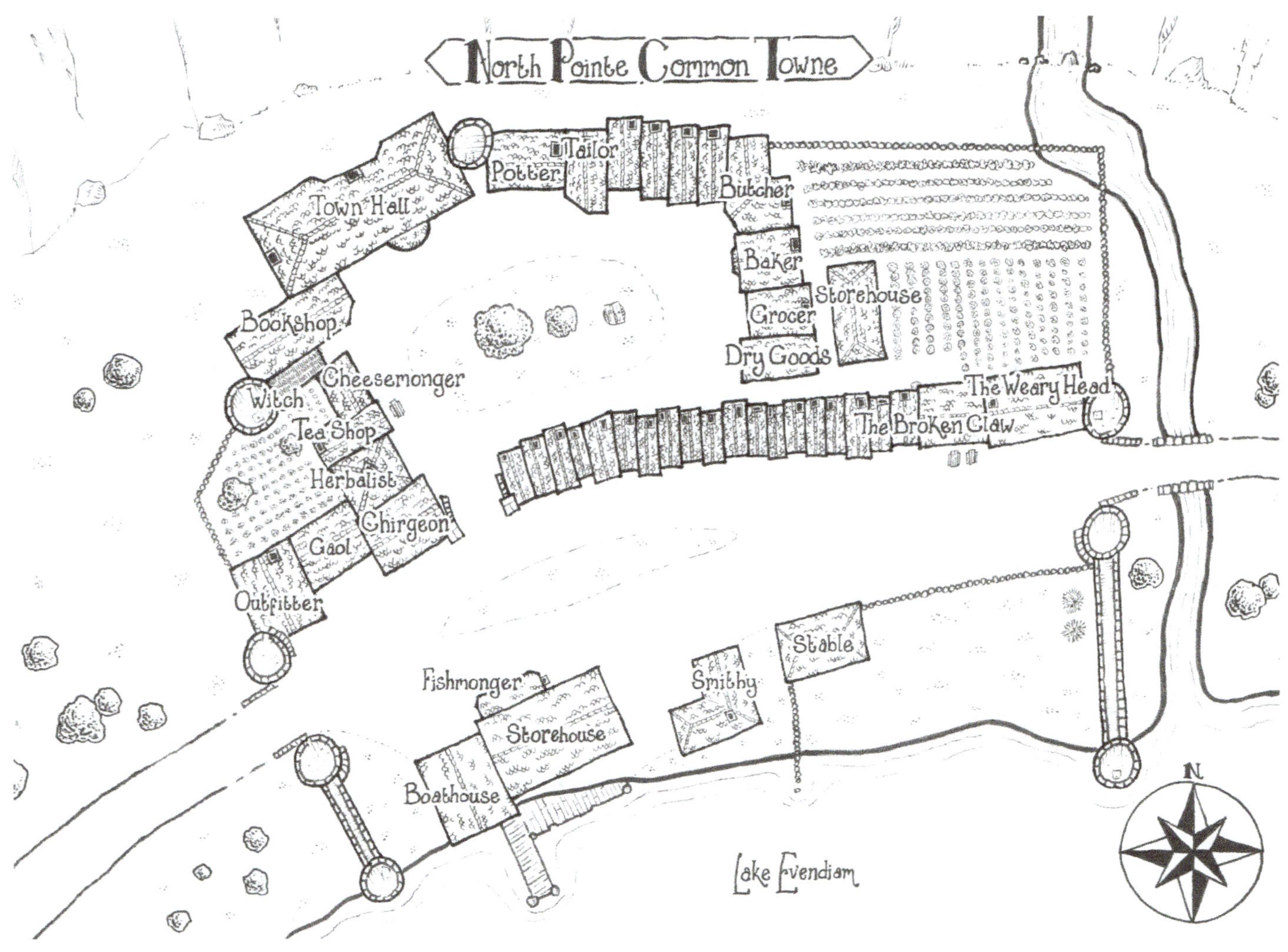

North Pointe Common Towne
Town Hall
Potter
Tailor
Butcher
Baker
Grocer
Dry Goods
Storehouse
Bookshop
Witch
Cheesemonger
Tea Shop
Herbalist
Chirgeon
Gaol
Outfitter
The Weary Head
The Broken Claw
Stable
Smithy
Fishmonger
Storehouse
Boathouse
Lake Evendiam
N

one

. . .

THE DREAM'S edges were as indistinct as the fading outlines of a watercolor painting, soft and blurred into a twilight mist—exactly as dreams always were. Warren had trained himself over the years to ignore those nebulous fringes, knowing that the swirling ambiguities held no importance; everything he required was boldly set in the center of his vision.

In that vivid core lay a sprawling battlefield. Two companies of foot soldiers clashed with brutal elegance—swords arcing in brilliant sweeps, shields flashing in desperate parries, and the ringing clamor of clashing armor reverberating like the drumbeats of war. In a real fight, one could have discerned each side by the vivid hues of their banners, the intricate crests emblazoned on their shields, or the detailed patterns woven into the heavy tabards draping their armored chests. Yet in this dreamscape, every detail was muted to a spectral gray; the distinctions were lost in amorphous vagueness, the crests melted into indistinct smudges, and the patterns hinted at stories too enigmatic to decipher.

But at the heart of the maelstrom stood a figure—a leader born of chaos and valor. He was an unmistakable "he," with broad, powerful shoulders, a towering, muscular build, and a thick, black beard cascading from his jaw like streams of ink. All eyes in the dream were drawn toward him, as if he were the sole nucleus around which the entire conflict orbited. In his grip, he wielded an enormous, twisted sword that looked forged from the very essence of nightmares. This heavy black weapon, dripping with the dark stains of his enemies' blood, moved with an almost sentient might. It crashed through helmets like brittle porcelain, shredded chain mail as though it were tattered cloth, and sliced through armor with the ease of cutting through delicate paper.

Without a shield or helm, what truly set him apart was the sinister crown that rested firmly upon his brow. Crafted from the same impenetrable darkness as his blade, the crown twisted in wicked loops and spirals—a complex latticework of barbs and elegant curves that seemed to pulse with a life of its own, shifting from sleek and refined one moment to grotesquely violent the next. It became a question that hovered in the smoky recesses of Warren's mind: was it the dark, writhing crown or the monstrous sword that posed the greater threat?

In the midst of this terror, a guttural roar tore through the fog of the dream. The leader had been wounded—a vicious spear had found a gap between the plates of his heavy armor. In response, he swung his massive, dread-forged sword with a savage flourish. The weapon sliced through the air, its brutal arc severing the spearhead from its shaft in a burst of crimson. With another sweeping motion, he nearly cleaved the soldier who had hurled the deadly weapon, missing him by a razor's breadth as the man staggered on the slick, blood-spattered field, tumbling backward in defeat just as the dark sword whistled dangerously close above his head.

And in that very moment, as the dream receded into a lingering haze, Warren's eyes snapped open, returning him at last from the vivid theatre of his subconscious.

Another Forge Dream concluded.

two

. . .

THE SMITH'S massive hammer fell again and again, pounding loudly and sharply at the sullen metal lying on his anvil. Sparks of black-red flew every time the hammer came down. The ringing sound echoed off the walls of the smithy, escaping through the wide-open windows and doors and reverberating off the other nearby buildings.

He'd started before first light, loading the furnace with fuel and carefully pumping it into an orange-yellow rage. When his son, Darby, had wandered sleepily out of their home and across the trade road just as the sun was rising, Warren had sent him through the smithy's impossibly small trapdoor to gather some of the ore that was there— from a pile that Darby insisted had never gotten smaller in all the time they'd been there. The ore that was used *only* to forge the items from Warren's dreams.

That ore had gone into the fury of the forge itself, heating until it had melted into a slick silver-black ooze. Warren had carefully considered his few simple sword-blank molds, ultimately choosing the largest one he had. The resulting sword would be enormous and difficult for all but the largest, strongest humans to wield; in Warren's hands it was *big,* certainly, but not all that disproportionate.

He'd poured the molten ore into the mold and then waited for it to cool, for the metal to begin congealing and hardening. Then he'd freed the simple bar from the mold and begun pounding, his hammer clamoring off it as the rest of the town roused itself.

He frowned at the current state of the thing.

The metal had already turned an unpleasant, sooty black. He had expected that; it matched the dream. He wasn't *happy* about it, but the moment he'd begun working the blade it had become clear that it was going to take on the finish that *it* wanted, not anything that *he* intended for it.

So, fine. A black, matte sword. Probably some people would pay extra for that, just for the novelty of it. Fine. Whatever.

What he hadn't expected was for the sword to be so stubbornly ugly. Instead of stretching into the long, symmetric, pointed blade that he intended, the thing had buckled and split into uneven prongs like a clawed hand reaching forward. With each crash of his hammer, the glistening metal rippled and curled back, arching around itself with a mischievous will.

Warren squinted at it, muttering under his breath. "Stubborn little beast." He'd managed to get the edges into something resembling a proper sword—thin edges that would take and hold a sharpening. But the spine of the sword looked more like a dead vine of some kind. It twisted and curled, and it was everything Warren could do to keep the edge itself even and straight.

"Don't worry," Susan called from the doorway, hands on her hips. "You're never going to let it win."

He grunted in reply, feigning confidence. The sword twisted again as if in protest, one side bulging outward into a jagged hook. He paused, wiped his brow with the back of one huge hand, and gave Susan a look.

His wife laughed. "You're used to making things pretty on the first try." Stepping into the forge's warm glow, she squinted at the rebellious shape on his anvil. "But it looks like it's *supposed* to be that way, doesn't it? You've got the edge straight, at least." She leaned in a bit further. "Mostly."

"Mmm." Warren turned it with his tongs. No matter how many times he struck at the misshapen thing, it refused to flatten out. It *refused* to stay straight. "Every time I hit it, some portion I *didn't* hit rolls out of shape, somehow."

"Is this the... special ore?"

Warren nodded. "I had Darby bring it up as soon as he got up this morning."

Susan glanced uneasily at the narrow trap door in the smithy's wood-planked floor. "I feel like I should go down there sometime."

"Why? I never have."

"You'd never fit."

Warren snorted. "Darby says it's just a dirt floor and a pile of ore chunks. Not much to see."

"Still." She turned back to the anvil, where the malcontent sword lay, its ruddy glow already diminishing. "Are you going to start over?"

Warren shook his enormous head. "No. Not yet. It can go another couple of rounds."

Repeatedly heating, hammering, and quenching the steel gave it structure and strength. It transformed from a relatively pliable metal into a hard, deadly weapon.

"Well, don't spend all day in here."

"Whoever this is for will probably be here in two, three days."

"Plenty of time."

Warren hesitated. "There's a crown, too. Or meant to be."

Susan's eyebrows arched. "A crown? Have you ever made a crown before?"

Once again, Warren's head swung slowly from side to side. "No. But they go together. I could tell."

"Well."

"If this sword doesn't work out, I can probably shape it into a crown. Strength won't matter as much."

"Maybe it would serve it right."

Susan stepped back as her husband's thick arm rose, the heavy hammer gripped tightly in one colossal fist. "Good luck." But Warren's attention had already refocused on the piece before him, so she turned and left.

After another blow that even to him seemed desultory, Warren's frown deepened. He set his hammer down on the floor and picked up the sword. It was still hot, but not hot enough to do more than make his thick, leathery skin slightly uncomfortable. He turned it this way and that, grudgingly admitting that the way the light caught the matte-black, scarred surface wasn't *wholly* displeasing. But the shape... the edges on both sides had subtle curves to them. The thing would be impossible to sharpen.

He turned and plunged it back into the forge. The smithy filled with the roar of the flames as the coals fanned to life, bathing the room in waves of heat. Warren watched intently, waiting for the ruddy glow to creep back across the metal's surface. When it was ready, he used tongs to pull it out again, laying it across the anvil as he resumed his work.

His hammer fell rhythmically, sending sparks skittering across the battered wooden floor. Warren focused on the spine of the sword, pounding each stray prong and hook and forcing them into a semblance of symmetry, or at least smoothness. But still, each time he hit one end of the blade, tendrils of metal danced willfully out of shape elsewhere.

"Like hammering a wiggling snake," he grumbled, pausing only briefly to lift the sword and inspect his progress. He went at it again with renewed vigor, this time concentrating on flattening the deeper curves that knotted along its length. Oddly enough, some of them seemed to be coming around by themselves—not losing their twist or bend entirely, but surrendering enough that they almost looked intentional.

"Ornamental," he muttered to himself. "That's what I'll call you. Ornamental."

The piece was cooling rapidly now—too rapidly—and he could tell that further hammering would do little good. He lifted it once more with the tongs and moved toward a heavy barrel in the corner of the workshop. He plunged it deep into oil that hissed and popped ferociously as the blade vanished beneath its surface.

Warren watched as bubbles rose from below, dark smudges spreading across his apron where splatters had landed. Once finished quenching, he pulled the sword free and examined it with a mixture of frustration and grudging admiration.

Completely black now, matte and dull from hilt to tip, it looked more like some piece of twisted art than a weapon. The long barbs at its end were sharp and menacing; Warren half expected them to move while he wasn't looking. But he'd at least gotten the edges straight, even if the spine of the thing writhed.

Maybe Susan had been right; maybe turning this thing into a crown would serve it right after all.

He laid the piece on his workbench and stretched, the joints in his shoulders and back popping loudly. "Time for a break." He should have another couple of days at least, and it shouldn't take more than a day to file and whet a proper edge on the thing.

Assuming it let him.

———

"Hey, Warren!" Sam, proprietor of The Broken Claw, the town's pub, waved from across the trade road.

"Hey, Sam," he called back, smiling gently. Even amongst the town's residents, who knew him well, Warren always avoided a full smile. The sight of all that ivory—including the one tusk that he refused to file down—tended to make people go a bit pale. "How's spring cleaning going?"

Sam set across the trade road as she answered. "Good enough. Got the fireplace sorted, at least. Gods, the soot. Totally worth it for the 'crackling winter fire' and all that, but sheesh. But from what Susan said when she came by, I should be asking you the same thing. How's it going?"

Warren cocked an eye at the sun, surprised that it was already well past mid-day. "At it longer than I thought," he sighed. "But well enough, I guess. I think I got the damnable thing into shape, at least. I'll sharpen it up tomorrow."

"Special commission?" That's what everyone called the pieces Warren forged after one of his dreams.

He nodded. "Should be through in two or three days, I guess. Felt about like that."

"Susan said it was... black?"

"Matte," Warren confirmed with a grimace. "Not a terrible color, mind, but it's all warped and bent... it's just..." He stopped, searching for the right word.

"Ominous?"

"Yeah, that's it."

"Well."

"Yeah."

Nothing more needed to be said: they all knew full well that the town had served some dangerous, even vicious, characters in its time. So long as those travelers came in peace, stayed in peace, and left in peace, the townspeople would play their part and serve them.

"Is he always like that this time of year?" Sam whispered, nodding down the road.

Warren turned to see Knodalon, keeper of the town's lakeside storehouse, sitting on his little bench, his back leaning on the rock wall. He was so still he could have been a statue, save for the gentle movement of his mussed hair and thick beard in the slight breeze. "Knodalon? Yeah. I mean, you know he's never all that social to begin with. But he spends all winter in his corner in the storehouse." Warren shrugged. "Takes him a while to come back out of it, once we start opening back up."

"You know, I must have gone in there a dozen times for supplies over the winter," Sam mused. "Never saw him."

"And don't go looking, either," Warren cautioned. "Winter is his... quiet time, I think."

"Huh."

"Had more folks through this winter than I'd expected," Warren said, pointedly changing the subject.

"Me too, from what you all had told me. But they were quick-in, quick-out, like you said. Minnie was bored."

"She always is," Warren grinned. "They roll through, get an ale and a quick bite, maybe buy a dagger or a horseshoe, and they roll on.

No sense risking being caught here in a snowstorm and stuck for days on end."

"Guess not."

"That's why we leave the gates to the square closed. No sense opening most of the shops, really, and so no sense having people wandering around in there."

"True. Although we did have folks after hard tack and stuff. Road provisions."

Warren shrugged. "Easy enough to bring it out to Tyran's place through the back. People expect an outfitter to carry that kind of thing anyway. How much ale did you wind up going through?"

"One of the plain stuff, almost one of the Dragon's Breath. Mainly had to go to the storehouse for food." She grinned. "Minnie did all of the cooking next door, but it was on the condition I brave the cold for supplies."

"Hah! Sounds like Minnie."

They stood for a moment in companionable silence, the busy sounds of the village rising from behind the pub as the residents aired out their homes, straightened their shops, and prepared for the coming season.

"Planning to help Cole?" Sam asked.

"In the farm? Absolutely. Everyone does." Warren allowed his grin to be a little larger this time, exposing his thick, yellow teeth. "I usually get to play ox, since we don't have one. Big ogre haul plow, big ogre make furrows in ground." His brown eyes sparkled at the joke.

"When will planting start?"

"After the spiders, usually."

Sam blinked in surprise. "Sorry, spiders?"

Warren lifted an eyebrow. "Nobody's told you?"

"Is this a bit? You all know I hate spiders."

"No, it's not a bit. They're big red spiders. Huge. Big as my head and bright red. They come down out of the Mistrals, a huge flood of them, usually a fortnight or two after thaw really sets in. They make straight for Lake Evendiam, and go skating across it, heading south. They won't eat crops, but they'll trample everything. No point even plowing until that's over."

"Spiders," Sam repeated carefully, her eyes scanning Warren's green, scarred face for signs of deceit. "Giant, red spiders."

"Yup."

"This is a bit."

"It isn't, I swear," Warren chuckled. "But look, it's not a big thing. They come straight down and head straight for the water. They'll pour right over the whole town, but that's why we get the main gate open so early. They'll funnel right out. Won't even turn around. A bunch of us sit under the overhangs and watch."

"Under no circumstances—" Sam began.

Warren's chuckle matured to a full laugh. "You don't have to. Just stay inside. Bar the door, if you want, although they won't even make an effort to get in. They go one direction only: toward the lake. Most will split around the storehouse, a few will just go up and over it. Trust me, you'll get plenty of notice—you'll hear the skittering a long bit before they show up. And then they're over and gone before you know it."

"I suspect I'll know it," Sam growled, clearly still suspecting this was all a prank.

"I'm telling you—oh, hello, ladies," Warren said.

Sam turned to see the town's dryadic thruple—and master cheese-makers—approaching. "Rinca, Clethra, Fennelis," she greeted them. "Have the shop all cleaned up?"

The three dryads were all but identical in appearance, although they took some steps to differentiate themselves for the benefit of their fellow townspeople. The small sprig of mistletoe behind one ear told Sam that it was Rinca who replied first. "More than usual. We're making the rounds."

Sam frowned. "The rounds?"

But Warren knew what they were talking about. "Time's finally come, then?"

The second—Clethra, from the crown of ivy she wore—nodded. "Our grove called over the winter, and we decided to set out once the road was fully clear. We'll leave under moonlight tonight."

Sam was blinking quickly. "But wait, you—"

"It's simply time," Fennelis said gently.

"Ladies," Warren said, cutting off Sam's retort, "I think Sam still thinks I'm teasing her about the spiders."

Rinca smiled. "The *Vael'ignis?*"

"Is that what they're called?" Warren asked.

"It's an elvish name," Clethra said. "But yes. And they're very real, Sam. And entirely harmless, if you stay out of their way."

"And... if someone doesn't?"

"Stung to death or possibly eaten alive," Fennelis replied in a matter-of-fact tone. "Happens in just moments, when they're swarming. But if you're behind them you're perfectly safe."

Sam's gaze flicked quickly between Warren and the three dryads. "I'll stay inside."

Clethrea shrugged. "Suit yourself, of course. But they're really quite lovely to watch."

"Right," Sam said, unconvinced.

"Warren," Rinca said, producing a small, paper-wrapped parcel from a pocket in her dress, "before we left, we wanted to bring you the last of your favorite."

Warren's eyes widened and his mouth filled with saliva. "The Parvottian Blue?"

"The one and the same," Clethra said with a wide smile. "Please enjoy it."

"Oh, I will," he said, accepting the pack with obvious relish.

"We've already told Susan we were bringing you some," Fennelis added.

Warren's expression fell a bit. "Oh. Of course."

Sam chuckled.

"Be well, both of you," the three said, turning and strolling unhurriedly back toward the town's main gates.

"I'm going to miss them," Sam said quietly as they left. "How long were they here?"

"Not that long, actually," Warren said, tilting his head in thought. "After me, obviously before you. Maybe three years? But we all knew they wouldn't stay long."

"I guess it's strange for dryads to settle down anywhere away from their tree," Sam allowed.

"Exactly. Took three of them together to stand the separation, but they all had a travel-itch. But you know, as they say. All good things."

"Yeah."

"But I'm going to miss the cheese," Warren sighed, looking at the tiny parcel is his giant hand. "This is barely two bites."

"Does it worry you?" Sam asked.

Warren sensed a tension in her voice. "Obviously. Susan's going to want a bite, and then there's hardly anything—"

"No, I mean them leaving."

Warren softened his tone. "I know. What about it should bother me?"

"It takes us below twenty shops."

Something cool and hard settled in Warren's stomach, and for a moment he forgot about the cheese. "Oh. The icosahedron."

"Right. Without it..."

"We'll just hope nothing nasty comes along the road, then," he said firmly. "We did well enough before last year, usually. And besides," he added more confidently, "you never know when someone's going to wander into your pub who belongs here. Maybe it'll be soon." He looked again at the small bundle of cheese lying in his palm. "Maybe they'll make cheese."

three

. . .

SUSAN HAD CORRECTLY CALLED it a crown, but Darby had called it a tiara, then laughed and said if he'd made an ogre-sized one, it wouldn't fit through their front door. Whatever it was, Warren just wanted it done and gone. The sooner the better. The first two rounds with it had ended with temperamental pieces of metal tossed in a pile of other, equally unsuccessful projects.

He'd melt them down later.

"How can this be so hard?" he muttered as he stared at the forge.

He'd called the third effort a complete restart. He'd broken it up, tossed the pieces into the largest crucible he had, and slid the whole mess back into the forge. Then he'd worked the bellows for a solid— no, he'd lost track of how long he'd pumped them. But now the forge was nearly white-hot, and the ore returned to a neutral, molten state.

"It's just a circle of metal," he muttered again.

Three tries down.

This one, though. *This* was the one that was going to work.

When he'd returned to the smithy, the moon still high in the sky, the forge had still held some heat from his work on the sword the day before, and it hadn't taken him long to get it roaring in the pre-dawn darkness.

While the forge had melted the lumps of ore into liquid, he'd worked on the sword nearly to completion. The strange shape had taken an edge more easily—almost *hungrily*, he thought—than he'd expected. He'd filed a rough edge onto it like it was butter, and then honed it even finer. A few test swipes at dried-up melons had split them like they'd never been whole in the first place. Warily, he'd finally set the sword aside. It still needed a grip, but that could wait until later. Today...

It would have been easier if his dreams had sent him another vision of the crown. He remembered its writhing, organic shape, but couldn't recall much of the *detail* of the thing. And so he'd taken some of the leftover ore Darby had brought up, melted it, and then started on the crown with a stubborn determination. Now, mid-morning, his heavy apron plastered to his chest and belly, he was waiting on his fourth attempt. Susan would scold him for forgetting to take the break she'd insisted on. *Maybe later,* he thought. *Maybe once the damn thing is done.*

Almost on automatic, he used tongs to pull the crucible from the forge and tipped the molten ore into a heavy mold.

When he'd woken yesterday, again before sunrise and with every detail of the original dream still burned into his memory, he hadn't thought the crown would be the more difficult of the two pieces. So he'd tackled the sword first, figuring it would be the more challenging. And it had certainly been *opinionated.*

It had put up a fight, the cooling metal buckling, twisting, stubbornly refusing to take the elegant shape he wanted. It hadn't given him much of a choice in how it looked, the sharp edges rippling and curving and arching forward as if it wanted to lunge at something. But that was what he'd dreamed. It's what Susan had said: That was what it was *supposed* to be.

But the crown...

The ore in the mold had cooled now, and he carefully levered it out of the mold and laid it on the anvil. He scowled at it, at the soot-black finish that had *already* crept over the brilliant silver of the ore. It wasn't just that the color matched the sword; he wouldn't have cared about the color at this point. The crown... it wanted to be *like* the sword. Parts of it were twisting and arching the same way, almost reaching into claws that would grip the wearer's head like a vise. It didn't move, of course, but the shape of it, the flow of its lines... strongly suggested that it *could*, if it wanted to.

On his first try, he'd started by molding the molten ore into a simple rod, which he then moved back and forth from forge to anvil, shaping and bending it. It refused to cooperate. The rod would slip out of his tongs, slip sideways on the anvil, even shattered a bit at one point. His shoulder ached from the number of times he'd swung his hammer and struck the anvil flat-out, missing the rod entirely.

So he'd thrown that first try into the scrap pile, figuring a sword like the one he'd made probably didn't need a crown to go with it. Forget about the crown. Probably it wasn't even an important, just an ancillary detail from the dream. The sword was what mattered.

But it immediately nagged at him. So he'd reached for the last of the ore that Darby had brought up and given it a second try. Melt. Mold. Shape. When whoever this was destined for finally showed up, he'd just throw the crown in with the sword and call it an extra. Didn't matter if it was perfect if it was free, right?

The second one had taken to the hammer beatings like a calf to milk, staying firmly in place. But that meant Warren's hammer had quickly beaten it out of the smooth, perfectly cylindrical rod shape with which he'd started. In its place, he found himself with a battered, beaten mess that curled around and around itself. You *could* have called it a crown, but Warren wouldn't have wanted to meet the king it was intended for.

Fourth time's the charm...

The sun was just up when his son came to check on him, and Darby had laughed when he'd gone down through the trapdoor for another batch of ore. He said Warren was going to end up with a whole collection of tiaras if he wasn't careful.

Warren's grumbled reply hadn't been a denial.

Then Susan had gotten on him for skipping breakfast, which was true, but when he said the forge wasn't going to run on pancakes, she'd told him the pancakes would be ready for the break he was going to take this morning.

"Uhh. Okay." He knew he wasn't sincere and she hadn't bought it, either.

The *last* thing he'd expected was for the crown to give him more trouble than the sword. But here he was, several iterations into what was supposed to be a simple crown that went with a sword, working with a furious focus on this last, blackened attempt.

The third attempt had gone even worse than the first two. It was like the metal was throwing a tantrum, that it was *bored*. The metal hadn't melted properly, he figured, because when he started pounding it on the anvil it just chipped and cracked. He'd given it a few dozen whacks before giving up and throwing the pieces back into the crucible.

And now it was ready.

Fourth time's the charm, he repeated to himself like a mantra.

He pulled the piece from the mold while it was still red-warm, ignoring the sizzling as the hot metal touched his tough skin. *Won't need to heat it back up to pound it,* he thought grimly.

This time, he'd forgone the simple rod shape of the first three tries, and instead gone with something he knew well: a horseshoe. He'd used the mold meant for the *clornesdells*, the largest breed of horse in the world, as far as anyone knew. Their shoes were the size of his own head, thick as one of his own fingers, and almost as heavy as his smallest hammer. Plenty of material to work with, and ugly as sin to start. Maybe the crown would emerge from *this* more readily.

Despite it still glowing a sullen red, he laid the thing gently in the forge, heating it back to orange-hot before pulling it out with his tongs and laying it gently on his much-abused anvil.

And then he'd raised his hammer, and his arm rose and fell with the tempo of an enormous metronome, ringing a clamor from the crown with each drop of his hammer.

This fourth try was stubborn like the sword, and that was putting it kindly. But at the same time, it was... *right*. This time, the crown had started imperfectly—his *clornesdell* shoe molds were old, the shoes rough and ready, their surface pitted and scarred at the start of it—and immediately begun *fighting* him. Not just slipping out of his grasp or refusing to cooperate, but trying to impose its own will, its own opinions, on its final shape.

"Like it's alive," he muttered.

He swung the hammer down in time with the echoes still bouncing off the walls, striking with a relentless, exasperated precision.

When Susan again wandered in, Warren had expected her to say something about that break he'd probably missed. "You were up early," she said instead, hands planted on her hips and her eyebrows arched in surprise.

"Technically late," Warren grunted. "Started before light. Moon was still up." He'd heard a soft rustle, in fact, as the dryads set out on their way home, wherever that was. *We'll leave under moonlight tonight.*

He almost smiled when Susan shook her head, but something that might have been a horn began curling out of the crown as the metal cooled. His jaw clenched, and he brought the hammer down hard enough to make the wood-planked floor rattle beneath his feet. "Damn thing," he muttered, and then paused to turn it with his tongs.

Susan peered at it. "It looks like it's supposed to be that way, doesn't it? Like the sword?"

He shrugged. He thought it did, too, but that didn't mean he was happy about it. "Mmm."

"Are you going to start over?" She sounded skeptical. "Again?"

Warren lowered his hammer, bending slightly to set it on the floor. The crown lay on the anvil, its edges rough instead of smooth, its shape irregular instead of even, its color black instead of bright silver. *Exactly like the sword,* he thought grimly. *They're made for each other.* Black, jagged edges of metal stood out here and there—sharp, for all that he'd made no effort to sharpen them—like unnatural thorns. Some of them even bent inward, promising blood and pain for whoever was stupid enough to wear this thing. As a crown it was an object, obvious failure.

And yet...

Warren looked up at her and decided she wasn't any more skeptical than he was. "No," he said. "Maybe this is it."

"You remember what I said," Susan told him.

He gave her a long, level look. "Which time?"

"Take a break. You're used to getting these right on the first try, but this one isn't going to beat you." She tilted her head. "You okay?"

"Yeah."

"One to ten." An old trick of hers: *Tell me how you're doing on a scale of one to ten.* It forced Warren to stop and actually think about it.

"Seven."

"Meaning six." Another playful grin.

"Okay, eight." He exhaled heavily. "You're right, you're right. I'll get it."

"You will." She headed back toward the house, and Warren looked back at the crown. *Maybe this actually is it.*

He raised his hammer, considering.

A shadow crossed over the double doors of the smithy.

Warren looked back to see Sam standing there, a wide smile on her face.

"Susan says you're going to have breakfast with us." She paused, then added, "Today. A bit late, perhaps."

"Not until it's done," Warren said.

"Food will be there when you're ready." She gave him a nod, seemed about to turn away, then reconsidered. "Minnie and I think you could use some help. Or at least some company."

"Or maybe some breakfast," a new voice called.

A short, round woman appeared from behind Sam. Minnie, the dumpling-like owner of the Weary Head, the town's sole, small inn, was in almost all white as usual. White apron, white dress, white bonnet... Warren wondered how she kept herself that way with all the work she and her son, Trevor had to do. If he and Darby had the inn, they'd have been coated in dust from the floors or flour from the kitchens, more than likely both.

He'd tried to make a hammer-wielding motion at Minnie, tried to indicate that he had his hands full. She didn't seem to get the message.

"He'll never take a break if you keep saying he has to," Minnie told Sam.

Sam shook her head, but the corners of her eyes crinkled into a smile.

"Didn't say he had to," she replied. "Just that it was ready."

"And I suppose," said Warren, "that Minnie just happened to be with you on your way over?"

Sam nodded. "Same as Susan running into me at the pub this morning. Just happened."

"Mmm," he said again.

"We were at the same place, is all," Minnie said.

Sam grinned.

Warren let the hammer drop to his side, pretending to give it some thought. Then he made a dismissive gesture toward the entrance of the forge and growled, "Ogre take break when shiny metal obey ogre."

That earned him a snort from Sam and rolled eyes from Minnie.

"You've got all the time you need to finish that," Sam said. "Two, maybe three days, the way we figure it. No?"

He didn't respond. They were right, but that wasn't the point. This crown didn't feel like one of the pieces that would take a long time to find its way. But this crown didn't feel right, either.

The women watched him expectantly.

The crown was starting to look like the other attempts. Susan and Darby had laughed when he said the ugly sword didn't win, he'd just stopped caring if it did; that one felt wrong until the very end, and when he'd admitted defeat, it instantly felt more right than anything he'd ever made. Was that what was happening with this? Did he just have to admit that it wanted to look like it did in the dream, instead of like he wanted?

"It doesn't feel right," he said slowly. Sam opened her mouth to respond, but he waved a hand to cut her off. "I don't think it's supposed to."

Sam blinked and closed her jaw with a *click*.

"Yeah," he said heavily. He picked the crown up, forgoing the tongs and relishing the heat against his thick skin. He tossed it onto his workbench, where it rattled loudly. "It's done."

———

"Figure there's no point plowing until the spiders have had their run," Cole said, eyeing the small farm with a calculating look. He leaned against the wooden stockade that formed the small field's outer barrier on three sides. The town's stone wall enclosed it on the fourth, and the whole thing looked more like a fort within a fort than a farm. But then, Warren thought, so did most of North Pointe Common Towne. Cole's four children were lined up next to him, each with a similar expression on their faces—though without the pipe that protruded from Cole's mouth and ended in a wild tangle of dark whiskers.

Breakfast had been exactly the break Warren had needed. Most of the tension had drained from his neck and shoulders over fresh, scrambled eggs, thick brown bread, and hot melted butter. The rasher of bacon on the side hadn't hurt one bit, either. Minnie had made an entire cauldron of hot tea, and then gentle ebb and flow of conversation in the pub had put Warren at ease. When he'd scraped the last off his plate, Cole asked if he could lend a hand in the field. Having no desire to return to the smithy just then, Warren quickly agreed.

The field itself was barren after the winter months; not much more than mud and mire stretched out in front of them. There was promise in it, though: The earth was soft beneath Warren's feet as he stood next to Cole. "So what are we doing, then?"

Cole jerked his chin at the dark brown skeletons of bushes. "Need to rip those out." He raised an eyebrow as he looked at Warren. "Be easier if you could do it, and figured you might could use the distraction, right now."

Warren snorted. "To say the least." Then he frowned. "But aren't those the rosefruits?"

"Yep."

"Everyone loves rosefruit."

"True. But you normally have to replant them every ten years or so. Their roots grow in on themselves after a while, and they just turn into a mass. Plant starts to die off. Now, our town's little gifts have kept these beauties going for twice that long, but they've hit the end. We'll rip 'em out now. I've got cuttings ready to go in, and—again, thanks to our little gifts—they'll grow up and be fruiting this Fall."

"Oh." Warren's fingers curled into a fist. "I'm on it."

He crouched low, gripping the base of the first bush. Thick, thorny branches reached out in all directions like a tangled web. Warren planted his feet and pulled. A low creak and the groan of straining roots met his effort, but the bush stayed stubbornly put.

He got lower and leaned back with all his weight, feeling it start to give—then lurch free with a spray of mud and tangled roots in its wake.

"Worth watching," Cole said, pipe clenched tightly between his teeth. "Looks like old man Warren hasn't slowed down a bit."

"Yeah!" one of the kids shouted. Warren thought it was probably Erich, but the voice came from somewhere down near his knees—a place that was currently occupied by four heads craning up at him. "Mom says we're helping Minnie with breakfast tomorrow. You gonna be there?"

Warren chuckled as he set to work on the next bush, this time getting his fingers far under before heaving it upward in another torrent of sodden earth. "Ogre do what ogre want," he growled.

"Trevor thinks you're funny when you talk like that!" Ivy—or maybe Willow—put in.

"Funny-looking!" another voice said, higher-pitched this time, definitely Willow.

Cole grinned as Warren methodically pulled up three more bushes and sent them sailing toward a growing pile of dirt-flecked brambles.

"They sure think your ogre jokes are funnier than your own kid does," Cole said as Warren dropped another mess of thorns onto the heap.

"Mmm." The sound came out somewhere between a grunt and a growl. Something about the bushes' roots had caught his attention.

Cole hadn't been kidding: although they'd clearly spread out initially, the roots had reached some predetermined limit and then started curling back in on themselves. The result was a dense, tightly woven ball of thick wood. He hunkered down, examining the root system as Cole's kids ran off and their father stood next to the ogre.

"You know," Cole said after a moment, "we come from out Holderdown way, west of Lake Milton."

"Oh?" Warren's eyes tracked one long root, starting where the soil level would have been and tracing it slowly as it wound down and around itself. "What brought you out here?"

"Governments out there are pretty informal. And they don't last long. Tend to start off well enough, usually someone from some village or another gets fed up with something and gets everyone to line up behind him. Works well for a generation or so. But then his kids, or their kids, start to get greedy. Start to think they *deserve* to be in charge. Start to give cushy jobs to their friends and family. But like that bush there, all curling back in on itself."

Something tickled Warren's brain. "And then what happens?"

"Fighting. Have to cut the whole thing down."

"Sounds pretty chaotic."

"Oh, aye. 'S why we left. No place to raise kids, until some villager takes it into his head to get everyone to line up behind him. Once people are sick of the chaos, you see."

"Yeah."

"Started calling 'em *rosebush councils*, a hundred or so years ago."

Warren snorted. "Because you have to rip them up every twenty years and start over?"

Cole nodded. "Thereabouts."

Then Warren's eye caught it. The main branch of the root, the taproot, had grown more or less straight down. Not *exactly* straight, of course; it still twisted this way and that, a bit. And where it had exited the soil and become the plant's main stem, little shards of wood stuck out at sharp angles. They were sharp, Warren knew, which is why it was easier—with his thick skin—for him to pull the plants out of the ground. "You know," he said slowly, reaching out and gently stroking one of the outer roots, "this looks a lot like the sword I just made."

four

· · ·

WARREN WIPED one meaty hand across his brow, smearing the sullen expression on his face. His sharp ears twitched at the faint, almost impudent whispering that came from the crown where it lay on his workbench. Or maybe it was the sword whispering at him. It didn't matter. What mattered was that it—they—would never win.

Or they already *had* won. Certainly, he was finished with them.

Still...

He picked up the crown, turning it over gently in one hand. The little pongs of metal sticking out at odd angles scraped against his rough palm. *I should probably sharpen those,* he thought idly as his other hand reached to his workbench where a file lay. Then he shook his head, snatching his hand back. "Stupid. Nobody wants their face cut open by this thing."

He set the glistening band of thorns aside and picked up his tongs. The sword still mocked him, its arched, dark spines reaching forward like a greedy hand. At least he'd managed to give it an edge, he thought, moving to toss it into the fire once more. It still didn't have the right shape, and with each piece he'd ever made, that was the most important part. And the color—that sooty, matte black. The very notion of it still irritated Warren. He'd finished the grip yesterday—

nothing more than a roughly carved piece of wood tightly wrapped with scarred strips of leather—but put off actually slipping it onto the sword.

The sword felt *wrong*, and for some reason that still felt *right*.

He contemplated tossing the thing back into the forge, melting it down, and trying again, but—

Darby's voice came echoing from the trade road. "Hullo the gate!" the boy called. "Hullo yourself!" came the muffled reply. Warren frowned and looked at his uncooperative creations one last time, weighing his options. "Bah." He took one last look at the pair. "Maybe I'll call you Rosefruit. The Rosefruit Sword and the Rosefruit Crown." He waited a moment, but neither piece responded. "Ogre eat stubborn sword," he growled as he turned to the smithy's open doors.

He stepped out into the bright day, the sun beaming down from a cloudless Spring sky, the scents of the season drifting by on the gentle lake breeze.

Darby was standing on the side of the trade road, watching the new arrival with an expression of bemusement.

The traveler was an old man, inexplicably on foot rather than mounted or in the back of a cart, shuffling along at a snail's pace. He wore a filthy gray robe whose hem was blackened and caked in mud. The robe's long hood was thrown back, revealing a balding pate that shone brightly above a thick, flowing gray beard. He was weaving slightly, his steps carrying him first this way and then that, but he seemed to be headed generally for the inn.

"Hullo," Darby said again as the man approached. "Welcome to North Pointe Common Towne." The boy had had politeness drilled into him from the moment they'd decided to stay in the town and come to understand what it was. "Can I help you?"

Warren crossed his arms and tried not to look dangerous.

Darby smiled as the spindly traveler stopped and squinted. The old man seemed to see everything in his first few seconds there, even things that weren't there. "Is that the lot of you?" he said, turning again to the inn. "Yes, I see now." His gnarled hand waved briefly toward Warren. "Hammers and ogres and noise." He resumed his course to the inn, but only for a few steps. "You know, I heard it from them. Heard it from your own small, dirty mouths." He pivoted sharply, suspicious eyes darting over to where Warren and Darby stood. They glinted in the sun like polished blades, like steel that had cooled on an ogre's workbench. "Tricksy and false!" he shouted, suddenly loud enough to fill the courtyard. "Then they were blue, and some had horns!" Warren gave a soft grunt of amusement and leaned in to murmur to his son. "Ogre eat crazy man?"

The boy nodded, grinning. "Ogre eat them all."

Warren stepped toward the old man, the massive bulk of him blocking out most of the sun as he approached. "Where are you coming from, sir? And how is it that you have no horse?"

The old man seemed to forget Warren and Darby's presence immediately. "Someone here would sell them?" he asked, rubbing his head in confusion. Darby watched as the old man resumed his way to the inn. Warren and his son exchanged a knowing look, then started toward the man again. "A young fool!" the old man cried, turning once more. "I knew a young fool here, once." He put a hand to his brow and shook his head. "Was it before the river? Or after? There was a river, and the fish were silver." The more he spoke, the less Warren and Darby seemed to understand. The less anyone would have understood. "You had some from that time. Even those?" the old man asked, furrowing his brows at Warren. Darby giggled.

Warren nodded. "Even those," he said, humoring him. "Especially those."

The old man confusion suddenly cleared, as did his suspicion. "And in the same plain way," he said. "Hmm."

"My name is Warren, sir," the ogre said gently. "This is my son, Darby."

The old man's eyebrows shot up. "I am... Aran." He seemed to consider this. "Yes, that's correct."

"What brings you to our town?"

"Hmph. Might as well here as anywhere else." He cocked his head to one side. "Is it still there? The old yellow one, with the roof and the window?"

Darby blinked. "Um. Which?"

"Yes," Aran said. "That's what I thought."

The door to the pub swung open and Sam stepped out. She was already wearing a grin, suggesting she'd heard everything so far. "Fancy an ale, traveler? Or a bite to eat? I've some hard cheese and fresh bread."

Aran turned to look at her. "Nasty scar, there. Cheese'll do that to a body."

Sam just stared.

Arun turned back to Warren. "You sell horseshoes?"

Now Warren blinked in confusion. "I, ah... yes. I do. But..."

"Yes, what?" Aran's mood shifted to impatience.

"I can't help but notice that you don't seem to have a... horse."

A wrinkled old hand waved away the concern. "Doesn't mean a thing. Have to be in the room where it happens, you know. I'll have two."

Warren worried he'd lost track of something. "Two... rooms?"

"Hah! Highway robbers! Sell an old man two rooms, plain as day I don't need more than three! No, you damn green fool, two horseshoes!"

"Darby," Warren said softly. His son dashed for the smithy. "They're two coppers each."

"Painstaking!" Aran cried, one hand rummaging around inside his robe. He withdrew a sparkling silver coin. "I'll not pay a chip more." He tossed the coin to Warren, he caught it in one meaty hand. "No more!" he added even more loudly as Warren opened his mouth to protest.

Darby was back in a moment, handing two standard-sized horseshoes to Aran.

Aran peered at the horseshoes, flipping them over and over in his hands. "Were they always this color?" he asked, holding one up to his ear and giving it a vigorous shake.

"They're iron," Warren explained. "They're supposed to be that color."

"No," Aran said, holding them at arm's length. "No, I don't think they are." He sniffed at one, then rapped it against the side of his head with a sound like a bell being struck. "Not how I remember them." He seemed to lose interest, dropping both shoes into the folds of his robe with a disappointed sigh. "Not special."

Warren exchanged an amused glance with Darby.

"I suppose I'll find it somewhere else," Aran said. He nodded to himself, then again to Warren. "Or maybe I won't!"

Minnie had come out of the inn without anyone noticing. She smiled broadly and waved as she approached. "Hello! Hello! Staying with us a while, traveler?"

Aran's eyes narrowed suspiciously. "You have rooms?" he asked.

"Yes indeed!" Minnie said cheerfully.

"Many of them?"

Minnie pursed her lips, pretending to think about it. "Some," she said at last.

Aran looked relieved. Or possibly troubled. "That's what I was afraid of."

"Well, we can put you up in one of the empty houses if you like! Make yourself comfortable for as long as you need!"

"Need?" Aran scratched his head. "I haven't had need since—" He stopped abruptly, staring at Minnie as if seeing her for the first time. "A fortnight."

"Oh?" Minnie asked, raising an eyebrow. "That long? We usually—"

"A fortnight," Aran repeated. "How long is that?"

It was Minnie's turn to blink as Sam stifled a chuckle. "Um. Two sennights?"

The old man frowned, and the fingers on one hand flicked madly for a moment. "So thirty nights?"

"That would be *two* fortnights," Minnie said. She glanced at Sam, who simply shrugged and smiled. "For that long, you might find one of the empty homes more comfortable than a room."

"Empty?" Aran said, tilting his head quizzically. "Empty, empty, empty, empty, or just empty?"

Minnie just stared, unsure of how to respond.

"A moon, then," Aran announced, seeming to come to some kind of decision. He nodded firmly. "Perhaps two. Although that's ridiculous, there's only one moon. How much? For the moon?"

"Um," Minnie said, trying to follow. "One of the homes for a... for thirty nights. Cleaning once a... every seven nights. Fresh towels for the asking. Three hot meals a day, either in the inn or the pub, your—"

"Oh, she'd like that very much wouldn't she just, then?" Aran sneered, his demeanor suddenly sly and vicious. He pointed at Sam. "Haul me in there and have with all my secrets, eh? Oh, no, Aran's too clever for that by a quarter!"

"The, ah... the inn then," Minnie said quickly. "Meals in the inn. Five coppers per night."

"No!" Aran said, his voice suddenly booming, his arm sweeping out in a wide arc. "No, no, no! Think I wouldn't see that coming? Do you take me for a fool?"

Minnie opened her mouth to reply, then thought better of it.

"There I am," the old man continued, the wrath and thunder pouring out of him. "Lying there under the bed instead of in it! Finding all the coppers left by children with teeth! It's an outrage!"

Warren nodded, rubbing his chin thoughtfully. "I see how that would upset a man."

"Eight coppers!" Aran said.

"Eight?" Minnie looked bewildered.

"A rotting pinecone!" Aran shouted.

"Oh," Minnie said. "You meant..."

"Clever by four quarters!" Aran snapped. "I'll pay it!"

"You could," Sam suggested brightly from her perch on the pub's porch, "you could do five silvers for thirty nights."

Aran turned and stared at her suspiciously, one eye narrowed to a slit and the other wide as a saucer. "Could I now?" he asked after a moment.

Warren shrugged. "Even ogre can do math."

Aran's eyes shifted rapidly back and forth between Sam and Warren before finally settling on Minnie. "Five?" he asked in a conspiratorial whisper.

"Yes," Minnie said slowly.

"One," Aran said stretching out an arm like he was about to throw something again.

"Four," Sam replied quickly.

"Done!" Aran shouted, jerking his hand back in triumph. He fished around in his robe for a moment, producing five silvers along with several nuts and what did indeed look like a rotting pinecone. All of them dropped to the ground as he handed over the coins. "The red one with the bushes, then?"

"The..." Minnie began.

"Yes," Warren cut her off with a wink at Darby. "That one."

Minnie laughed and caught Warren's eye as she pocketed the money.

"It's always an adventure," she said softly.

Aran was bent over double, grunting as he gathered up what had fallen. He held a finger to his lips before scuttling off toward town with surprising speed. He paused at the gate and turned back toward them.

"Our little secret!" he called hoarsely before vanishing from sight.

Warren let out a deep breath that was half sigh and half chuckle. "Darby, go show him around. Which one, Min?"

"Three. Between you and Calder. Just aired it out yesterday."

"Three, Darby."

Darby chuckled and dashed off after the old man.

Sam hopped down from the porch and joined them near the inn's door. "Another customer satisfied?" she asked innocently.

"He's quite something," Minnie agreed with a grin.

"You're sure about this one?" Warren asked her seriously.

She nodded emphatically. "Trevor will be so excited when I tell him we have someone staying for more than just a night or two! Besides," she added slyly, "I think this one might pay us in gold if I confuse him enough."

———

Darby caught up with Aran, who'd stopped just inside the gates. "What's this, then?" the old man demanded.

"Welcome to North Pointe Common Towne," Darby said carefully, feeling it bore repeating. "Let me show you around."

The town was a series of connected stone buildings, roofed in slate, with a wide overhang running along the front of it all. A sturdy wooden walkway stood beneath the overhang, which provided shelter from whatever weather the lake and the mountains threw at them. The entire structure formed a rough rectangle around a grassy green in the middle. "That's the town green," Darby said, pointing. "From our left," he added, pointing to the first doorway inside the gate, "The chirgeon's, the herbalist, her tea shop, the—ah," he stammered, remembering that the dryads had left. "That was our cheese shop. Closed now. Then—" and he paused again, remembering that he wasn't supposed to refer to Leota as a witch, "our town wise woman, the—"

"Witch, you mean," Aran said in a surprising lucid, matter-of-fact tone. "It's fine."

Darby blushed. "Yes. Um. There's a bookshop, then our town hall. We have school there. The potter, then the tailor." His finger tracked past several empty doors—travelers were never put up in those. "The mapmaker. The menagerie. That's animals. Butcher, baker—"

"Candlestick maker," Aran mused.

"Um, no. Don't have one of those. Sorry. Then it's the grocer and the dry goods shop, he might have candles. I know he does, I mean."

"Can't abide candles."

"Oh. Um, out on the trade road, you saw the inn and the pub. My dad's the blacksmith. Fishing boat dock is out on the lake."

"Stupid place for it."

"Ah, sure. Yeah. Outfitter's shop is next to the other gate, next to the gaol." Darby finished quickly, unsure of where to go next.

"I'm tired," Aran said suddenly.

"Oh! Okay. You're in number three. Right this way." Darby led the old man to the door of the narrow two-story home, one of nearly twenty that formed the wall between the town's center and the trade road. "We live in four, so if you need anything at night, just knock. Calder's in two, on the other side, but he gets up really early to go out on the lake."

"So just empty, then," Aran said wearily.

"Sure." Darby opened the door and showed Aran in. "Bedroom's upstairs. These places... ah, they stay pretty warm? You shouldn't need a fire, but if you do, go see Minnie in the inn." He didn't mention that almost nobody ever lit a fire for heat as the town's gifts kept every home perfectly snug. Fires were more for ambiance.

"Buggerit," Aran sighed. He stepped in and closed the door behind him, almost catching Darby in the face.

"Huh," the boy said thoughtfully.

———

Warren sat upright in bed, startled out of a deep sleep by a loud commotion. He blinked furiously to clear the sleep from his eyes, and realized he was alone in bed—and the morning sun was streaming through the bedroom window. "Haven't done that in a while," he chuckled as he pulled himself out of bed, dressed, and straightened the bedclothes.

The commotion was still going on when he stepped out into the town square, and it sounded like it was coming from—the trade road? He walked to the town gates. *Yeah, sounds like a fuss at Tyran's.* It was a tradition in the town that, whenever a traveler set up a fuss of some kind, Warren would casually wander over and... lurk. The sight of an ogre would often calm people down.

Not so much this time.

Aran was standing just inside Tyran's shop, Mistral Adventures. It was an outfitter's shop, stocked with almost anything that an adventurer might need on their quest—clothing, equipment, even hard tack and other rations. Of course, given the town's gifts, Tyran generally had more exotic items if a traveler was destined to have them, but this time...

"Lies!" Aran was yelling. "Tricks and deceits! You all think you're so clever!"

The old man's voice echoed across the trade road. Several townsfolk were watching with bemusement, and Sam, lounging outside the pub, gave Warren a friendly wave as he walked to the shop.

Tyran's big, booming laugh greeted him as he opened the heavy door. "And then there were two!" Tyran roared cheerfully.

"The jig is up! The cat is out of the bag! The dice have been loaded!" Aran shouted, jabbing a bony finger in Tyran's direction.

Warren caught Tyran's eye and quirked a brow. His friend winked back conspiratorially and waved him over. "What's going on?" Warren asked in feigned innocence.

"This scoundrel!" Aran howled. "This scurrilous rapscallion! He doesn't have what I need!"

"What do you need?" Tyran asked, smiling broadly.

Aran paused, his mouth working soundlessly for a moment. "Something," he exclaimed at last. "Something... else!"

"We could start with some travel rations!" Tyran suggested energetically, holding out a burlap sack that rustled softly with the sound of full water skins and dried meat.

"Too salty!" Aran snapped without inspecting them.

"How about this fine bedroll?" A tapestry of colorful fabric unfolded before him.

"Too blue!"

"An elegant cloak for those rainy nights?"

"Too... cloaky."

Warren stifled a chuckle as Aran threw his hands up in frustration and stormed around the shop in an erratic pattern. The old man grabbed at random items, dismissing each with increasing fury.

"Everyone else gets what they want," Tyran said with playful exasperation. "Why can't I fit this one?"

Aran stopped dead in his tracks and fixed Tyran with a blazing glare. "Because I'm not everyone else!" he declared triumphantly, as if unmasking a dastardly villain.

Tyran nodded sagely. "That part's true," he admitted with another booming laugh.

"I knew it!" Aran cried triumphantly before turning on his heel and making for the door, an elaborate shuffle that had him zigzagging past every shelf along the way. He shoved it open with surprising force, nearly knocking down another bemused traveler who had just arrived on horseback.

Warren could almost sense the tension in the shop. Generally, the shelves and the items on them would rearrange themselves, presenting whatever the current customer needed or was destined to have. But now, the entire place seemed to tremble, as if poised on a dangerous precipice.

"Watch your step!" Aran shouted over his shoulder as he marched off toward the town gates.

The shop seemed to sigh and relax, and Warren thought her heard the soft sounds of a few items settling back into place.

"Well," Warren said after catching his breath from suppressed laughter, "I hope Minnie knows what she signed up for."

Tyran clasped Warren's shoulder with one massive hand and grinned from ear to ear. "I've got a side bet that he'll be back here demanding something ridiculous within two days."

"No bet," Warren replied over his shoulder as he turned to leave.

Before he reached the door, Tyran called after him. "I know you're working on that big commission—"

"It's almost done!" Warren cut him off quickly.

"That's great!"

Warren let the door *thud* closed behind him, and began trudging to the smithy. *Today, I will make horseshoes,* he promised himself firmly. *And nothing else.*

five

. . .

THE DREAM WAS like an apocalyptic in shades of gray, stripped of color yet saturated with the stench of raw desperation and uncontrollable panic. It ignited a beastly, primal instinct deep in Warren's hindbrain—a savage urge from his primeval ancestors, an urge to *chase* and *kill*. At the searing center of the vision raced the image of a woman astride a powerful horse. Warren strained his eyes desperately to see her face, but the details dissolved into a thick, unyielding mist. It wasn't her armored chest or the head of her furious steed that held his attention—it was her hands.

One hand, shrouded in a gauntlet, gripped her mount's reins with iron resolve, while her other hand, bare, was held tight against her armored abdomen. Its gauntlet must have been lost or shattered. The blurred, chaotic landscape whipped past in violent strokes of greens and browns as she fled.

Because she *was* fleeing. Warren was certain of it.

Shouted in a guttural, savage tongue, the voice of pursuit thundered: *Skutt Zog! Nok snag!* Warren's heart hammered as the sound jolted him—sound was rare in his dreams, and the significance of this sound in particular pierced him like shrapnel. *Ruk! Ruk! Ruk! Ruk!*

It was ogreish, a language Warren hadn't heard since he and Susan had set out, the infant Darby sleeping peacefully against his mother's chest.

This lone warrior with one gauntlet was not alone: she was being hunted by ogres.

With defiant fury, she raised her bare fist beside her armored one, never once loosening her grip on the reins. In one desperate, almost ritualistic moment, she brought her fists together in a gesture that teetered between challenge and invocation, only to drop them immediately—a stark portrayal of missing strength. The lost gauntlet, then. Together the armor pieces must have given her some advantage, some protection, but with one of them missing—

Grak-a-blok!

Circle 'round! Block her off! A common ogre tactic when dealing with false prey, Warren knew. His parents had, after all, met in one of the many mercenary companies who maintained an ogre platoon.

Her relentless pursuers began closing in, their savage words like daggers in the chaotic gale of the dream. Warren couldn't make them out, focused as the dream was on her hands, but he could *sense* them. Even as the furious ogreish cries sliced through the air, she hunkered lower, drawing closer to the back of her steed. A tactical move to maximize speed.

Krag climb! Skutt Zog! Nok Grog!

She must have surged forward into a treacherous terrain that the heavy ogres, on their even heavier mounts, could barely navigate; the margins of the dream blurred into a harsh, ashen gray and Warren could hear the rough skitter of loose shale. A risk on her part, but one worth taking, as the ogres would be at an even greater disadvantage.

For a heartbeat, the woman's face snapped into razor-sharp focus, terror etched deep beneath an unyielding resolve. With reflexes honed by desperation, she ducked lower as a deadly projectile—a spear or perhaps even an arrow—whistled past her head, its threat tangible and immediate.

Rida Stuk!

The cacophony of ogreish shouts receded into a distant clamor as their pursuit faltered. In that fleeting moment, her eyes blazed with a ferocity that pierced the veil of the dream—locking onto something just beyond reach.

Then, as if struck by lightning, Warren jolted awake, lungs burning and heart racing.

———

Warren had always enjoyed making armor pieces, even though he didn't often get the opportunity. Gauntlets in particular demanded a level of finesse and precision that he loved, with their fine points of articulation and thin plates of metal. He'd long ago made himself a set of tools to help bridge the gap between those tiny details and his giant hands: clamps, tweezers, tongs, miniature hammers, and more. He'd even devised a special bench to accommodate his long, blunt knees, so that he could hunch over close to his work without jabbing himself in the chin. The supple leather inlay on the seat had been Susan's idea, and it made a surprising difference in how long he could sit before his legs went numb.

At the moment, though, he wasn't sitting at all.

The gauntlet in Warren's dream had been worked with a design that seemed to glow an ominous orange, and he wanted this one to be an exact match. He knew just how to achieve it: there was a mineral in his stores that was a dull, plain gray when raw, but which burned with color when worked properly. He'd gotten Darby out of bed at first light to bring up some of the special ore from the trapdoor as well. His son had grumbled a bit, but brightened when Warren told him he could beg an early morning treat from Makota. She'd likely spoil him with more than one.

"One to ten?" Susan had asked softly, giving him a peck on the cheek as he herded his son out of the house.

"Solid nine," he'd replied.

He'd spent the rest of the night going over every detail of the dream—every inch of the gauntlet was seared into his mind, now—before finalizing his own design. As soon as Darby brought up a few chunks of the special ore, they'd ransacked the smithy for all of the other materials Warren needed to start work. They were scattered about him now like pieces of an intricate puzzle: cut sheets of tempered metal waiting to be hammered into shape; lengths of thin wire for fastening plates together; a dozen tiny hinges for joining each articulated finger to its neighbor.

He'd begun by stoking the forge back to full heat, its coals glowing hot and white as the morning sun climbed lazily into the sky. The smithy's special ore had gone into a set of crucibles, rendering the near-black metal into a silvery liquid and burning off the few impurities that it contained. While the forge did its work, Warren prepared for the next step, setting up one of his sturdiest work tables in a way that only an ogre could have managed. Pressing out sheets of metal—which he'd need for the gauntlet pieces—was a difficult thing to do by hand. Most blacksmiths wouldn't even attempt it, and instead would simply buy sheets from a larger smith who'd invested in a proper rolling press. But Warren didn't have that luxury—not when he needed to use the special ore.

But what he did have was a massive amount of strength.

As the ore liquified, Warren added small chunks of the orange mineral, watching with fascination as it too melted, never quite merging with the silvery ore, but threading its way throughout. As it heated, its bright orange color emerged, mirroring that of the fiery forge.

After it was all a molten mass, Warren used his heavy tongs to pull the first crucible from the forge and pour the liquid material into the work table he'd prepared, pooling it at one end. Heavy metal bars kept the material from spilling off the table while Warren set the crucible and tongs aside and picked up his heavy roller.

This, he'd purchased—he didn't have the means to make a roller so perfectly cylindrical, with a mirrored surface so perfectly smooth. He withdrew it carefully from its wooden crate, puling aside the thick cloths that protected it. A human couldn't even have accomplished that much, not even with a friend—or two. Warren's muscles bulged under his green skin as he maneuvered the roller to the table, where it fit perfectly between the thick bars along the sides.

He began rolling, as Darby looked on in fascination.

The glowing liquid resisted at first, but soft as it was it was no match for the weight of the roller combined with Warren's own strength. Back and forth, back and forth, he rolled the liquid thinner and thinner, until it evenly covered the table's surface. It had just cooled to a dull red when Warren removed the roller with satisfaction, setting it into a purpose-made wooden cradle to cool. He poured a light oil over the metal to temper it, and then waited for it to finish cooling. Once it did, he pulled it out, admiring it with satisfaction: it had settled into a dark, matte grey, streaked through with rivers of deep orange that would glow when they caught the light.

He repeated the process for two more sheets.

The process of cutting out the individual gauntlet pieces was straightforward, given the power in his hands, and before long another workbench was covered with neatly arranged pieces of intricately cut metal. Now, Warren grabbed a short length of coarse-grained charcoal from a barrel beside his forge and marked each piece with its intended position: forearm, wrist, thumb, knuckle, fingertip. With a single-minded determination, he set aside any piece that didn't meet his standard. At some point, Darby wandered off for his promised treats.

For the rest of the morning, he ignored everything else—the loud creak and bang of wagonloads arriving outside; the chatter and bustle from Sam's pub across the road; even young Darby's persistent knock on the doorframe as he left a mid-morning meal on a workbench. *Gauntlet for woman bigger than lunch for hungry ogre!* Warren joked to himself with a toothy grin when he finally noticed the meal some hours later.

Allowing himself to sink into an almost fugue-like focus, he fit pieces together one by one, testing each joint and seam for strength and flexibility before taking them apart again to refine them even further. The plates were small but not thick enough yet to hold up under pressure—they needed layering, welding, more hammering.

There was a rhythm to it all: fire hissed as he plunged metal into snow-white coals; metal clanged against iron as he hammered it deftly into shape; oil sizzled and spat when it quenched each finished piece.

By late afternoon he had assembled most of its structure: an elegant latticework of thin, orange-streaked plates that overlapped like dragon scales across forearm and wrist.

Another ogre might have lost patience halfway through such delicate work, or lost hope when faced with so many tiny details. But Warren was both patient and determined.

And incredibly hungry.

He thought again about Susan's stew waiting on the workbench and decided maybe there was time for one more bite before getting back to work.

"Dad!"

Warren blinked, his intense focus dropping away. "Darb?"

"Dad, there's a guy out here."

Warren's eyes darted to the dark, twisted shapes of the sword and crown, still lying where he'd left them on the far side of the smithy. Foul things, and something told him their owner had arrived.

He stepped out into the late afternoon sun, brushing off his heavy leather apron. *Yeah, that has to be the guy.*

There were eight in the party, most of them already dismounting and brushing the road dust from their clothes. Darby had already scurried back to them and started leading horses into the stables that sat next to the smithy. Minnie and Sam had already stepped out of their establishments, eyeing the newcomers warily.

The leader—and there was no question he was the leader, as the others exuded deference without saying a word—slipped off his horse and looked around.

His eyes locked on Warren's.

He didn't look much like the man in Warren's dream, but they almost never did. He was shorter than Warren would have imagined, barely Susan's height. His raven-colored hair was pulled back into a neat tail, his pale, roughened skin darkened only by a day's stubble scattered across his chin.

But his eyes.

His eyes were *dead.* Flat, cool, and uncaring. Hard and focused.

"Ogre," he said, his voice low and sharp. "Are you the smith here?"

Warren gave a silent nod, his stomach tightening into a cold knot.

Aran had wandered out of the town and was standing a short way from Sam, eyeing the proceedings. He seemed calmer now, more focused.

"I've ridden a long way," the newcomer said, his voice cutting through the air. "There are tales that—"

"This way," Warren grunted, turning back to the smithy.

"I require a weapon," the man was saying as he hurried after Warren. "One that can strike—"

"It's this one," Warren grumbled, pointing to the dark, twisted sword and crown that lay in the corner.

The man's jaw snapped shut and he walked to the table. He lifted the sword almost reverentially, carefully running the pad of one thumb across its edge. He pulled his finger back sharply, nodding in satisfaction at the thin line of blood he'd drawn. Then he frowned. "A crown? I didn't—"

"They're a set," Warren said flatly, his tone brooking no discussion.

The man seemed about to protest, but then he simply nodded. "Do they have names?"

When he'd first come to the town, when he'd first started having the dreams, Warren didn't understand why *everyone* expected his creations to have names. It wasn't just the swords, or even the other weapons he'd made over the years. *Anything* that people needed for their quest apparently had to have grand names.

Vamir, the town's bookseller and scholar, had tried to explain. "Names leave an impression on the world. They fill a space, and create an aura. They define a thing, give it its... purpose, you could say."

It made a kind of sense.

And Warren had indeed considered many names for the set. *Dark-sword*, which he'd immediately discarded as being overly dramatic. *Rosefruit*, which seemed inappropriately whimsical. *Thornbiter*. Susan had suggested *Twist*, while Darby liked *Tiara*.

Fortunately, the smithy had always had its own ideas about names.

"The Grieving Crown," Warren said, the words spilling out his mouth. He leaned forward a bit as if he could bite them back out of the air. "The sword is Avarice."

The man's eyes glittered now, no longer dead but very much full of death. "How much?"

Again, the smithy always set the price. "Five hundred gold," Warren blurted, his own eyebrows rising even as he said it. An astronomical sum, an impossible sum, more than double any price he'd ever set before.

"Would you accept a platinum piece?"

Warren almost took a step back. An astronomical sum indeed, worth far more than he'd asked. But then he shook his head. "We use the money to buy food. Cloth for clothes. We've no use for platinum out here."

The man's lips pursed slightly before he nodded. He took up Avarice and the Grieving Crown in each hand and stalked past Warren out of the smithy. This time, it was Warren's turn to hurry after.

He barked a few, low words to his men, who began rummaging in their saddle bags. Two of them even jogged into the stable yard, where Darby had led their horses. In moments, a pile of ten heavy leather bags lay in the middle of the trade road.

"Fifty in each," the man said evenly, giving Warren an even stare. "Do you need to count them?"

Warren shook his head. Nobody ever cheated the townspeople of North Pointe Common Towne.

"Then we ride," the man said. Warren turned at a noise and saw Darby scurrying over with the small wheelbarrow. His son began loading the heavy bags of gold.

"But we thought—" one of the other men began to protest.

"We ride," the leader insisted in exactly the same tone. "Merrick, give me your oil cloth." He considered the sword he was holding. "Tommin, yours as well."

As Darby grunted the bags into the wheelbarrow, Warren, Minnie, Sam, and Aran watched as the dark-haired man wrapped Avarice in oiled clothes and fastened it over his saddlebags. Warren had never even considered making a scabbard for the thing, couldn't even imagine how such a thing would be constructed. The twisted sword wasn't meant to be convenient, didn't *want* to be straightforward. The

Grieving Crown went into a saddlebag on the horse's other side, swaddled in more cloth.

At some silent signal, the men all swung into their saddles, wheeling their horses. The leader threaded his horse through them until he was at the front of the pack, gave his horse a light kick, and they set off at a ground-devouring trot.

Aran wandered over from in front of the pub. "That wasn't a nice man," he said softly.

Warren shook his head silently.

"And he's not going to do nice things with that sword."

"It's not a nice sword."

"So why, then?"

Warren sighed. "It's what we do. If they come in peace, stay in peace, and leave in peace, we serve. Whatever their quest. The town gives us many gifts, and that's the price."

"He'll kill, with that thing."

Sam had wandered over as well. "And maybe a hero will rise to stop him."

"Maybe?"

"As Warren said, it's part of... the agreement. With this place. Those men, they have a story ahead them. Behind them, too, obviously. They're the players in it. Not us."

Aran was still frowning.

"Look at it this way," Warren said wearily. "That sword, and the crown—they were going to come into the world. One way or another. We're just the outlet." He shook his head, suddenly overcome with fatigue. "I've got a stew to eat," he sighed as he turned back to the smithy. "Darb, get all that inside," he called to his son.

"What's he mean?" Warren heard Aran ask.

"Everything we make here, we share," Sam replied simply. "C'mon, I'll buy you an ale."

"Not setting foot in that pub."

"I'll bring it out to you."

Warren ignored them and trudged back into the smithy. The stew had gone cold, and so he held it near the forge for a bit to warm it. It tasted heavenly, rich and earthy.

"You all right?"

He turned to see Susan leaning against one of the open doors. "Yeah." He gave her a small shrug. "Six out of ten, right now. The stew's helping."

"It's a lot."

He flashed her a toothy grin. "It's actually kind of a small bowl."

She smiled back. "The sword, I mean. All of it."

"Yeah." He lifted another large spoon of stew to his mouth. The spices Susan used spread over his tongue, and he felt his shoulders unknot a bit.

"You know," she said softly, "Darby's older now. We could... you know."

"Move on?" She nodded, but Warren just shook his head a bit as he swallowed another spoonful. "No. We're safe here. You know how much grief we got when we married, even from the other ogres. An orge and a human? Ridiculous. But Darb's starting to show. You've seen his ears." A soft smile played across Susan's lips. "A half-breed would be even more unwelcome, most places." He slurped the last of the stew directly from the bowl and walked over to the doors to hand it to her. "We're safe here. Welcomed. And the price isn't much. Not usually. That sword," he said with a deep sigh. "That's unusual."

She nodded to the workbench where the assembled gauntlet lay, its threads of orange catching the sun, which was beginning its trek toward the horizon. "That's next?"

Warren eyed the gauntlet, nodding with satisfaction. "That one I'm proud of."

"Well," Susan said. "Good." Then she looked up at him, tilting her head and grinning. "Fancy an ale?"

Warren grinned back, his tusks showing. "Only if it's in that giant bucket Sam keeps for me."

six

. . .

THAT NIGHT, Warren had a blessedly dream-free sleep—for which Susan was equally grateful. She'd found that he tended to toss a bit when he was having one of Those Dreams, and lying in bed next to a tossing ogre wasn't necessarily the safest place to be. The dreams tended to come just before sunup; she tended to just decamp and go help Minnie or Makota with their morning cooking and chores.

So after a restful sleep, a leisurely breakfast with Susan and Darby, and a few long moments standing in the town green simply breathing in the cool morning air, Warren made for his smithy with no pressing business. The place seemed brighter and cheerier with the sword and crown gone, and so he spent a bit of time polishing the gauntlet, cleaning up after the past few days' efforts, and taking an inventory. The ore that came from beneath the trapdoor was self-replenishing, but he was getting low on clean sand, and he had a notion of replacing the quenching oil. That, he'd need to order, but the current barrel was looking a bit murky, and the last thing he'd need would be for it to sludge up.

Something pricked at his ears.

He stopped and turned this way and that, trying to identify it. It

was almost like a distant scratching, like the sound of metal against...
rock?

He stepped out of the smithy.

It was louder now. Someone coming down the road? It was a bit
early, but if they'd set out when it was still dark... but no, it didn't
sound like wagon wheels.

He'd heard the sound before, but...

"Spiders," he whispered.

———

Fortunately, the *aral'pyra* made a *lot* of noise, the hard surfaces of the
Mistral Mountains echoed and amplified it, and both ogres and Fellis
had excellent hearing. There was more than enough time to "sound
the alarm," so to speak, and for everyone to put away whatever they'd
been working on, batten their doors and windows, and gather under
the northern overhang in the town square, lining themselves up in
front of Lucy's, Prudence's, Barnaba's, and Dooley's. They sat on
whatever chairs they could pull from everyone's shops and homes.

Even Sam had made it, although she looked paler and more jittery
than usual. She sat stiffly in a straight-backed chair Dardrad had
pulled out, next to Jen. Jen had one hand resting on Sam's thigh, grinning slightly at her friend's discomfort.

The *scritching* from the mountains grew louder, until it became a
skittering and then a *clacking*, accompanied by a near-continuous high-
pitched chirping, like that of a flock of demented one-note birds.

Then the spiders arrived.

Like a wave of bright red nightmare, the spiders cascaded from the
foothills and over the roofs of the town. Hundreds of them. Thousands. Each as big as a small dog or a large cat. They plummeted to the
grassy ground just in front of the townspeople, their long legs
absorbing the impact with eerie grace before they skittered directly for
the town's open gates.

At exactly that moment, across the square, Aran stepped out of his
rented town home, closed the door behind them, and then turned to
see the rapidly approaching wave of arachnids.

"Nope," he said quickly, hurrying to his right.

Everyone held their breath as he scurried along the covered walkway in front of the town homes, passing eight of them before stopping.

Warren tensed, and noticed Tyran and Dardrad doing the same.

Aran looked to his left, eyeing the massive tide of red carapaces, but the spiders seemed to pay him no attention, focused as they were on funneling through the gates. Aran leapt to the grass, and in three quick strides was under the overhang in front of Alred's dry goods shop. Everyone released their breath at once as the old man walked quickly to join them.

"Might have told a soul," he muttered as Calder stood and offered his stool. Aran sank onto it, nodding gratitude before turning his eyes to the ongoing swarm.

Susan held Darby tightly, murmuring quiet reassurances more for herself than for him, while Dardrad, next to them, watched with wide eyes and open mouth as the swarm galloped past, up and over one another in their frenzy. The spiders bounded through the gates in a single-minded rush toward Lake Evendiam.

"Never seen them this bad," Jen said, shouting to be heard over the clacking and chirping. Her hand remained steady on Sam's leg.

"Never seen them at all," Sam said through gritted teeth.

The wave went on and on.

Sam looked around in sudden concern. "Where's Knodalon? Did he—"

"He's fine," Jen said with a chuckle. "He'll be out on his bench as usual."

"But you said—"

"They'll give him a wide berth, trust me."

The spiders were still coming. The front rank had finally reached the storehouse and fishmonger's counter, where they split, flowing to the left and right. A few hardier—or more determined—ones simply skittered straight up the vertical stone walls of the storehouse, intent on reaching the lake as quickly as possible.

They poured around the boathouse to the right, and between the storehouse and smithy to the left, and the watchers could now hear the frantic sloshing of water as the spiders reached their goal.

"Won't they drown?" Sam wondered aloud.

"No," Vamir said, taking a bit out of one of the pastries Makota had brought out for the occasion. They were cherry tarts, each heaped high with bright red fruit that resembled the spiders themselves. Despite loving Makota's baking, Sam had taken one look at them, shuddered, and declined. "The tips of their legs are incredibly sharp. Once they get off the shore itself the surface tension of the water will support them. They'll spread out a good bit as well, which helps."

"They walk on water," Sam said, shaking her head in disbelief.

"Oh, indeed," Vamir replied with a smile. "Once we see the back of the pack, it's perfectly safe to go look. They won't turn back for anything."

They watched for a bit longer, and the swarm seemed to be thinning.

"How many *are* there?" Sam murmured.

"Tens of thousands, usually," Jen said easily. "Not all in one pack, mind. But this is a big crowd this year, for a single group. Winter must have been light up there."

"And where do they go?"

"Everywhere," Vamir answered. "They'll spread out along the lake. There are actually four or five points where they come down from the mountains. They'll spend the summer feeding, although most of them will be killed by predators, believe it or not. Singly or even in small groups, there are a lot of animals that'll go after them. Not to mention whatever humans they run across. Whichever ones survive will head back up in the fall, although you'll almost never notice them by then. On their own, they tend to keep low and travel at night."

"Back into the Mistrals?"

"Correct. They'll be fed up by then, and they'll have mated. Most of the males die during mating, so it's the females heading back. And they'll be exhausted. They'll make their way back into the mountains, lay several thousand eggs apiece in giant egg sacs, and then die."

Most of the spiders had cleared out by now, leaving only a few stragglers scampering after their brethren on ungainly legs. A chorus of relieved sighs came from the townsfolk as they shifted back to normal conversation. Folks went inside to fetch cups and mugs and some drinks appeared.

Sam seemed undecided about whether she wanted to relax or bolt for her life.

"Don't worry," Jen said with a chuckle, "they're really only interested in the lake." She gave Sam's thigh two reassuring pats.

Sam scowled back at her.

"I know," Jen said dryly. "Reassurance doesn't help if you're still scared."

"It's less scared," Sam insisted, "and more creeped out."

A particularly large spider made its way over Barnaba's shop at that moment, dropping to the grass and pausing right in front of Sam as if considering its options.

She froze.

Jen snorted in amusement.

The spider found its bearings and scurried toward the gates.

Another clacking sound rose up from some distance away; this time it was accompanied by increasingly frantic splashing noises.

"They'll be gone soon," Warren said, his bulk casting a long shadow across those still seated outside.

"Oh good," Sam muttered. "Then there will be ten times more next year."

The crowd on the covered walkway started thinning as people fetched drinks inside or went back to their interrupted tasks. The noise from down by the lake intensified briefly before beginning to fade off into silence.

"Want to go see?" Warren asked Darby.

"I'll go if Sam goes," Darby said reluctantly.

"Hah!" Susan laughed. "That's the closest we've ever gotten him to a yes. He's bluffing by the way."

Sam considered for a moment, and then stood. "I call."

"Truly?" Jen asked, her face full of surprise.

"Yeah, I actually do want to see it."

Darby groaned, but fell in behind her as she stepped off the walkway. Jen, Warren, Susan, and a few others hurried behind.

They walked through the gates and headed left, passing between the smithy and the storehouse.

The sight of the lake made Sam stop in her tracks. The spiders spread across its surface like a giant, creeping stain. From a distance they looked almost beautiful, an undulating carpet catching the sun on their glistening bodies as they flowed out into the world. Thousands of them moved with perfect coordination, cutting parallel wakes that shimmered on the smooth waters of Lake Evendiam.

"It's like some kind of dance," Sam said, half in awe and half in horror.

"Pretty much," Jen agreed. "The big finale is that island over there —takes them a while to clear it."

She directed Sam's attention to a tiny landmass just off the shore. Spiders were already swarming its shoreline, splitting into two groups to circumvent obstacles before converging again along the far side and spilling back into the water.

"You weren't kidding," Sam said, "they really don't turn back for anything."

"Not even for you," Darby noted hopefully.

"Oh, they're all yours," she replied. "Say, Calder, will you take the boat out tomorrow?"

The old fisherman shook his head. "No. Always a straggler or two and when they're alone, in this mood, they're dangerous. Scuttle right up the ship's hull and lay into whoever they find." He considered. "Day after should be safe, though. Weather's even."

The sun climbed higher, casting stark shadows over the town as it reached its zenith. The spiders appeared even more frenzied, driven by some mysterious urgency across the lake's reflective expanse. The breeze picked up slightly but did nothing to mar the water's glassy surface or slow the swarm's relentless pace.

"See?" Warren said. "Harmless."

"That's not exactly what I'd call it," Sam said under her breath as they watched in fascination.

Warren grinned his wide ogre grin at her and laughed. "Indifferent, then?"

"Better," Sam admitted grudgingly.

"Well, now we know what to threaten Darby with when he misbehaves next." Susan grinned.

"I didn't even want to come!" Darby protested.

"Looks like you got twice your wish," Jen observed wryly. "You'll get home with no spiders and no Sam!"

Sam shook her head in mock frustration and started making her way back toward town. "I should have known better than to bring you all with me."

"We can leave you behind if you prefer!" Warren called after her.

"They're headed everywhere," she called back over her shoulder, "so I guess nowhere is safe!"

Laughter followed her until she was through the gates once more and had retaken her seat on the walkway. She leaned back against the wall and closed her eyes, letting out a long breath as she listened to the clacking rhythm of thousands upon thousands of legs slowly making their way out of earshot.

"You know, it's funny," Dooley said as he sipped a mug of hot tea that Galhani had provided.

"What's that?" Tyran asked.

"Well, you know I can understand them."

Sam blinked. "Under—you mean, they were... *saying* something?"

Dooley shrugged. "All animals speak. These ones were just saying *Go, go, go, go* over and over and over. But, like, all of them at once, in perfect synchronization. It was like the loudest whisper you've ever heard." He cocked his head. "I can still hear it, a bit."

"Fascinating," Vamir murmured.

"*Hên gond, hên menel*," someone said.

Everyone turned to see Aran standing on the edge of the walkway, his eyes unfocused and staring toward the lake.

"Togo-lîn în-gûl e-Ered.
  Sui raid renia- hae o aegas,
  Rin i vâr, i vellas hen ped."

On the last line, Aran's voice fell to a whisper.

"You know Elvish?" Vamir asked softly when he'd finished.

The old man shook himself and turned to the elf. "What's that?"

"That blessing you just spoke. It was in Elvish."

"Was it? Hmph." Aran turned back to stare at—through—the town gates.

"What did it mean?" Darby asked.

Vamir considered for a moment before speaking.

"Child of stone, child of sky,

> Let mountain wisdom be your guide.
>
> Though paths may wander far from peaks,
>
> Remember home, the strength it speaks."

Vamir cleared his throat. "It's a blessing, of sorts, as I said."

"Of the Mountain Elves," Alred murmured.

Sam raised an eyebrow. "I've never heard of Mountain Elves."

"Extinct, now," Vamir said sadly. "But once there were four races of elves. Forest and Plains, Mountain and Sea."

"I've never heard of Sea Elves, either," Jen said.

"The Mountain Elves were..." Vamir began.

"Hunted," Alred finished quietly. "To extinction."

"And the Sea Elves?" Susan asked.

Vamir shrugged and managed a small smile. "Vanished. Legends say they're still out there, somewhere."

"Oh."

"Where did you hear that blessing, Aran?" Vamir asked.

But the old man gave no indication he'd heard.

seven

. . .

WARREN SLEPT QUIETLY AGAIN that night, undisturbed by unsettling dreams. Susan was a comforting warmth next to him, snuggled tightly to his chest and breathing the deep, easy breaths of someone who is totally at peace.

The next morning, he took a leisurely breakfast with his family at the Weary Head, where Minnie, in a fit of inspiration, had laid on an incredible spread of eggs, roasted vegetables, sharp cheese, and hot, flavorful tea from Galhani's shop. "Full ten," Warren had whispered to his wife.

Satiated and energized, he returned to the smithy, Darby in tow, while Susan stayed behind to help clean up. He pointedly ignored the red-black gauntlet, well aware that its destined owner would likely turn up soon, and instead turned to the task he loved the most: making horseshoes.

It wasn't so much that the town was constantly inundated by shoeless equines, although thrown or damaged shoes were common enough for the travelers along the trade road. It's that Warren welcomed working with simple iron, which was much less opinionated than the ore that came from beneath the smithy. And horseshoes were simple enough that Darby could help—and, now that he was starting to shoot up and put on weight, even try making them himself.

An unconscious grin flitted across Warren's expression as he watched his son. He'd grown at least half a head this past winter, and put on a good bit of weight in his shoulders and chest. His skin was starting to take on a light emerald tint, and the tips of his ears were definitely growing to points—although they were, thankfully, not nearly as long as his father's. *The perfect mix of Susan and me,* Warren mused. *Although hopefully he'll stick more with her as he grows.* A deep-green human boy with long ears wouldn't have an easy time of things in the world.

Darby's face was a mask of concentration, his brow furrowed and his lips pressed into a thin line as he worked the metal over the anvil. Warren held back, mindful of the boy's growing independence, though he watched every swing of the hammer with the gentle vigilance of someone who'd gone through the same motions a thousand times.

"Like this?" Darby asked, holding up a rough, glowing crescent of iron with an eagerness that bordered on impatience.

Warren stepped in and examined it with the air of an expert appraiser. "Mmm. A little long here," he said, pointing to one end. "Just give it another few taps, but you don't want to lose that curve."

Darby nodded and set back to work, his hammer striking down with rhythmic precision. The sound rang out into the morning air, mingling with birdsong and the distant hum of town life. After each blow, he paused to inspect his progress, occasionally glancing up at his father for silent approval.

Warren melted at those glances. "Time to shape it," he offered when Darby seemed satisfied with lengthening and shortening. Darby shifted his grip on the tongs and moved to a smaller anvil, designed more for a gnome or a hobbit than an ogre-sized smith like Warren. He started shaping the shoe to fit a more delicate hoof than they usually saw at North Pointe Common Towne—a palfrey's hoof rather than a draft horse's.

Warren marveled at his son's determination. Most travelers along the trade road had great beasts of burden or hardy riding horses; they rarely saw finer animals like palfreys passing through. But it was good practice, and Warren liked that Darby was willing to try something different even if no one ever bought it.

"Watch your heat," Warren reminded gently as Darby continued shaping.

"I got it!" Darby insisted, dipping the shoe back into the forge until it glowed just right for fine-tuning.

As much as Warren loved teaching him—and loved seeing how natural his son's instinct for iron was—he also loved seeing those flashes of confidence where Darby asserted himself. It was so much like Susan: that quiet strength that settled into certainty.

They worked in companionable silence until finally Darby plunged the shoe into water with a hiss of steam and satisfaction. "How's that?" he asked, holding up his work again.

"Perfect," Warren said with pride swelling in his chest. And then, because too much praise could be its own kind of burden: "Almost as good as mine."

Darby laughed and set down the shoe among their morning's work: sturdy C-shapes big enough to fit ogre feet. The sound warmed Warren from his bones outward; it softened even those parts of him that still felt a raw edge from not having dreamed anything useful last night.

His thoughts drifted back to the gauntlet waiting on its shelf in the smithy. He wondered what manner of person it would bring through their stout wooden gates—and whether they'd have use for a well-made palfrey shoe by way of thanks when they left again.

His ears twitched.

"Someone on the road, Dad?"

"Sounds like it. Let's go see." The *clump-clump* of hooves on the packed earthen road sounded... tense. Hurried. Warren stepped outside and eyed the open gates even as the rattling sound of a cart began echoing ahead of its arrival.

There was a subtle tension in the air. *Not danger*, Warren thought, inhaling deeply and considering the scents. He wasn't the only one who noticed it, though: Minnie had stepped out of the inn, Susan just behind her. The door to the pub open and Sam walked out, blinking in the morning sun and eyeing the gates. Warren turned and saw that even Knodalon had taken notice, turning his shaggy head in their direction.

There: his sharp eyes caught it now, a simple buckboard emerging from the dust. It was pulled by a single horse, who seemed to be on its last legs. Its flanks were slick with foam, and its head was held low. It was still surging forward with every erg of energy it had left, but the poor thing had clearly been hard-pressed. Already, Darby was stepping out in the road, ready to grab the traces.

A man sat on the bench seat. He looked to Warren to be just past middle-aged, with salt-and-pepper hair and weathered skin. He too looked exhausted, his hands holding the reins in a death grip, but his arms slack.

Something made Warren glance behind him again, and he saw Jen standing there, her posture tense.

"Please!" the man bellowed in a hoarse, drawn voice as he pulled through the gates. Darby rushed forward, grabbing the traces and slowing the beleaguered horse. "Please, it's my wife! These spiders, giant red spiders—"

"Dexter," Jen snapped, leaping toward the wagon.

Sam was barely a step behind her as the two of them quickly pulled a woman from the cart. Like her husband, she had salt-and-pepper hair pulled back into what had once been a neat tail, but was now a tangled mess. Her face was a ghastly white, sheened with sweat. They laid her gently on the road.

Dexter, the town chirurgeon, had always been oddly attuned to his name. He arrived just as the Jen and Sam were lowering the woman to the ground, appearing seemingly out of nowhere and accompanied by a light gust of wind. He knelt, leaning over the woman. "Venom," he said in a low voice. He began rummaging through the black leather bag he seemed to always carry, quickly withdrawing a vial full of an inky-red fluid. He reached under the woman's head, tilting it back a bit so that he jaw fell open slightly, and then poured the contents of the vial down her throat. "I always have some ready this time of year," he murmured, watching the woman carefully.

"They ran right over us," the man said as he clambered down from the cart. Darby was already unhitching the horse. "It was a nightmare. They—"

"Happens this time of year," Jen said, standing and helping the man down. He was trembling like a leaf in a gale.

"She'll be fine," Dexter said. Indeed, the woman's face had already regained a trace of color, and her breathing seemed easier. He looked up, his sharp features a contrast of light and shadow in the late-morning sun. "She'll do better in my office."

Warren leaned down, easily scooping the woman up.

"Easy," Jen said. The old man obviously hadn't noticed Warren until the ogre picked up his wife. "He's a good man. She'll be fine."

The man's jaw worked silently as Jen and Sam supported him. Minnie was hurrying back out of the inn, having gone in for a cup of hot tea, which she now offered the man. Darby was leading the horse into the stable yard, where buckets of cool water awaited the poor animal.

Warren hurried after Dexter, past the pub and the backs of the town homes, through the town gates, and into the chirurgery tucked just inside the town's stone wall. Warren ducked through the narrow doorway and detected a sudden change as they entered. He paused for a moment, readjusting to the cool, dim interior. The air was still and quiet, as if holding its breath, and the only sound was the soft shuffle of Dexter moving ahead to clear a space on one of the low wooden cots along the far wall. Sunlight filtered through a small window, casting soft shadows over shelves neatly lined with jars and vials. It was peaceful in an immediate way that eased even Warren's hurried pulse, like stepping out of chaos into calm.

"Here," Dexter said gently, motioning to an empty cot draped with a clean linen sheet. Warren placed the woman down carefully; her eyes fluttered open for a moment before closing again. He stepped back to allow Dexter room, watching as the chirurgeon checked her pulse with long, delicate fingers.

Warren noted how quiet it was here compared to the bustle outside. He knew this peace was part of what made the place special, part of its gift along with easing pain: that sense of well-being that helped healing along its way.

"I'll make something more potent," Dexter said absently, already turning toward his shelves and gathering supplies.

Warren nodded, glad for the man's focus and skill. "You need anything else?" he asked.

Dexter shook his head without looking up, busy mixing ingredients with practiced precision.

Warren stood for another moment before slipping back out into the sunlight. The tension from earlier had begun to dissolve like mist under a warm sun: Minnie buzzed around the woman's husband, while Sam and Jen had each taken an elbow and were leading him into the pub. Their horse was already gulping water from a pail, and Warren noted with satisfaction that Darby was monitoring the beast to keep it from making itself sick. With a sigh, he realized he'd have to move the cart out of the road.

The back of the cart was packed with neatly made wooden crates, all carefully stacked. The two must have planned to take turns driving and resting, for the narrow area where the sick woman had lain was set up as a pallet of sorts, with soft blankets to ease the jostling ride. Warren considered, and decided to push the thing from behind. With a grunt, he got it into motion, and by leaning hard into one side managed to get the thing to turn. He pushed it just off the road, along the fence that defined the stable yard, before wiping his hands and turning to the pub.

Jen and the man were seated at one of the sturdy trestle tables inside, while Sam was fussing behind the bar. At Warren't entrance, the man's eyes flew wide again.

"Easy," Jen said. "He's a friend."

"Ogre no eat nice man," Warren said calmly, reminding himself not to smile.

The man's eyebrows beetled together.

"Not the right time for jokes, Warren," Jen sighed.

"Sorry. You okay, sir?"

"Meh—me?" the man stammered.

"You. My name's Warren. What's yours?" The ogre pulled a sturdy chair away form the wall near the door—a chair he'd made himself, to avoid stressing the tables and benches in the pub—and eased into it. "That's my son, Darby, out there with your horse. She'll be fine."

"Wilem," he said after a moment. "Cyntia is my wife."

"Your wife will also be fine," Warren assured him. "Dexter's the best there is. She's already looking better."

"When can I see her?"

"Dexter will let us know," Sam said, easing a mug of ale onto the table in front of Wilem. "He works best when he's got quiet, though, so we'll leave him to it."

"The spiders," Wilem said with a shudder.

"Yeah," Sam said, nodding emphatically as she sat next to Wilem. "Tell me about it. I'd hate to have been caught on the road when a swarm came down."

"You're welcome to stay in town for as long as you need," Jen assured him. "In fact, we can put you up in one of the empty homes inside the walls, if you'd prefer. Make you both a bit more comfortable until you're ready to move on."

Sam leaned back and gave Jen a sharp look over Wilem's back, shaking her head slightly.

Warren's eyebrows rose, and he resisted the urge to glance back at the clock-like contraption that hung over the pub's door. It helped Sam understand a traveler's destiny, and Warren had a sudden, uneasy feeling that this Wilem and his wife *had* a destiny.

Jen blinked and stammered a bit before continuing. "And of course we'll make sure you're both—you know. We have plenty of food, I mean."

Warren almost snickered at the constable's uncharacteristic stumble.

"There's no problem getting you into one of the houses," Sam said, earning a black look from Jen. "Can we help unload your things?"

Wilem was just staring at the mug of ale.

"Wilem," Warren said gently, leaning forward. The man's head snapped up. "Cyntia is going to be *fine*. This happens every couple of years or so, someone gets caught in a swarm and gets stung. Dexter's used to dealing with it. Jen, when was the last time? Three, maybe four years?"

"Three," Jen confirmed. Then she grinned. "It was a band of high-waymen, remember? I'm not saying Dexter took his time with them or anything, but we certainly sent them on their way as soon as they could walk."

"And they were fine," Warren prompted.

"Oh, aye. Nothing more wrong with them that a good stew and a night's rest wouldn't cure. Your Cyntia will probably be up and about for dinner, in fact. Although we do welcome you to stay to make sure she's fully healed."

"Where were you heading to?" Sam asked, her eyes flicking toward the door.

"Don't know," Wilem sighed, finally taking a sip of ale. "We were more heading *away*."

"From?" Jen asked.

"The East," he said, shaking his head sadly. "We had quite a busi-ness just east of Magefell, a little town called Threadneedle. We are—were—cartwrights."

"Let me guess," Sam said quietly. "Rosefruit towns?"

"Aye," he said heavily. "But it's been so peaceful for so long, we just figured... well. Old Baggum was a good leader, took after his father. But his son... no strength to the boy, and he'd developed a habit for strong drink and gambling. Got himself killed, and that's when it started."

"The fighting," Jen said flatly.

"So much of it," Wilem said, taking a longer swallow of ale. "At first, we thought the town miller, Calum, would take charge, but this horror of a man from out past Holderdown rode in one night. Killed Calum and his whole family." He shook his head again. "That's when Cyntia and I decided we would leave. No children to worry about, so we packed up that night and left at first light."

"You're safe here," Sam said firmly, putting a hand on his forearm. "And you can stay for as long as you like."

"We've money—"

"Absolutely not," Sam insisted before anyone else could speak up. "Folks along the Mistrals care for one another, when we can. And we can. If someone comes in with a busted wheel on their wagon, you can return the favor."

Wilem's eyes had moistened. "Thank you."

"Ahem."

Warren turned as everyone else's eyes snapped to the door. Dexter stood there, silhouetted by the bright sun that had just climbed near its zenith. "Your wife is doing well, sir," he said in his cool, hollow voice. "She is sleeping peacefully. I suggest we leave her to rest for a few hours at least. I've spoken to Galhani about a restorative tincture when she wakes."

The tears were running hot down Wilem's face now. "Thank you, sir," he said, his voice cracking a bit. "I can't repay you enough—"

"I don't accept money in any regard," Dexter breathed. He gave a quick nod to everyone in the pub, and then slipped away.

Wilem took a moment to regain his composure and wiped his eyes. "I know it's an imposition," he began, "but I find that I'm near the end of my own strength at the moment. Could—"

"Let's get you into the inn," Sam said, rising and helping Wilem up. "We'll need to clean out one of the empty homes anyway, and I'm sure you could use the nap. Come." She led him out the door, turning left toward the inn's entrance.

"She's sensed something," Jen said quietly as the two left.

"I figured as much," Warren said. "Reckon those two stay?"

Jen blinked a couple of times. "I hadn't thought—ah. I'd said, 'until you're ready to move on.' That's when she shot those daggers out of her eyes." The old constable smiled. "Might be that's what she's picked up."

"We are short a shop."

"For the icosahedron, yes. So perhaps." Last summer, they'd all learned that North Pointe Common Towne could only be fully functional, in possession of its gifts and powers, with exactly twenty shops open for business. With the dryads gone, they were down to nineteen.

"We could use a cartwright here."

Jen arched an eyebrow. "Go help your boy with that poor horse."

Warren chuckled as he stood, pushed his chair back against the wall, and stepped out into the noonday light.

As he walked across the trade road to the stable, he noticed Aran, standing at the gates to the town proper. The old man stared keenly at the ogre before nodding once and stepping back into the town square.

eight

. . .

WARREN STARED at the closed doors of the smithy, an unfamiliar anxiety crawling up and down his spine. He'd slept fitfully, but not because of the Forge Dreams. No, he'd simply tossed and turned, woken up and fallen back asleep, pushed the covers off and pulled them up again. He'd been blearily aware of Susan leaving sometime in the middle of the night, retreating to the tiny sitting room at the front of the town home, but rather than say anything he'd simply relapsed into a half-slumber filled with unease.

The first dim, drab rays of sunlight had finally managed to penetrate the small window in the bedroom, and he'd gratefully hauled himself out of bed, stripped the bed of its sweat-soaked, rumpled sheets, remade the bed with fresh linens, and eased quietly out of the house. Susan was still snoring lightly in the sitting room, and he managed to latch the front door silently behind him.

"Dad?"

Warren started, and turned to see Darby standing next to him, rubbing one still-sleepy eye with a closed fist. His hair—tousled on the best of days—was completely mussed. "You sleep okay, kiddo?"

His son shrugged.

"I keep you up?"

"Maybe a little."

"Hmm."

"Another dream?"

"No. Just... couldn't sleep, I guess."

"We going to make horseshoes?"

No. The feeling came to Warren hard and fast, as the vague dread that had been worrying at his guts came into sharper focus. "No. No, I think... we should inventory the place."

"You need some of the ore brought up?"

Warren hesitated long enough for a stab of restlessness to knot his guts. "Yeah, I think we should."

"Okay."

Darby swung open the doors, and cool morning air rattled through the smithy. Warren followed, feeling the slight chill against his skin. The forge was black, still breathing out warmth from yesterday's work but not yet stoked for today's.

"Let's start with what we've got in stock," Warren said, trying to keep the wobble of urgency out of his voice. Darby nodded, already moving toward the corner where iron bars were stacked like firewood.

Warren grabbed a thick ledger and a charred stub of charcoal. "Good stock or scrap?" he asked as Darby hefted a bundle of bars.

"Good," Darby replied, with the certainty that only an eleven-year-old could muster.

Warren made a tally mark. Darby set the bars back down with a clang that rattled Warren's teeth. More marks followed: good, scrap, good... Warren's mind buzzed through the inventory as they made their way through raw iron stock, tools hanging along the walls, half-finished projects from before his dreams had started coming with such frequency.

"Anvils next?" Darby asked when Warren seemed to hesitate.

"Yes." Warren moved to a pair of anvils he'd made a year ago; they had been too large and too heavy for anyone to buy. His own work-bench was built out of three others.

Darby heaved at one end, and Warren steadied him with a hand on his shoulder. "Careful there."

Darby grinned at him from beneath the weight.

They cleared off bins of rivets. Buckles. Hinges and latches and hooks and spikes. They set aside a stack of iron bands and hoops, counted shield and sword blanks, and carefully moved stacks of unused hammers. "How many hammers you need anyway?" Darby asked. Warren chuckled, the knot in his stomach loosening.

"Depends how many arms you got," he said.

The corner of Darby's mouth twitched up in a crooked smile as he scribbled another tally: eight hammers, two arms. "What about these?" he asked, pointing at a row of metal helms, some polished to a dull sheen, others still rough.

Warren squinted playfully. "I'd say... dragon helmets."

"That's not even a thing."

"Not here." Warren tapped the side of his nose with one thick finger. He added helmets to their list and looked around the smithy, now strewn with supplies like an ironmonger's dream. The air was still cool but growing warmer now, less heavy with worry.

Darby pushed an errant lock of hair out of his eyes and reached for another bundle of bars, his sleeves slipping up to reveal wrists that seemed thicker than they'd been just last week. A twinge—something between pride and apprehension—tugged at Warren's heart before melting away into a softer feeling of contentment.

"So what are we going to make?" Darby asked again.

"Good question." Warren wiped charcoal dust from his hands onto his apron, thoughtful lines creasing his forehead but not his voice this time. "Guess we'll start when we know."

"That's never stopped you before," Darby said.

"True, I—"

"You two skipping breakfast?"

Father and son turned to see Susan standing in the doorway, a wide grin on her face and the morning sun spilling around her.

"Didn't realize how late it had got," Warren admitted sheepishly. His stomach growled—this time the honest grumble of an empty gut, and not the churning anxiety he'd suffered with all night. "What's on?"

"Minnie's preoccupied with Wilem. Bread and cheese in the pub. Galahani's brought tea, and Makota has a basket of pas—whoa!" At the start of the word *pastries*, Darby had bolted past her, grinning madly. "Pastries," she finished with a chuckle. "And Dardrad's promised grilled venison for dinner tonight."

"Town cookout?" Warren asked with a smile as he let Susan lead him across the street.

"Sounds like it. Cole says he's going to break out the last of the—oh."

Warren's ears, perhaps duller for not having slept much the night prior, had still alerted him and he was already staring toward the East gate. A rider on a brown horse was coming in at a hard gallop, leaned over low against the animal's neck, her hands—

One hand, shrouded in a gauntlet, gripped her mount's reins with iron resolve, while her other hand, bare, was held tight against her armored abdomen. Its gauntlet must have been lost or shattered.

"Go on in," Warren told his wife in a low voice. "Send Jen out, if she's in there."

Susan complied immediately, hurrying into the pub. The constable stepped out a moment later, looking first at Warren and then following his gaze toward the gate. She reached behind her and pulled the pub's door closed. "Big dumb ogre?" she asked in a low voice as the newcomer pounded to a halt in front of the stable yard.

Warren simply nodded.

"Ho, traveler," Jen called, stepping in front of Warren as the woman dismounted.

She ignored the constable, looking wildly from left to right until her gaze settled on the smithy. Then her head whipped back to the two townsfolk. "I... don't know why I've come. Or I mean, I do, but I don't know why *here*. You have a blacksmith?" She jerked her head toward the smithy.

"Aye," Jen said calmly. "And we're happy to help you. Provided you've come in peace and mean to stay and leave that way."

The woman exhaled heavily. "Yes, yes, of course. *Peace* is all I've been looking for these past fortnights. Please, can you call your black-smith? And, is there someone who could care for my horse?"

"Warren," the ogre rumbled, nodding. "I'm the smith here. Darb!"

he called. He waited a moment until the pub door swung open and his son's head poked out. "Take the lady's horse."

"Thank you," the woman said as Darby darted over to lead the horse to water. The cartwrights' horse eyed it warily, moving to the far end of the yard as the heavy beast began steadily gulping water from a stone trough. "My name is Lydia. I've ridden hard from the Skyreaches. There's... trouble."

"We've heard," Jen said with a cautious nod. "Rosefruit towns all in disruption, no?"

"That and more. It's different this time." Lydia looked down at herself, made a halfhearted attempt to brush some of the thick road dust from her riding leathers, and then looked back up with a sheepish grin. "Now that I'm here, is there someplace I can clean up? Maybe get a bite to eat? I've coin."

"In what order?" Warren asked.

"The food first, honestly." She looked toward the pub and nodded at the trestle table situated out front. "I can stay outside so as to not—"

"Nonsense," Jen said. "It's simple this morning, but we've plenty. Step right this way."

Warren cocked an eyebrow. *Ah,* he realized at once. *She wants Sam to get a reading on her. Fair enough.* He turned the other way, striding quickly to the smithy and walking to the side table where the lone gauntlet lay. Now that he'd seen the original in person, he was more pleased with his work. It was a true twin to the first.

"Dad?" Darby asked, stepping in from the yard.

"Stay clear 'til we're sure, son."

"Is this the gauntlet?"

"Yeah."

"Okay. I'll go help—"

"See if Minnie needs any help with Wilem. As far as I know he slept all day and through the night—if he's ready to move into one of the homes, he'll need help unloading their boxes."

"Okay. And the lady?"

"No word from Dexter yet."

Darby rushed off without another word.

Warren stared at the gauntlet for a while longer, letting the glow of the red-orange material mesmerize him. He shook himself when another voice interrupted him.

"That healer of yours."

It was Aran, his expression both tight and thoughtful.

"Chirurgeon," Warren corrected.

"Known him long?"

"As long as I've lived here."

Aran's face twisted for a moment, and then relaxed as his eyes seemed to glaze over. "Foxes in the middens!" he exclaimed sharply. "Buggerit!" He spun on one heel, flapping his arms loosely at his sides as he stalked away.

"Okay," Warren muttered.

He stood quietly for a while before walking back out of the smithy.

"Morning, Warren!" Minnie waved from across the road, clearly making for the pub.

"Morning, Minnie," he called back. "Darby come see you?"

"Aye, I've got him airing out one of the empties. Cleaned it up last night, didn't need much more than a dusting."

Warren strode across the road. "How's Wilem?"

"Fine, fine. Dexter says he'll bring the wife to the house once it's ready. Says she'll mostly sleep a day or two, but we're to keep her fed and watered." She lowered her voice to a conspiring whisper. "Sam says they're meant for here, and I think he had the dream last night." The inn's gift: Spend a night under its roof and it would send you dreams of your destiny. "Not sure he's convinced, though."

"We've got a few days for them to come around, if that's their destiny. Darb can help unload their crates, too," Warren offered.

"Oh, good. Trevor's starting to get the vibe, you know, and we both think there'll be crowds due through in the next day or two. He's beside himself checking the supplies."

"He's not the only one," Warren murmured darkly.

"Hmm?"

"Nothing, nothing. Let's go in."

The Broken Claw was bustling. A long, battered bar ran the length of one wall, with trestle tables scattered across the room. They were well-worn but scrubbed clean, and they echoed with the sounds of cutlery against plates and soft laughter into mugs of hot tea. Sam dashed from table to table, refilling tea and platters. Galahani and Makota sat together near the hearth, their backs to the fire that staved off the morning chill, while Cole poured himself more tea at a low table close by.

"It's not just the rosefruit towns," Lydia was saying, her voice low but intense. "They've reached as far south as the Silvering settlements."

"Farms burning?" Cole asked, his eyes bright with curiosity.

"Some," Lydia admitted. "But more often they just collapse in on themselves. Like they were built on quicksand."

"That's strange," Susan said around a mouthful of cheese. She swallowed and continued: "There's been nothing like that up this way."

"Yet," Jen added pointedly.

"Some of the would-be barons," Lydia said softly, giving Warren a hard glance as he pulled his chair away from the wall and nearer to a table, "have enlisted the ogres of the Skyreaches."

So she was *pursued*, Warren thought. "More than a few ogre young take jobs as mercs and more," he said easily, nodding thanks as Sam set a plate of food and a mug of tea in front of him. "Considered it myself, for a while, until I met that lady there." Susan dimpled.

Lydia blinked, and then frowned in confusion, but said nothing.

"So how bad is it, exactly?" Jen asked.

"You're likely to get a lot more custom," Lydia said with a sigh. "Whole towns emptying out, people scattering as far and wide as they can. Looking for somewhere that'll take them in, let them start over. Most are staying, to be sure. The bigger towns are seeing a lot less fighting."

"And where were you heading?" Sam asked, taking up her position behind the bar and polishing a mug.

"Here. Although I don't know why." Lydia's voice was heavy with frustration. "I... I'm not proud, but I gave a coin to a fortune-teller, of sorts. She said I'd find... *it*. Here."

"A fortune-teller sent you to North Pointe Common Towne specifically?" Galhani asked from by the fire. "Well, aren't we getting famous!"

Jen's expression hardened.

"Yes, but... I don't know why I even listened. The orges found me not long after, and I just—rode."

"The gauntlet is done," Warren said quietly.

A hush fell over the room as Lydia stared at him.

"I can take you to see it," he offered.

"Impossible," she whispered, but she rose almost without conscious thought.

"Save me some of this cheese, Sam," Warren said as he rose.

"Leave the chair," Jen told him.

"Appreciate it." He strode out of the pub, Lydia trailing in his wake.

Darby was there, pulling a crate from the cartwrights' wagon. He caught sight of his father's expression and paused, waiting until the two adults had passed before hurrying toward the town gates with his burden.

"How could you possibly have known—" Lydia began as they stepped into the smithy.

"I get dreams," Warren replied. "It's there." He nodded to the gauntlet.

Lydia walked toward it slow, as if in a dream. She stared at it for several long moments before reaching out to touch it with a single finger, pulling back sharply when it didn't... vanish? Give her some kind of magical shock? Warren wasn't sure what she'd been expecting.

She'd removed her other gauntlet to eat, but now detached it from where it hung from her belt, pulling it on with the speed of long practice. Then she reached for the other, hesitantly at first, but with growing confidence as she slipped it onto her bare hand.

It fit perfectly.

"How?" she breathed.

Warren simply shrugged.

She turned to him. "What do I owe you?"

"Nothing." The answer came to him all at once, as it always did. "You're going to ride back, aren't you?"

"Yes."

"Will it hurt to wait a night?"

She frowned. "Why?"

"Your horse. He's spent."

Her eyes widened. "Oh. Yes. Yes, of course."

"We'll feed him, clean him up."

"Yes. Yes, thank you."

"It's three coppers for the horse and a room at the inn. Five with meals."

She blinked rapidly. "Yes, of course, she repeated. "But the gauntlet..."

Warren shrugged again, his massive shoulders nearly stirring the still air of the smithy. "I don't set the prices on special commissions."

"I see."

"Can I ask you a question?"

"Yes."

"What do they do?"

Something about her posture, her entire bearing, changed in an instant. She went from a tired horsewoman who'd ridden hard to flee attackers—*ogres!*—to someone that Warren profoundly believed might be royalty. "They've been in my family for generations. But my father had no son. He was the headman of Little Neck, a bit south of Holderdown. He was... killed." She looked around. "Is there a path to the lake?"

"Sure." Warren turned out of the smithy, and Lydia hurried to follow. The smithy actually sat right on the edge of the lake, not a dozen strides from where the water lapped gently against the rocky shore.

Lydia stepped right to that edge and stood tall, her feet at shoulder width and her back straight as a new pike. She held her gauntleted hands in front of her, closed them into fists, and banged them together —exactly as Warren had seen her attempt in his dream.

Something cut a furrow into the lake. It started just past her feet, slicing the height of a full-grown man into the calm waters, frothing a tall wave on either side and stretching almost instantly to the horizon.

Warren took a step back as Lydia turned. "They're called the Hands of Fate. They can do much more. Protect me. Protect the people of Littleneck. But one of them was stolen when my father was killed. I expect they thought they'd gotten both, but we never kept them together. The other one was destroyed. I... felt it. I knew." She shook her head. "How is it possible to made another?"

"We're... special, here," Warren admitted.

"I can't thank you enough. Not ever. This will help me free my people."

"It sounds like you'll have a lot of fights to keep them free."

"I may. And we may simply leave, once they're out from under the thumb of whatever war-baron has the town today."

"Just leave?"

"We're a people together. It doesn't matter where that is."

"I see. You know—"

He was interrupted by screaming.

The screams of children.

nine

. . .

WARREN DASHED TOWARD THE ROAD, Lydia hot on his heels. Everyone left in the pub had spilled into the road as well, and were rushing toward the town gates.

Ogres were built for endurance rather than than speed; the feline Makota quickly pulled ahead of the group while Warren found himself pounding along at the back, next to the diminutive Galhani, whose legs were moving even faster than Makota's but simply not carrying her as far with each step.

When he arrived at the gate a moment behind everyone else, his height let him see over everyone's heads.

The town's children, who'd obviously been playing an energetic ball game on the grassy square, had swiftly retreated to the safety of the covered walkways. Their laughter and shouts were suddenly replaced by a tense silence. Adults emerged hastily from their shops and homes, their expressions a mix of urgency and determination. They quickly shepherded the little ones indoors, or stood protectively in front of them, forming a barrier between the children and whatever unseen threat had caused such a rapid change in the atmosphere.

Oddly, Aran was there, standing in front of his borrowed home, arms crossed and looking curiously at the square. Wilem had also stepped out at the noise, and was standing in his open doorway, a look of horror on his face.

It took Warren a moment to spot it, and when he did his blood ran cold.

It was one of the giant spiders, its abdomen a dull red, crouched in the middle of the square. Warren's brain had at first mistaken it one of the kids' balls, but as he watched it moved in a slow pirouette, its stick-thin legs rustling eerily along its carapace as it spun.

"I got it," Warren said cooly, pushing through the others.

"Warren!" Susan gasped.

"I'll be fine." He suspected he would be: ogre skin was legendarily thick and dense; even ferocious dire cats could do little more than scratch him. And while he wasn't as quick as one of these spiders, he'd only need to land a single blow to squash it.

He *hated* gore.

"Leota!" Jen called.

Warren looked to see the town witch, young but frail, standing in front of her own doorway. But she was shaking her head. "It's natural and it's native," she called back. "The defenses won't do anything about it, any more than they would the whole swarm."

Someone—Warren thought it might have been Aran—snorted with what sounded like derision.

"Wait!"

Warren looked back. Dooley and Ella had emerged from their shop at the first sound of screaming, and now Dooley was edging off the walkway and onto the grass. The spider turned instantly, lowering itself further to the ground as its spindly legs tensed for a jump.

"Dooley, don't!" someone cried.

"Just wait!" the man called back. He took another step forward and the spider chittered threateningly, sending chills up Warren's spine.

"Höhvaktar! Skjalde uns vor dem Dunkelzorn! Mögen eure Lichtstrahlen die Schatten brechen!"

That was from Wilem. Warren didn't understand the words, but thought they sounded a bit like the tongue of Stormport, far to the West past the Demonbane Range.

"Just wait!" Dooley repeated. Then, he lowered his voice and seemed to address the spider directly. "We're not going to hurt you. Not if you don't hurt us. You're injured, aren't you? Or... different?"

The spider skittered backward a bit, and Warren realized it was moving unevenly. One of its legs didn't move properly—it was shorter than the rest. *That's why it fell behind the rest of the swarm,* he thought.

The spider chittered again.

"We have a saying here," Dooley continued, moving more easily now as he took another step forward. "Come in peace, stay in peace, leave in peace. You've harmed nobody here, so we can call that coming in peace. If you want to leave, we'll let you." He looked up at the crowd blocking the gates, and everyone quickly moved to one side or the other, leaving Warren standing in the middle of the wide opening. "And if you want to stay in peace, we'll have you."

Wilem made a choking sound. Someone—again, Warren thought it sounded like Aran—started humming.

The spider pivoted first to its left, and then to its right, as if surveying the scene. It chittered again.

"I know. But you're on your own, and you're not going to survive the lake, if you'll pardon me saying so."

He's actually talking to it, Warren thought. He'd understood that to be the menagerie shop's gift, but this wasn't some cuddly bird-creature out of the Mistrals. This was a deadly, venomous—

More chittering.

"With me. Although Knodalon might welcome you in the storehouse now and then. He lost his cat over the winter and the vermin aren't completely cowed."

Chittering.

"Yes, of course. We don't suffer much from voles and the like, but there's ample hunting in the foothills."

Chittering.

"You can leave at any time, yes."

Chittering.

"It will take some time for everyone to get used to you. We do have a... visitor who was hurt by your kin. On the road. Caught in the swarm."

Loud chittering.

"Oh, we know. Wrong place, wrong time. It was an accident. There's no blame to lay."

More choking noises from Wilem.

More chittering.

"Very well. Would you like to come inside and meet everyone, then?"

The spider stood rock-still for a long moment, and then took one or two tentative steps forward. Its body twisted left and right, as if assessing the threat from the nearby townsfolk.

"Here," Dooley offered. He turned, walked casually back to his door, and pushed it open. He stood to one side.

Again, the spider seemed to freeze while it considered, and then it dashed forward with a speed Warren wouldn't have credited. It darted in a crooked line due to its one short leg, but it was inside the menagerie in an eyeblink.

"I'll introduce you all later, once everyone's had a moment to calm down," Dooley said, smiling as he stepped inside his shop and pushed the door closed behind him.

"What," Jen breathed to Warren's left, "in the name of the little gods just happened."

"I believe Dooley made friends with a venomous mountain spider," Vamir said, stepping off the walkway to stand next to Jen.

"Unbelievable." The constable shook her head, but Warren thought he detected a hint of admiration in her tone.

Everyone was moving toward the west of the gates, including the few older children who hadn't been rushed inside.

"Wilem," Vamir said, nodding a greeting to the cartwright. "We haven't met, yet. I'm Vamir. I run the bookshop, and have the honor to teach our children."

Wilem nodded, but his face was almost gray with fright and stress.

"May I ask—was that Stormtongue you spoke? It sounded like a Call to the Watchers."

Wilem blinked a couple of times. "You know Stormtongue?"

"Oh, languages are a hobby. My people have a similar saying—*Ai Laegthiriel! Varyamen o Lómorn! Nai calanar lya i gwathrim terhata.*" Everyone gave Vamir a blank stare. "It translates to... oh, roughly something like, 'Oh Green-Guardians! Shield us from the Gloom-Wraith! May your beams of light shatter the shadows.'"

"Exalted Watchers! Shield us from the Dark-Wraith! May your light-rays break the shadows!" Wilem murmured his own translation.

Vamir's smile widened. "Yes, very close. My people originally settled the foothills of the Demonbanes when they came to this continent. And I'm pretty sure we picked up the notion of the 'Dark-Wraith' from the Stormporters."

"My family came from Stormport, generations ago. They crossed the Demonbanes to escape the constant turmoil, back when settling east of here was safe." Wilem shook his head. "I'm sorry, but who was that man who just invited the *krasnagornik* into his home?"

"That was Dooley," Sam put in. "He and his wife Ella run the menagerie. He can..." She paused, and looked at the assembled crowd, especially Lydia. "Well," she said, noting the gauntlets on her hands, "I supposed it's no secret that we've been given some... gifts, here. Being able to understand animals is Dooley's."

"Gifts," Lydia breathed, looking at Warren.

"We'd very much appreciate that not getting out," Jen said cooly.

"No, no. Of course," Lydia said. "I'll... I should see to Charger. My horse." She slipped through the crowd.

"I know your wife was hurt by one of them," Vamir said, "but they really do tend to keep to themselves apart from the spring swarms. You really were just in the wrong place at the wrong time." He tilted his head. "I may not help to say this, but if they'd actually attacked you, neither of you would be here."

"And your wife is already healed." Everyone turned to see Dexter standing in his doorway, his soft, chill voice drifting to them in the still late-morning air. "Another night's rest and you'll be ready to move on."

"If you choose to move on," Sam put in quickly, giving Dexter a glare.

"I..." Wilem began. He stopped, and swallowed heavily. "We spoke, just now. We wanted to inquire what it could cost to... perhaps stay longer. To rent this home we're in. We could perhaps rent some space in the stable yard, I could work on carts, we assume surely travelers must come through with some damage, and perhaps—"

"To be clear," Warren said, his deep, gravelly voice cutting through before anyone else could reply, "we don't rent things to each other here. Or charge each other, either. We're a family as much as a town. And to be clearer, I've always been terrible at repairing carts. Your skills would be welcome."

Wilem blinked a few more times. "That's... but then there's the *krasnagornik.*"

"Do you know what they're called in Elgindam?" Vamir asked.

Wilem shook his head.

"*Skarnúlfr,*" the elf said. "It means 'Saving Knives.'"

"I don't... you said Elgindam?" Wilem asked.

"Yes. It's far to the east, on the coast, through a pass where the Mistrals meet the Skyreaches. You see, one of the biggest threats Elgindam faces every year is from rodents who push through the town in enormous masses, descending from the foothills when the spring rains begin. The *Skarnúlfr* swarm after them, paralyzing them and carrying them back to their burrows in the mountains. The residents of Elgindam prepare well in advance, and the spiders are well-known for not attacking humans—provided they stay out of the way."

"Oh."

"Just south of Lake Evendiam," Vamir continued, "there is an ancient volcano caldera. Dormant for ages, but still hot. It's believed that's where the spiders go each spring. In a sort of mating frenzy, if you will."

"Really," Dardrad murmured.

"We would love to have you," Sam pleaded.

"If," Jen added, "you can be at peace with the spider who apparently lives here now."

"I doubt we'll see much of it," Vamir put in.

"I..." Once again, warm tears began trickling down Wilem's cheek. "You are too generous."

Aran *harummphed.*

"But," Wilem said, slowly meeting each of their eyes, "what is to be our gift?"

"The gifts are an obligation," Jen warned. "We serve all. *All.* Our gifts are for everyone who follows the rules: Come in peace, stay in peace, leave in peace."

Aran *harummphed* again.

"And I don't think we've had a cartwright here that anyone remembers," Cole said. "So it's hard to tell what your gift will be. Or what obligations it will bring."

"Also, we are not so generous," Dardrad said in his rough voice, although there was a hint of a smile beneath his thick black beard. "I'm going to make you tend the fire for tonight's dinner."

"Well then," Wilem said, his voice quavering just a bit. "I suppose I should let my wife know."

————

Nearly everyone turned out for the cookout—save for Lydia, who proclaimed herself too tired and eager to get a start at first light. Darby ensured her horse was comfortable in the stable, and then joined the rest of the town in the square.

Everyone contributed to these events: Minnie took charge of cooking up sides on a wood-fired planchette set up specifically for the evening. She stirred pots of beans, pans of greens, and trays of root vegetables, liberally basting the latter with a savory sauce she and Galhani had concocted. Alred and Tyran set up most of the tables and cooking areas, drawing from the goods in their stores, while Cole had brought out the last of the winter's dried fruits and vegetables, soaking them in a succulent butter sauce to soften them before adding them to Minnie's grill.

Makota, of course, had produced trays and trays of fresh brown bread, curly pastries, and fruit-filled tarts for dessert—tarts she and her mate were laughingly protecting from the town's children. "After your dinner, dears," they chuckled as child after child tried to wheedle an early treat from them.

Dardrad had the crown jewel of the event, of course, with fresh venison he'd only hung and butchered a couple of days before. Thick-cut filets, marbled steaks, and small chunks of marinated meat more suitable for the smaller children all sizzled merrily on a grill, while Wilem—as promised—kept the fire beneath stoked and fed. A second grill, kept at a lower heat by Wilem, featured fresh and salted fish brought in my Calder and his family.

Dooley's contribution was to keep the children occupied, with a quartet of fluff-covered ambulatory balls he called Snow Burrows. They were covered in deep, white fur, and could easily have vanished into a snowbank with no effort and no discomfort from the cold. Here in the grassy square, they stood out sharply, and chirped and squealed as they chased the children in a mad game of tag.

Barnaba, proprietor of the map shop, had turned out to be a deft hand with flavorful cocktails, and so he and Sam were busily making up bright-tasting drinks, with the help of several tart syrups Galhani had prepared. One, made with clearspirit, tartroot, mint, and muddled zofruit, had proven to be especially popular with the adults, and Sam had resorted to mixing the stuff by the pitcher.

Prudence had brought out a set of fresh table linens she'd made to while away the quiet winter hours, while Lucy produced a new set of plates and bowls that had occupied her time over the season.

Vamir was a bit at loose ends, given that everyone already had their recipes memorized, and so he busied himself flitting from grill to grill, helping where he could, and helping Trevor set the trestle tables that had been carried into the square. Galhani trailed after him, replenishing supplies of herbs and spices for the cooks.

Leota managed to slowly make her way to one of the tables, smiling gently and chatting with anyone who came near. She'd spent her magic putting a bubble of gentle warmth over the entire square, taking the edge off the chill evening air.

Jen presided over it all, wandering the perimeter of the square and chatting up the adults. Even Knodalon had left his bench in front of the storehouse to take up a position at one of the trestle tables, smiling gently at the children's antics. Only Dexter failed to put in an appearance, but he rarely turned out for community gatherings, solitary as he was.

Aran pulled a chair out of his town home, and sat in front of his door, arms crossed and a vague scowl on his face. Jen had made an attempt to engage him in conversation, but she'd elicited no response and only deepened his frown, so she left off. Whether he'd eventually partake of the community meal was up to him.

Aran aside, the atmosphere was one of gentle joviality, a welcome respite from the day to day business of the town, and a chance to spend some time in the fresh air as a large, extended family. But beneath it all ran a tight current of nervous anticipation. Most of the adults hid it well, having grown used to it over the years, but Trevor and Wilem—both new to the sensation—showed it in the tension of their shoulders. Wilem at least likely didn't know the cause, and might have attributed it to worry for his wife, who had emerged from their town home and seated herself next to Leota. But the real cause was upcoming business: every shop owner could sense the town's expectation of incoming travelers, and it felt like it would be a lot of them.

"Let's go, then!" Dardrad called, turning the steaks and chops with his stubby fingers before nodding to Wilem. "Kid! Get the sauce on these and we'll be ready!"

Trevor, startled by being addressed as 'kid,' was slow to react. He gathered his wits a moment later, though, and rushed to Minnie's cooking station for the basting brush and pot.

"Here," he said breathlessly, holding them out for Dardrad.

"Do I look like I have time for that?" the dwarf said. He gave Trevor an amused glare, but took the brush and pot anyway. "Next grill is yours," he promised.

"It... it is?"

"If you're not shy of heat."

Trevor blinked in surprise, leaving him no chance to reply before Minnie drew him into her own flurry of activity with a quick hug and instructions to fetch serving spoons and trivets. As he dashed off again, she turned to where the kits Kene and Sora were helping their mother Makota wrestle with their many trays of bread and pastries. "Can you two take a break from guarding those wonderful tarts? I think everyone's ready!"

"Go ahead," Makota said, laughing as she caught them each by a shoulder before they could dash off. "But don't you be eating all of those curly buns on the way." She released her hold on them, and the two skittered off toward one of the trestle tables.

The other children quickly got wind of what was happening, and soon flocked around Trevor as he returned with utensils.

"Looks like you've got a whole crew there, son," Minnie called to him as every single child demanded to set the table and be first in line. "This way! This way!" she shouted as they took off through the crowd. Galhani was already there and had a line formed before the kids reached her, but she simply laughed and motioned them over.

Trevor followed them more slowly, watching wide-eyed as they swarmed around the table she'd set with Minnie's finished sides and his mouth-watering filets. "One of each, now! Leave room for bread!" Galhani warned.

The adults followed in a more orderly fashion, lining up behind the children. They gave each other knowing looks and teasing smiles as they watched their little ones pile their plates and rush off for pastries and curly buns.

"They'll be asleep by sunset after all that," Lucy predicted to Prudence as the two women made their way to the line, arms linked.

"It's going to be almost worth it," Prudence replied with a wry smile, eying the stacks of tarts at Makota's station.

Dardrad turned one last steak on the grill, examined it critically, and tossed it to Wilem with an approving nod before joining Sam at Barnaba's impromptu bar setup.

"Should have seen this coming," Barnaba said congenially as he mixed something fresh and bright for Jen. He handed it over when Sam started to help Dardrad with his drink. "Might have been ready with something different."

"It's fine just like it is," Jen assured him with a laugh.

Barnaba poured another drink for himself and leaned on the edge of his table. "Thought we'd have at least a few weeks before starting up."

"It's that time of year," Jen said. "You'll get used to it."

"Worse than it usually feels, though," Sam put in.

Wilelm joined them as they made their way toward the trestle tables, cradling his own laden plate close to his chest. "You mean there were even more people here last summer?" he asked incredulously.

"And fall," Barnaba said. "Although I just got here last summer."

"And part of winter," Dardrad added.

At one of the tables closest to Dooley and Ella's shop, Vamir sat with Cyntia and Leota. The elf had a large plate before him, but most of his attention was focused on an animated discussion with Cyntia about repairing carts and wagons; Leota listened quietly but interestedly as she picked at one of Calder's fish filets and took long sips from one of Barnaba's refreshing cocktails.

Several tables away, Warren shared space Knodalon, forgoing conversation for quiet companionship.

And so the evening went as the sun set in a blaze of oranges and reds: Soft conversation punctuated by the occasional laugh, a gathering of friends and families whose gifts would once again find heavy use in the near future.

And apart from it all sat Aran, although his scowl had transformed into an expression of soft curiosity.

ten

. . .

IT WAS unusual for Warren's Forge Dreams to be so... unfocused. In fact, they were usually *too* focused, if anything, often tempting Warren with details that fuzzed and hazed, forcing him to focus on the *one thing*.

But not this dream.

In this dream, his mind's eye was whisked from one vivid scene to another: a ramshackle cart, its wooden sides creaking and barely clinging together, threatened to collapse under the weight of its load. Then, a small, robust home appeared, its walls sturdy and straight, with an iron door knocker gleaming dully in the middle of the solid wooden front door. Next, a stout fence emerged, its weathered planks encircling a modest piece of land where chickens clucked and pecked contentedly at the ground. Finally, a raised platform loomed, from which someone—Warren could only discern their feet—stood as a silent sentinel, vigilantly surveying the rolling countryside that stretched out beneath a sky painted in hues of twilight.

Cart. House. Fence. Platform. Cart. House. Fence. Platform. Over and over, the little scenes looped through Warren's brain. Some part of his sleepy mind managed to find it amusing: *What exactly am I supposed to do with this?* But, as usual, the dream wouldn't tell him, and instead just kept flipping from scene to scene. *Cart. House. Fence. Platform.*

In the rare moments when the dream offered him vivid details, they were breathtaking. Take the door knocker, for instance; it was crafted into an elegant, uncomplicated form, yet the hand-hammered surface transformed it into a mesmerizing tapestry of undulating textures that caught the light in fascinating ways. The cart's sidewalls were a patchwork of weathered wood, precariously held together with coarse, fraying twine. The original nails had surrendered long ago to the relentless march of time, their iron bodies reduced to flaky rust and decayed remnants.

Cart. House. Fence. Platform.

Finally, exhausted by it all, Warren forced his eyes open.

The deep blue of pre-dawn seeped in through the window, casting a soft, grainy light over the room. Beside him, Susan slept undisturbed, her hair spilling across the pillow like autumn leaves. The gentle rise and fall of her breath made it clear that this strange dream hadn't sent Warren into his usual fits of tossing and turning. He lay still, listening to the quiet breathe of their home. A floorboard creaking quietly as it settled. The distant echo of a water bird calling mournfully from the lake. The rhythmic mumble of crickets beginning to still as they wound down their night-long song.

Outside, the air was cool and fresh, scented with pine and the earthy hint of fading night. Warren turned his head toward the window, listening as a few brave birds began to test their morning calls in tentative little bursts: Is it time yet?

He tried to piece together what he'd just seen. Beyond the muddle —cart, house, fence, platform—there was something new here. Something different from all his past Forge Dreams that had fixed themselves so firmly on a single object. Was he supposed to build each of these things? That seemed impossible; he only had hands enough for one task at a time.

A cart? A fence? Warren sighed deeply and closed his eyes again, trying to pull the vision back into clarity and precision. Instead, he heard a soft murmur from Susan as she rolled closer, draping an arm across his barrel chest. He wondered if perhaps this dream wasn't so much about what he'd seen as what it meant for him to do—whoever needed these things must be desperate for so many at once.

The sky outside continued to lighten, shading slowly from indigo to grey, hinting at pink in the east where the sun would soon rise above the mountains. A new breeze rustled in through the cracked window frame with a cool whisper that was like a promise: there was something important here if he could only figure out what.

Warren's resolve solidified like cooling iron; he would start with what he knew best—iron—even if it meant guessing blindly until one guess struck true.

With another sigh, this one softer and more resigned than before, he let himself settle back against the mattress. What would Susan say when she woke up to find him hunched over an anvil with such nonsense swirling in his head? He chuckled quietly to himself as he imagined her bemused smile. "Nine out of ten," he whispered as he let his eyelids settle closed.

———

"I don't think I've ever seen you mold something like this," Darby said, his voice full of fascination. "You use sand?"

Warren nodded. The sand was fine and white as it sifted through Warren's wide fingers. It flowed like water, pooling smooth and bright over the wooden workbench. "Sand's just the beginning," he said, kneading more into a small metal frame to start building the mold.

Darby leaned in closer, his eyes aglow with curiosity. "Is it like casting? The way you did that sword for—what was her name?"

"Rhea?" Warren chuckled while packing the sand tight. "Only vaguely. This way's slower." He scraped the surface of the mold with a flat blade, revealing an intricate network of lines beneath. "But worth it when you want something just so."

The forge blazed hot behind them, its hungry glow bathing everything in shades of orange and gold. A crucible sat ready, filled with the special ore that simmered like a pot about to boil over.

"So you pour the ore into this?" Darby pointed at the sand.

"Not quite yet." Warren dusted his hands and reached for a small wax form shaped exactly like the door knocker from his dream: elegant and simple, its surface already imitating the hammered texture he'd seen so clearly in his mind. "First comes this." He placed the wax carefully into its sandy nest.

Darby watched as Warren covered the wax piece completely, layer after careful layer, until it was hidden deep inside. "How does it turn into iron?"

"The wax melts away," Warren explained, sealing up the mold with a deft twist of wire before setting it by the heat to bake. "Leaves an empty space behind. Then we fill 'er up."

"Like magic." Darby's voice held a note of awe.

Warren grinned wide enough for his tusks to show. "Or like patience," he said.

They stood side by side, father and son, both absorbing the comfortable heat that radiated from the forge. As they waited for the mold to dry, Warren cast a sidelong glance at Darby's increasingly large hands and feet and wondered if they might be able to tackle more than one thing at a time after all.

Just then, Susan's voice floated in from outside: "Breakfast before you two set anything on fire?"

"Coming!" Darby shouted back while Warren gave another hearty laugh.

As they left the shop together, Warren glanced once more at the glowing crucible. The doorknob was obvious, but... a cart? Would he be asked to repair one? Was Wilem's arrival... fated? And where did the fence fit in?

He shook his head and wandered across the street to the pub.

———

"Another big crowd today," Minnie said. "I can feel it."

Trevor, sitting beside her, nodded as he scooped more eggs into his mouth. He looked... *Not nervous,* Warren thought. *He's excited for it, now.*

"Seems like the big crowds just keep coming," Dardrad growled.

"Good for business," Lucy countered with a grin. "That group yesterday bought every pot I had ready. I'm going to fire the kiln up in a bit and start in on another batch."

Warren reached over to grab the last Ram's-Horn pastry from what had started as a large, overflowing platter of them. Soft and buttery, just a bit chewy, and delightful when covered with redberry preserves, they hadn't lasted long. "Had a weird one, this morning." Everyone knew what he meant, and he briefly explained the vignettes. "Started on a mold for the door knocker, but bash me in the head if I know what the others mean."

"You said the cart was falling apart?" Wilem asked. Cyntia, sitting next to him, tilted her head.

"Held together by twine, from the looks of it. And it was a big point that the nails had rusted out." Warren could still see it in his mind: the red-black stains of rust on the wood where the nail heads had once held the cart's boards together.

"Sounds like you'll need nails, then," Wilem said.

Cyntia nodded. "We've a small crate of them. Our hope was to go along to the west side of Lake Evendiam, maybe find a small plot of land. Build a little house." She grinned. "Didn't consider a door knocker."

"Nails," Warren breathed. The dream flashed back at him now, the focus pulled out a bit as he discovered the key. Nails to repair the cart, to carry them on their way. Nails to frame their home, to keep it sturdy and strong. Nails for the fence, to contain their flock and keep big animals out. Nails for a platform... so they could see the danger coming. And the door knocker... Warren knew it would play a role. He didn't need to know what it would be. "C'mon, Darb," he said, pushing his heavy chair back. "We've got nails to make."

"We've a crate—" Cyntia started to repeat.

"Not of the ones I'll make."

———

The forge roared and hissed as Warren and Darby worked. The mold with the door knocker sat cooling on the workbench, still too hot to touch but slowly darkening from its fiery glow. Darby circled it with impatience, leaning in close as if his eyes could will it to cool faster.

"Not quite yet," Warren said, reaching over to ruffle Darby's hair. "We've got plenty of time to make a crate of nails before that's ready."

Darby straightened, wiping sweat from his brow. "So many? Why not just buy some?"

Warren set a handful of dark ore pieces into the crucible where they gleamed like unpolished gems. "Not every day you have special metal like this," he said. "And when you do, best use it right."

They worked in tandem, father and son flowing through familiar patterns of heat and hammering; while one poured, the other prepared. Warren filled a small ingot mold from the crucible, pouring molten ore that gleamed a pure, polished silver until it cooled and dulled.

"See if she's ready now," Darby said, nodding at the door knocker as he used a small pair of tongs to pry an ingot free.

"Try again later," Warren suggested. He laughed as Darby sighed dramatically and dropped the ingot into a waiting pail of cold water with a steamy hiss.

Soon they had a stack of ingots piled high on the corner of the bench: dull grey blocks of promise and possibility. They glowed faintly in the forge's light like coals not yet catching fire.

Warren pulled one loose from the pile. "Ready for magic?" he asked with a grin.

"Or patience?" Darby replied.

They clamped each ingot one at a time into the vise, stretching them long and thin under hammer blows that rang sharp and high among the lower notes of crackling flame. The nails took shape rapidly; slender and strong, they piled up by dozens on the work-bench where Darby gathered them quickly into bunches.

"How many?"

Warren eyed the growing heap with approval. "I'll know," he said.

Darby nodded but glanced again at the cooling mold with longing. He picked up another handful of nails while Warren fastened together a rough-hewn crate from scraps lying about the shop.

"Dad, where do ogres come from?" Darby asked.

Warren almost dropped his hammer.

"Not you, I mean. Ogres generally."

"Oh. Well, I guess that's easy enough." He returned to hammering, raising his voice to be heard over the ringing blows. "Our legends say that we were created on the Forbidden Continent, easily a trip of many moons across the Salten Seas. We dominated the entire continent, domesticating its most dangerous beasts, farming its fertile land, and building ever-bigger villages and towns. Eventually, everything was at peace, and ogres started picking up other pastimes. Art, poetry, architecture—it was supposed to have been a beautiful place. A paradise. Nobody wanted for anything."

"So why'd the leave?"

Warren sighed as he passed over another handful of finished nails. "Ogres have a wanderlust in them. Not all, but plenty. According to the stories, a lot of them just got... bored. And so they came here, to this continent. They founded Ogrehame, a great city in the Skyreaches. And they found plenty to keep them busy: orcs, terrible winters, you name it. But, just like back home, they eventually carved out a paradise for themselves, and they turned back to gentler pursuits."

"Art and stuff?"

"Yes, and song, I'm told."

"Have you been to Ogrehame?"

Warren shook his head. "No, but my parents came from there. Filled with the wanderlust. They say something like more than half the young adults leave the city, and most never return."

"What do they do?"

"Become mercenaries, mostly. That's what your grandparents did. They survived it, saved enough money to buy a little place down on Lake Trenton. Big town, very cosmopolitan. Or so they thought."

"Is that where I was born?"

Warren nodded sadly and passed over another batch of nails. "When I married your mother, it raised eyebrows, but most everyone we knew treated us normally. But when we had you... things changed. Your grandparents promised to protect us, but neither your mom nor I wanted the trouble. And so we packed up and moved out."

"Did I know my grandparents? Your parents, I mean?"

"Yes, but you were so young. We'll go back one day and visit."

"Will you ever go to Ogrehame?"

Warren's heart fell a bit, and he missed a beat in his hammering. "I dreamed of it, once. I was born in Trenton, and I think ever ogre thinks about going. But... it wouldn't be easy." A half-human, half-ogre would *certainly* raise eyebrows in Ogrehame. At the least.

"Because of the mountains?"

Now Warren's heart wrenched at his son's simple innocence. "Yeah. They're tough mountains. Here, take this last batch."

With nimble fingers—even larger than last week—Darby packed the final handful tightly the crate inside until there was no room left at all except for one lone nail sitting atop like decoration on a cake.

He held it aloft triumphantly before slipping it in place and closing up the lid. "Done?"

"Done," Warren said. He'd started to go into tunnel-vision again as he worked, but having Darby there helped him pull out of it. A modicum of tension was already draining out of his shoulders, confirming that his work here was finished. "Let's have a look at that knocker."

He unclamped the mold and pried it open. The door knocker sat snugly inside, a gleaming silver crescent still hugged by its sandy cast, radiant with warmth. The old ogre's fingers were steady and sure as he brushed the sand away. "Just right," he murmured, holding up the steaming piece.

Darby watched, wide-eyed, as Warren took a soft cloth and started to polish. "Wow," Darby said as the knocker's surface came alive under Warren's careful touch, light dancing over its hammered textures.

"Still warm," Warren said with a wink, "but not too warm."

He gripped it in one hand while he polished with the other, turning it over and around until every facet shimmered like moonlight on water. The elegant simplicity of the design seemed to catch Warren in a moment of thought; his face softened into something almost reverent, as if he were seeing more than just metal.

"Does it look just like your dream?" Darby asked.

"Yeah," Warren replied, setting it down with satisfaction that shone as brightly as the silver. He washed his hands in a basin of water gone grey from soot and metal dust. He stretched, holding his arms high overhead, his fingertips almost brushing the rafters, his spine popping with pleasure. Then he caught something out of the corner of one eye, and turned quickly: Aran stood there, looking... thoughtful. "Aran?"

The old man simply turned and walked away, not saying a word.

Darby cocked his head. "Sounds like carts."

Warren listened. "Yeah. You'd better go help Trevor with the horses." Ever since Darby had been spending more time inside the smithy, Minnie's son had stepped in to help travelers with their beasts, but Darby still loved the giant animals. He grinned at his dad and rushed out.

Warren laid his hammer down on the anvil and rubbed his eyes. This had already been a busier spring than any he could remember, and it showed no sign of slacking off. He stepped out of the smithy and eyed the sun, already well into its descent toward the far horizon. His stomach growled—he and Darby had both missed lunch. *Maybe I'll see if Dardrad has any leftovers.* A piece of venison would go down well, right now.

He glanced back inside the smithy, at the still-raging forge, at the small, heavy wooden box of nails. *Magic nails,* he grinned to himself. *Might as well admit it.* The door knocker lay on a workbench. *I'll see if Cole has any old rags I can wrap it in.* Again rubbing his eyes, he headed across the road to the town gate.

———

The sun sank low, casting long shadows over the trade road. Warren sat on a bench outside the pub, a ceramic mug of ale—a huge one that Lucy had made specially for him—cradled in his large hands. Bawdy songs spill out through the open door, mixing with the evening air. A dozen voices belt out: "The maiden did cry, 'Tis too much!' but he said with a leer, 'Never fear!'" Laughter followed, rolling out like waves over the quiet town.

With the inn full, one pair of travelers had set up camp by their wagon along the road. They'd even considered the possibility of letting people lay out their bedrolls on the town square, but the influx of visitors had tapered off quickly as the sun went lower.

Warren leaned back against the cool stone wall of the pub with a deep sigh. His eyes felt heavy. He sipped his ale and watched as Susan makes her way down the road toward him, her face soft with concern and love.

"Busy day?" she asked as she settled next to him, tucking her legs up onto the bench.

"Busy spring," he corrects with a wry smile. "But we're caught up for the moment."

"You look exhausted." She reached over to smooth the hair where it stood wild and white against his green skin.

"One to ten?"

"Oh, an eight at least," he assured her. "Nothing bad, just not as young as I once was."

"Or as old as you think," Susan countered gently. She leaned her head on his shoulder and glances toward the inn where, inside, Minnie flitted between tables packed with visitors. Trevor hustled in her wake, already burdened with trays of mugs and platters despite his size and apparent youth. "They've been coming more. And harder, haven't they? The Forge Dreams."

A cheerful din rose from inside the pub: "So come take my hand / Let me show you my land / Where the ale flows like water!" Warren shook his head at this last line—they're doing Sam's brew no justice with that one—and took another sip.

"Yeah."

"What's it mean, do you think?"

"All the strife out East, I'm guessing. People are running."

"Have you noticed that Aran is still here?" Susan asked after a moment. "I thought he'd be long gone by now."

"He showed up at the smithy earlier," Warren replied. "Just looked at me and left."

"What do you think he wants?"

"Dunno. Maybe he's waiting for someone to come along who'll take him with them. We should probably put up a warning sign."

Susan laughed softly, then turned serious again as she studied his face, lined and shadowed by more than just fading light. "Promise me you'll take it easy for a bit?" she asked.

"I'll try," though even now he wondered what tomorrow will bring.

"And eat something tonight?"

"I'm counting on it," Warren chuckled. "If Darby left anything." He stretched again, working stiffness from muscles worn by work and worry both. His long arms wrapped around Susan briefly before pulling away so she could stand.

"They'll come looking for you if you stay out here," she teased.

"This is true." He finished his ale and sets the mug down with a contented thunk as she headed back into the pub to help Sam corral the crowd. He watched until she disappeared among them and then closed his eyes, listening to the songs and laughter echo through twilight's gathering hush.

eleven

· · ·

THE NEXT MORNING was unexpectedly moist—*dewy,* Susan had insisted—which had at once the effect of cooling the air and making the smithy noticeably more humid. Warren noted the difference, but didn't really mind either way—ogres' bodies regulated their heat more readily than humans, making them comfortable in a much wider range of climates.

He'd resisted the urge to follow that morning's dream directly to the forge, instead forcing himself to step into Makota's for a baked treat, Darby following close on his heels. His son had become more sensitive to Warren's more-frequent nighttime tossing and turning, and had met him in the front room of their little home just as the sun was peeking above the distant horizon.

The bakery was alive with the smell of yeast and sugar, the heat from the ovens mingling with the morning's dampness. Inside, the air was a cozy blanket, wrapping around Warren and Darby as they entered. Shelves lined the walls, steadily filling with the day's offerings. Makota, her striped tail flicking back and forth, deftly maneuvered trays of rising dough. Her kits, Kene and Sora, were already at work, their small hands dusted in flour.

"Good morning, Warren, Darby!" Makota called, her voice as

bright as the sun streaming through the window. "You're early! I have just the thing for you."

She disappeared into the back, emerging with a tray of Cloud Buns so fresh that steam curled from their golden surfaces. They glistened like sunrise clouds, impossibly light and promising sweetness.

"Here! Try one before they float away," she laughed, setting the tray on the counter.

Darby reached eagerly, his eyes wide. "Thanks, Makota!" he exclaimed, taking a big bite. Warren followed suit, the sugary, buttery bite dissolving on his tongue. It was a moment of bliss before the work ahead.

Already, the townfolk were stirring outside, their chatter filled with a mixture of excitement and anticipation... and concern. The tales of unrest in the east had continued to pour in, and the influx of travelers seeking refuge and resupply was noticeable. Many had the wearied look of those who had been on the road too long, and with too little preparation, their clothes dusty and their eyes searching.

Makota's buns, still warm and fragrant, began to vanish as fast as her family could make them.

The bell above the door jangled, announcing a small parade of new arrivals. One of Cole's kids, wild-haired and bright-eyed, bounded in with the energy of a puppy. "Dad said I should grab a dozen sticky twists!" he shouted over the noise, already halfway to the counter.

Jen followed on his heels, chuckling. "Better make that two dozen, Makota. He'll eat half before he's back."

Vamir lingered by the door, his gaze sweeping the room. He nodded to Warren and Darby, a quiet hello, before shuffling up to the counter. "Morning, Makota," he said, his smile gentle. "Heard you've got some new kind of turnover?"

"Pear-berry and cream!" Makota answered, her eyes twinkling. "And don't worry, Senan—I've got your sticky twists here." She handed over a bundle, each pastry oozing with syrup.

The boy grinned, clutching the package like treasure. "Thanks!" he said, already munching his first as he ran out the door.

"And make it two for me as well," Jen said.

"Two dozen?" Makota asked, starting to fill a large box. "Planning on company?"

"Two dozen," Jen confirmed, exchanging a knowing smile with Makota. "I'm under strict instructions from Tyran. You know he likes to keep them out on the counter when it's going to be busy."

The bakery filled with easy chatter, speculation on what the day would bring, and recollections of the last batch of travelers, some of whom were just now getting underway. The clattering of pans and the hum of conversation turned the morning into a whirl of comforting noise. Beneath it all was a sense of urgency and worry: it had already been one of the busiest seasons in memory, and everyone was silently wondering if whatever was brewing out east would make its way this far to the north and west to spill trouble at their gates.

Then, with a creak and a bang, the door swung open again. Galhani, her cheeks pink with exertion, appeared with her ever-present cheer. "Morning, friends!" she announced, pulling a small wagon behind her. A large crock of chilled tea sloshed gently inside. "Thought the workers and travelers might like some refreshment today."

Makota's ears perked up. "Perfect timing, Galhani! I'll trade you a dozen buns for it."

"Make it a dozen and a half," Galhani laughed. "It's going to be a busy day. But do you have the shortbread cookies instead?"

Makota chuckled, a sound halfway between a hiss and a purr. "Don't I always?"

Kene and Sora rushed over, eager to help. They lifted the crock together, their tails flicking in unison. Darby and Warren exchanged looks, the kind only family could, a shared moment of peace before the bustle outside claimed them again.

Makota handed Galhani a box of crisp cookies wrapped in brown paper, her hands moving quickly and efficiently. "Here you go!" she said. "And I saved your favorite," she added with a wink.

Galhani beamed. "You're the best, Makota!"

Aran wander in so quietly that nobody noticed him until he asked, "Any chance of a brown loaf?"

Everyone turned and stared at him. He met each of their eyes, his own glinting with sharp awareness. Warren frowned slightly as, for just a moment, the old man's expression seemed to loosen and drift, but it snapped back to the present so quickly that it could have been a trick of the light.

"Yes, of course," Makota said easily, each to one of the trays behind her. "I've hot butter as well, if you like."

"Please. How much?"

"On the house," the Fellis said, her whiskers twitching.

"You said it was on the house yesterday," Aran grumbled.

Makota shrugged. "You can settle up when you're ready to move on, then."

"Hrmph." But he accepted the hot, hearty brown loaf, twice as long as his hand and glistening with warm butter. He took his first bite, nodded appreciatively, and then headed back out of the shop.

"Odd duck, that," Galhani mused.

"Mmm," Vamir murmured, his eyes following Aran out the door as the old man walked slowly across the grassy square to the town gates. "Puts me in mind of someone, but... I can't quite put a finger on it."

Outside, the sun rose higher, casting long shadows across the town square. Inside, the light grew warmer, brighter, as the day stretched its arms open wide, welcoming whatever might come next.

"C'mon, Darb," Warren said at last, having put it off as long as possible. "Let's get to work."

"Warren?"

The ogre blinked at the interruption, turning to see Wilem standing in the smithy's doorway. Both he and Darby had been so focused on their work—molding a set of pots and pans—that he hadn't even heard the cartwright approach.

That morning's Forge Dream had been... *different*. Rather than a chase, or a battle scene, or even the montage of cart-fence-house, he'd been presented with a simple wooden wall, where cast-iron pots and pans hung from stout wooden hooks.

The dream had been *deeply* boring, so much so that Warren had been fully aware of his mild tossing and turning—which hadn't even been bad enough to drive Susan out of bed, this time.

In the dream, the wall had loomed large: bare wood planks, every knot and grain a stark reminder of its simplicity. Pots and pans had hung silent and still. He had seen them in such detail that it was almost absurd—every imperfection, every speck of cast-iron texture. They were simply *there*, unmoving and eternal, as if mocking his expectations.

If it's going to be this boring, he remembered thinking, *I might as well be allowed to sleep.*

A window not far off had let in thin, pale light, casting shadows that crawled across the wall. Warren had watched them stretch with the slow deliberation of a passing day, turning from morning's grey to harsh noon glare, then softening into the dim amber of evening. The pots and pans remained unchanged through it all, dull sentinels in the fading light. Warren had even imagined he could even hear the faint creak of the wooden hooks as they shifted under the weight, an almost-audible sigh of monotony.

Pans. Light. Pots. Shadow.

Boring.

He shook himself. The banality of the dream had made it easier to try and have a normal morning, to stop in Makota's for a bite, to josh with his son as they finally made their way to the smithy and began stoking the forge. But although it was subtle, the pressure was still there.

Pots. Pans.

"What can I do for you, Wilem?" he asked as he laid his tongs aside. "Knock off for a bit, Darb," he told his son. He quickly eyed the shadow pooling around Wilem's feet. "Looks like it might be lunch anyway. Go see what your mother is up to."

"Got it, Dad!" Darby scurried past Wilem in the direction of the inn.

That's when Warren noticed Aran standing just outside the open doors. Darby darted past him, almost brushing one elbow, but the old man didn't notice. His eyes were locked on Warren.

"Maybe got a job for you out here, Warren," Wilem said, jerking his chin toward the roadside.

Warren tore his gaze away from Aran. "Let's see what we've got."

The ogre followed the cartwright to the trade road. There, pulled up along the stable yard's fence, was the most battered, beaten-down cart Warren had ever seen.

"They've offered to buy my cart," Wilem said, nodding toward his much sturdier vehicle, which was now parked inside the yard, "but I'm not so sure I'm willing to part with it." He shrugged. "They're not going to get much further in that thing, though."

Warren eyed the cart, even as its passengers eyed him back, their expressions wary. "Ogre no eat friendly strangers," he told them mildly. "Can't you fix it?" he asked Wilem.

"If I had some good nails, perhaps," the man said. "And if—"

Cart. Fence. House. Platform. "Right, right. I forgot," Warren sighed. "Nails?"

"Nails. Be right back."

Warren stumped back inside the smithy, picked up the heavy crate of nails in one hand, and brought it back out. He handed it to Wilem, who grunted softly as he took the thing in both hands. "So many? I won't need half of these to—"

"Yeah." He raised his voice. "Wilem here is a cartwright. He's going to fix your cart. No," he added more firmly as the oldest man in the cart opened his mouth to protest, "you'll have to trust me, this is for the best. These are the best nails on the continent. Guaranteed. You're all headed in from the east?"

"Powerful trouble out there," one of the cart's passengers acknowledged.

"Right. So Wilem will fix your cart, and you'll head on. Spend the night here if you need, but no longer. Find where you're going to settle. Save these nails—and pull the ones out of the cart as well. Use them to build a new home. Use them in your fence, too. They'll hold fast. Understand me?" The people on the cart nodded slowly, clearly *not* understanding, but just as clearly not willing to argue with an ogre. "Good. I'm off to grab a bite," he added to Wilem. "You need any help?"

"Some tools?"

"Take whatever you need," Warren said, waving at the smithy. "Made Darby a set of hammers that should suit you." He set off across the road with another sigh. "Food, then back to pots and pans." He shook his head and let his shoulders slump. "Pots and pans."

Aran's sharp gaze tracked the ogre as he shuffled across the road to the inn.

———

Warren watched the ore melt, the heat transforming it into a glowing river. He poured with careful precision, the liquid metal flowing smoothly into the sand molds, filling the shapes of pots and pans. Darby stood close, his eyes wide and attentive, absorbing each detail of his father's practiced movements. Steam rose from the molds, hissing quietly, curling like a phantom mist in the humid air.

The forge blazed hot and bright, casting a golden hue over the smithy. Shadows danced along the walls, flickering with the rhythm of the fire. The silence between Warren and Darby was thick with concentration, the only sound the gentle roar of the flames and the occasional crackle of cooling metal. Ordinarily, Warren loved this—the sense of focus, shutting out the world, his entire universe narrowed to the forge, to the metal, to what it would become.

It was a bit spoiled today, because Aran had invited himself into the smithy, and was now leaning against the far wall. Warren had to continually resist the urge to look over his shoulder at the gray-robed old man, but for some reason who couldn't bring himself to simply ask Aran to leave.

Focus. Warren set the empty crucible down, his hands steady and sure. The molds sat in neat rows, already beginning to darken and cool. Darby's gaze lingered on the edges of the sand, where the metal had spilled in thin, silvery lines. "Should I start on the next batch?" he asked, eager to help.

"Not yet," Warren replied, his voice calm and deliberate. He knew the weight of the Forge Dreams, knew their stubborn insistence, and he knew that rushing wouldn't ease the strange pressure on his mind. "These need time to set. Patience, Darb."

Darby nodded, though his fingers twitched with the urge to work. He picked up a set of tongs and carefully tidied the forge, arranging tools and clearing the worktable. Warren began to turn the molds, inspecting each for flaws, ensuring the metal had settled just right.

Aran's eyes tracked him all the while, itching at the back of Warren's head.

"Think we'll need more molds?" Darby asked, glancing at the growing stack of filled ones.

"Probably," Warren said, allowing himself a small smile. He knew they would need more molds. They always did. The Forge Dreams had a way of expanding until every corner of the smithy was filled with their demands. "But let's see how far these get us." With luck, most this first batch would set perfectly and there wouldn't be a need for too many more attempts.

He moved with the confidence of experience, but the set of his jaw betrayed his lingering uncertainty. Pots and pans. They seemed too simple, too ordinary, for the weight the dream had placed on them. He wondered who would come for them.

At the back of the smithy, Aran shifted his weight from one foot to the other.

Darby watched Warren closely, sensing his father's unease. "This is the most we've ever done at once," he said, trying to lighten the mood. "Maybe even more than the nails!"

Warren laughed, a deep rumble that softened the tension in his shoulders. "That's a safe bet, son." He moved to the forge, preparing to melt the next batch of ore, eyeing the barrel of clean sand to judge how much was left. "We'll keep on until it's done. Until it's all done."

He *had* made an awful lot of them. He'd set out to make four sizes of pot and three different-sized pans, but he wasn't truly a master of this casting technique. In the past, about half of them had cooled unevenly, forcing him to make a new mold out of fresh sand, melt down the failure, and begin again. So this time, the dream pushing insistently in his mind, he'd decided to just begin with twice as many. Two large hearth-ovens, two large stew pots, two mid-sized sauce pot, and two smaller pots. They were all cooling nicely now, alongside the two large skillets, the two heavier pans, and the two smaller pans.

They worked on in the heat and silence, the clink of metal and scrape of sand their steady companions. The day stretched long and bright outside, the sun inching its way across the town square. The shadows in the smithy shifted and grew, marking the passage of time as Warren and Darby labored on, intent and tireless.

They watched as the pots and pans slowly lost their molten glow, settling into rich, earthen hues. The cast-iron surfaces, still faintly warm, transformed into a tapestry of dark greys and blacks, their textures raw and inviting. Each piece bore the unique stamp of its making, a delicate pattern of tiny divots and bumps that caught the dimming light in subtle ways.

One pot, its edges cooling faster than its center, gave a sudden, sharp crack, the sound ringing dully through the smithy. Darby jumped at the noise, his eyes wide as the flawed piece splintered across its surface.

"Ah, well," Warren said, a touch of resignation in his voice. "One more round, just to be sure."

"We've got the spare," Darby reminded him.

"True," Warren sighed. "But I'd hoped to have two full sets. We can always sell the second set"

In the back of the smithy, Aran frowned.

"Better too many than not enough," Darby replied cheerfully, already moving to gather more sand.

"Maybe," Warren said, though he wasn't entirely convinced. The Forge Dreams were never this simple, and never this subtle. If they were, he thought, we'd have left here long ago. He watched his son's growing skill with a surge of pride, but also a sting of worry, knowing that one day Darby might feel the same strange pressure, might be drawn into the same unending cycle.

"Darb," Warren said suddenly, "leave it."

"Dad?"

"We'll get one good set. Everything else, we'll break up and use for the next project."

Darby looked confused, but he let his scoop of sand pour back into the barrel. "You sure?"

Unnoticed, Aran rose an eyebrow.

"I don't... we can make another set out of ordinary iron to sell. Probably should keep a couple of sets on hand anyway. So... yes. I'm sure. Let's see if we can get a full set out of these."

If someone had been watching, they may have noticed Aran's expression soften slightly, before he gave a slight shake of his head and slipped out of the smithy.

———

As the afternoon crawled toward evening, Warren paused to wipe the sweat from his brow. He surveyed the rows of molds, the metal in the last ones finally cooled enough to no longer glow. "That's it Darb," he told his son, who'd already begun tidying up the smithy. "Think we can knock off for the day." Only one more pan had developed a slight crack, which meant he had more than the single full set he needed.

"Okay." The boy continued puttering around, putting tools away and carefully staying away from the cooling ore. "When can we open these?"

Warren considered. "Morning, I think." The pressure in his mind had largely abated, meaning the dream was satisfied with what they'd done so far. "Give them plenty of time. Pull them too early and we're likely to get another crack, which means starting over." Again, he tested his sense of the dream, and it seemed to agree. Morning would be fine. "C'mon, let's go see what's what."

The trade road had grown busy—Warren had been dimly aware of the noise of travelers all day—and several carts stood along its edges. Trevor had clearly been leading horses into the stable yard, for easily a dozen were standing around munching the last of the winter hay and slurping water from the trough. Wilem was still busy on the broken-down cart, although it was looking substantially less broken-down than it had. As Warren watched, Wilem made a few final hits with the hammer he'd borrowed, before standing back and surveying his work with satisfaction. "That should hold you."

"Too late to keep going tonight, though," the older man—the head of the family who owned the cart, Warren supposed—grumbled.

"Put up in the inn if there's room," Warren rumbled, making the man jump a bit in surprise. "Or pull through outside the road gates and camp. Should be a pleasant enough evening, and we leave the gates open should you need anything."

"Aye," the man murmured, nodding thanks to Wilem. He began calling directions to his family, bidding them to bring the horses back around.

Wilem wiped his hands as he stepped closer to the ogre. "Pretty dire tales out of this lot. Everyone coming through today, really."

"Oh?"

"Seems the danger's some sort of war-cult sprung up back east. That's what kicked off the first of the rosefruit towns falling."

"Figured it was just the last headman in the lineage dying off."

"It usually is," Wilem agreed. "But Charls—that's the old man's name—says it was started a town over from his. Some upstart calling himself Lord Vennit, started gathering other young men to his side. Bullies the lot of them, but they started sacrificing animals, chanting, dancing around bonfires, all that. Then they set off against the next town over, and have kept repeating. Keeps drawing the young, the second sons, the disaffected, those with more muscle than brain."

Warren frowned.

"Should tell you that Cyntia and I have decided to stay." He snorted. "Should have just sold those folks our cart."

"They need their own cart," Warren rumbled. "And the nails."

Wilem stared at him for a moment, and then nodded. "Something to do with your gift."

"The smithy's gift, really. I'm just the current occupant."

"So what's the cartwright's gift?"

Warren raised one heavy eyebrow. "No idea, actually. We haven't had a cartwright. Not since we've been here, at least."

"Well, to begin, I'll need some stout log we can saw some planks from. And some proper tools. Saws, different hammers, that kind of thing."

"Wood won't be a problem," Warren mused. "Everpine?"

"Everpine, oaken, ironwood. Any or all."

"Everpine and oaken grow in the foothills," Warren offered, gesturing toward the hills that rose gently at the back of the town. He eyed the sun. "Shouldn't be a problem felling one or two before sundown. Tyran's got a saw and a stout back. Let's see if he's amenable."

———

"Timber!" Tyran's voice boomed through the foothills as the second tree began to crack and sway. It fell with a slow majesty, the branches rustling in a final protest before crashing to the ground. The air filled with the fresh, green scent of pine, and Warren let himself breathe it in, savoring the moment.

The three of them stood for a moment, admiring their work. Wilem wiped the sweat from his brow and grinned. "Not bad for a half-day's effort."

Warren hefted the first tree onto his shoulder. It was massive, but he carried it with ease, his steps deliberate and steady. He felt a deep satisfaction in the work, the simplicity of it. No dreams, no pressure, just the honest labor of felling trees with friends.

Tyran clapped him on the back with a heavy hand. "You're a natural, Warren! Maybe you should take up lumberjacking." He laughed, a loud, cheerful sound that echoed off the hills.

"Don't tempt me," Warren said, his voice a low rumble. They set off down the slope, Wilem and Tyran dragging the second tree behind them, its branches leaving a trail through the grass.

The sun dipped lower, casting long shadows that stretched toward the lake. Their path wound through patches of wildflowers and young saplings, the ground firm beneath their feet. The day was cooling, the air crisp and clean, a welcome change from the heat of the forge and the bustle of the town.

"Cyntia's not going to believe we're going to be building carts again," Wilem said, a note of wonder in his voice. "We thought we'd left that life behind."

"Sure she will," Tyran replied, his tone confident.

"And you'll likely have help," Warren added. "The kids in town haven't had something new to turn to for a while. You'll be fending off the little ones."

"Hah! Until their arms tire from the sawing," Wilem chuckled. "That's the hardest part of it."

"Frankly wouldn't mind mine learning how to make a proper wheel," Tyran said.

"Well, that *is* the fun part..."

Warren listened to his friends' easy banter, a quiet contentment settling over him. He felt the weight of the tree on his shoulder, solid and reassuring. It was good to be out here, away from the clamor of the town and the demands of the forge, even if just for a little while.

The rooftops of North Pointe Common Towne came into view, the slate gleaming in the evening light. They passed the inn, where travelers had gathered on the porch, sipping Galhani's chilled tea and swapping stories. Jen waved as they walked by, a slight smile on her face. Warren nodded back, his expression as close to a grin as it ever got.

They reached the stable yard, where Warren dropped the tree with a heavy thud. "Need to grab a rope?" he asked Wilem, gesturing at the other tree.

"Got it," Wilem said, dragging the tree alongside its twin. "I'll bring the tools back in the morning. Thanks, Warren. Wouldn't have managed without you."

"Don't mention it." Warren's voice was a gentle rumble, the kind that seemed to absorb all the weight of the world and leave it soft and light. "Glad to have something to keep me busy."

"Come on over to the inn when you're done here!" Tyran called, already halfway to the pub. "We'll save you a seat."

Warren and Tyran mingled with the day's visitors for a bit, until by ones and twos they retired, each eager to set out early in the morning. As the sun's last rays twinkled away under the horizon, they moved into the pub, where the rest of the townfolk had gathered for a meal.

"Worrying news," Jen said as she plunked down next to Sam, spooning a healthy portion of stew out of the common pot.

"The war cult?" Tyran said with a frown. "Aye. Not the best news."

"Normally those rosefruit towns go through a bit of angst and then settle down," Cole agreed, his expression troubled. "But for someone to be... conquering them all."

"Conquering, or just disrupting," Sam said quietly, shaking her head.

"It's the cult part that worries me," Jen said. "Those things have a way of spreading until someone stops them. And if they've found some actual little god to back them... it could take some doing to stop them."

"Surely they won't come this far," Galhani protested.

"Not easily. Certainly not this year," Sam said, shaking her head. "Magefell won't be easily taken. And if they skip that and head more northerly, Smallhaven is well-defended, despite the name. Celestrum is the last bastion of the great mages, unlikely even a little god would mess with them."

"And Strongfast is *very* well-named," Dardrad said.

"Aye, but a small enough crew could slip by unnoticed," Cole said darkly.

"But why?" Makota asked with a soft purr. "There are few towns along Lake Evendiam, and fewer riches."

"War cult won't be after riches," Warren muttered, drawing a look of concern from Susan.

"But still, there's more for them east of here—" Alred began.

"He's worried about the oracle," Vamir said quietly. Everyone turned to the elf, who shrugged. "We've all heard it. Someone—maybe more than one, but I'm inclined to think not—has sent people here. Specifically here, for specific goals."

"A sword. A gauntlet. Who knows what's next?" Warren said.

"There was that woman who commissioned the two pots from me," Lucy added. "She didn't say, but they would be perfect for those goblin fire-bombs. Round, almost spheres, or as close as I could get to it. She said they were for carrying water, but..." The dark-skinned old woman shrugged. "Nobody carries water like that."

"And I've sold more than a few... *unusual* books, in the past days," Vamir agreed.

"Aye, and no small number of ordinary pikes and daggers," Tyran sighed heavily. "And that man did say he'd been told by a fortune-teller that he'd find what he needed here."

"Just so," Warren said, nodding. "And so what if this war cult gets wind of us? Gets the idea that we're some source of magical weapons and treasures, and heads here specifically?"

"Anybody had any... signs?" Jen asked slowly.

Around the pub, heads shook.

"Well, that's encouraging," she said. "But... still. Best we keep an eye on the road."

Everyone finished their dinner quietly, as a heavy pall settled over the room.

twelve

· · ·

THE DAGGER CAUGHT the light in a dull, muted flash. It was an ordinary blade—notched, plain, its steel stained with time and use. But in Warren's dream, it pulsed with an unsettling energy, a dark ambition that clung to it like a shroud. The focus—a pair of rough, scarred hands—gripped the hilt tightly. The hands were strong and calloused, the fingers curled with grim determination. They moved with a practiced, unsettling ease, as if the dagger was an extension of their will.

Then, the dream shifted.

The dagger struck with brutal efficiency. The hands plunged it into shadows, where the vague outlines of people—friends or foes, Warren couldn't tell—crumpled silently. The blade gleamed red, then black, then red again. Each movement was a precise and devastating blow, each target falling before they could even scream.

The dream shifted again.

The hands wiped the dagger clean on a ragged piece of cloth. Their movements were calm and deliberate, as if death was a routine they had long since mastered. The cloth was stained with more than just blood; it held the same ugly vibe as the dagger, a dark thread that wove through the entire vision. It thrummed through the ogre like a relentless, dissonant chord.

The dream shifted once more.

The hands held the blade aloft, the light catching its edge. The dagger looked so simple, so ordinary, yet it was more deadly than anything Warren had ever seen. Its plainness was its power, its deception. It was ambition and misery forged into steel, and it terrified him.

The dream lingered, refusing to release him. The hands, the dagger, the quiet, terrible deaths they dealt. Warren tried to wrench himself awake, but the dream clung to him like a second skin, smothering him with its insistence.

When he finally forced his eyes open, Susan was gone. She must have left while he thrashed in his sleep, as the air was still thick and warm with the aftertaste of his nightmare. He lay still, trying to calm the pounding of his heart and slow the racing thoughts that tangled through his mind. The memory of the dream was a raw wound, refusing to fade. The weight of it pressing down on him, and knew he wouldn't find rest again today.

He rose and dressed, his movements sharp and irritable. He thought of the dream's relentless focus, the way it had honed in on those rough hands and that dreadful dagger. He could see it so clearly: the ugly way it glinted, the horrible surety with which it killed. He knew what he'd have to make, and the thought sickened him.

Susan was nowhere to be found, likely already across the road at the inn, helping Minnie and Trevor. *Good,* Warren snarled to himself, immediately regretting it. They both paid a price for the smithy's gift, for the town's protection and acceptance.

He left the house, the door slamming behind him with a force he didn't intend. The town square was quiet in the early morning, the sky still dim with the retreating night. He crossed to the smithy, his mind a storm of anxiety and frustration. As he stepped inside, the air was stifling, as if the dream itself had seeped into the walls, thick and suffocating.

Warren stoked the forge with a kind of fury, the flames leaping to life under his rough hands. He wanted nothing more than to *make* the damn thing, to finish it and exorcise the dream from his mind. He worked with abrupt, anger-filled movements, clattering his tools reck-lessly across the workbench. He realized, with great irritation, that he didn't have any of the special ore stockpiled, and he was in no mood to go wake Darby.

Then his eyes fell on the pots and pans, still sitting in their molds. He de-molded them carefully but quickly, brushing the molding sand away from each piece. Another had cracked in the night, but he still had more than a full set of perfect pieces, and the others contained more than enough metal to craft the dagger he'd seen.

He reached for his hammer.

———

The smithy was oppressive, the air heavy with heat and unspent words. Warren had left the doors closed, a barrier to curious eyes and a refusal to the world outside. He worked with single-minded preci-sion, the clanging of his hammer a fierce, rhythmic punctuation to his own unsettled thoughts.

The dagger took shape with a speed that surprised Warren. He had chased Darby away, unable to stomach the idea of his son witnessing this creation. The look on Darby's face—hurt, confused—clung to him, a fresh wound atop the weight of the dream. But Warren had been unwilling to explain, unable to let those young eyes watch as this thing came into being.

"Not now," he'd barked as Aran slipped into the forge. The old man ignored the warning, lingering near the door with his inscrutable gaze fixed on Warren's work.

Warren hunched over the anvil, the dagger slowly emerging under his relentless hands. His anger was a palpable force, each strike of the hammer a blow against the vision that had haunted him. The ore from the cracked pots melted smoothly, as if complicit in the task. He watched the metal stretch and form, its surface dark and unpolished, exactly as he'd seen it.

The process of making it dug at him like a betrayal. Warren was a craftsman of protection, of aid. He had never forged anything this... irritating. The dagger was plain, but foul, and the Forge Dream had demanded it with a terrible clarity. It wasn't like the sword and crown. No, those pieces had been foul but *honest,* pretending to be nothing they weren't. This piece...

Outwardly, it was so plain as to be unremarkable.

The blade was long and narrow, tapering to a wicked point. Its spine was thick, plain, and straight, giving it a sturdiness that belied its simple shape. It gleamed a dull silver, the color of ash and death, with a surface marred by uneven textures. These imperfections caught the light in strange ways, making the dagger seem alive and shifting, as if it held a dozen secrets in its forged steel. Warren knew they weren't accidental; the Dream had shown them with brutal precision.

He crafted the tang to extend deep into the handle, ensuring that the blade would hold even under the most vicious use. The handle itself would be simple, wrapped in a thin, unremarkable black leather from a spool lying on the edge of a work table.

The guard was almost nonexistent, a small, curved piece of metal that barely separated blade from grip. It was a parry and a trick, a whisper of protection that would fail in the end. Warren hated the way it laid in his hand, hated the ease with which it came together. Each piece was a lie, plain and lethal.

He began wrapping the handle, pulling the leather tightly using nothing but his thick, strong fingers. 'Round and 'round, overlapping just slightly to provide a better grip. The smell of hot leather—*I really should have let this cool more*—bullied its way into his nostrils.

Why the urgency? Why the rush? He'd always advocated for patience, always told Darby to—

"Warren?"

Susan's voice, through the cracked opening of the smithy door.

"Out!" Warren snapped, his powerful ogre's voice filling the smithy.

The door clicked shut and Warren immediately felt terrible. *I should apologize. Explain.* But no, first he would finish this irritating, intrusive, insistent weapon.

He finished the last binding on the handle, setting the dagger down with a finality that echoed his frustration. He stared at it, the ugly thing, knowing it was complete, knowing it was perfect in its deadly simplicity. A cold dread settled over him, the certainty that this piece would draw more than its fair share of blood.

Aran watched silently, his eyes flicking from the dagger to Warren's face.

Warren ran a hand through his white hair, his fingers catching in the sweat and grime. "It's done," he said, his voice flat and hollow. But the relief he'd expected didn't come.

"Seems you've had a rough time of it," Aran said, his tone almost sympathetic.

Warren looked at the old man, his expression a mix of anger and resignation. "You could say that."

"What's it for?" Aran asked, nodding at the dagger.

"Trouble," Warren replied. The word was thick in his mouth, filled with truth and portent. His gaze lingered on the blade, its uneven surface catching the light like a promise and a curse.

Aran gave a small, knowing nod. "You're not wrong." He turned to leave, pausing at the door. He turned back. "Why?"

"Why what?"

"Why not stick with... nails? Horseshoes? Pots and pans, even?"

"Not my choice."

"You always have a choice."

"Our choice was to stay here. After that..."

Aran nodded slowly before slipping out and closing the door behind him.

Warren grunted, watching as the old man stepped out into the morning light. The smithy was too quiet, the clamor of his work replaced by a silence that pressed in on him. He sat for a moment, his head in his hands, before wrapping the dagger in a thick cloth and tucking it away on a high shelf. Out of sight, but not out of mind. Never out of mind.

He pushed the door open, letting the morning air rush in and sweep away the heat and the memory of the Dream. He needed to get out, to breathe, to see Susan and Darby and remind himself of the things that mattered. The dagger would wait.

———

"I can only offer you two silver," the woman said regretfully.

At some point—Warren couldn't have said when—Susan, or Darby, or both had snuck into the smithy and liberated the finished pots and pans. Susan was showing them now, spread out on one of the tables in front of the pub. A young woman stood next to her, eyeing the simple, cast-iron items with obvious desire. But her expression wasn't one of greed or even avarice—it was pure desperation.

"Two is fine," Susan said gently. She looked up, raising an eyebrow at Warren, who flushed a deep green.

"But you can't—"

"We don't get much call for items like this," Susan lied easily. "Please, you'll be doing me a favor by taking them."

The young woman hesitated only another moment before nodding. She reached into a small pouch at her waist, carefully picked out to shining, precious silver coins, and laid them gently into Susan's palm.

"Now," Warren's wife said, "let's get you all some provisions, as well."

"We can't—"

"You'll find prices here to be quite a bit less than what you may have encountered along the way," Susan said firmly. She looked up, making eye contact with Warren. "This is my husband, Warren." The young woman followed Susan's gaze and her eyes widened. "He'll help you negotiate a good price. Right, dear?"

"Of course," Warren rumbled. *She's already forgiven me*, he realized, a tension he hadn't realized he'd been carrying slipping off his shoulders. "What are you most in need of first? And what should I call you?"

"Mayd," the young woman said, clearly still more than a bit in awe of speaking to an ogre. "And thank you. Foodstuffs—something simple. Sturdy. We've a long way to go."

"Let's go see Cole, then."

As he led her toward the town gates, he asked, "How many are you? And how far are you going?"

"Six. My husband, Jace, and we have four children, eight to twelve. And we're... we're going to the Demonbanes."

Warren almost stumbled at that. "To Westhold, then?"

She shook her head. "All the way to Stormport."

Now Warren stopped and looked at her. She stopped as well, craning her head back to meet his eyes. "Things are that dire?" he said softly.

Her eyes almost filled with tears as she nodded. "Whatever sea-demons exist beyond Stormport, they cannot be as terrible as what we've seen. There's this... I can't call it anything but what it is, a cult. They tried to conscript our children. *Our children!* Even little Jala, she's only *eight*..."

Warren put one heavy hand on her shoulder as she fought back tears. "Those pots and pans you bought," he said softly, leaning down to speak more quietly. "I made them."

"Thank you so much," she whispered. "They're so much more—"

"They're more than you know," he interrupted, a certainly settling over him like a blanket of chain mail. "They'll keep you fed. Keep your food safe. Cook everything in them. You'll get more out than you put in."

She blinked away a last tear. "But, how...?"

"Just trust. There are... good powers in the world, as well. Keep to the trade road around Evendiam. Leave the shore at first light on the road to Westhold. If you're bound to cross the Demonbanes, do so in the light, and move fast as you can. In fact, camp at the foothills—they're safe enough—so you can enter the pass at first light." He spoke quickly now, urgently. "Do you have a map?" She shook her head. "See Barnaba." He pointed to the mapmaker's shop. "He'll have one. It's ten hours through the pass—if you set in at first light, you'll make it through by dusk. Don't camp there, though—ride through the night until you reach Stormport. Stick to the shore of the bay, then." Warren didn't know where all of this was coming from—he'd only been to Stormport once himself, and it had been with a band of ogres—they'd had little to fear in the pass. "There will be brigands on the road to Westhold. Travel with others if you can. Carry as little of value as you—"

"We've little enough left," Mayd said bitterly. "And thank you."

Warren nodded, all his urgent instructions out and an emptiness sitting in his chest. "C'mon. This is Cole's." Then he tilted his head. "Did you come here on purpose?"

"What do you mean?"

"You came through Strongfast?"

"Yes."

"The southern route would have been faster. More comfortable."

She hesitated, and then nodded. "We met a fortune-teller on the road to Stronghold. She advised we take the northern route around the lake. She said we'd... that we'd find friends. Things we'd need."

"Mmm. Come, let's see what Cole has for you."

————

He left Mayd in Cole's care and stepped back into the grassy square. Jen was standing there, giving him a wary look. "Customer of yours?"

"For the post and pans," he nodded, suddenly overcome with fatigue.

"Not whatever secret thing you were pounding away at all morning."

"Dagger," Warren sighed. "No, not that. If things go as they have, that'll be tomorrow's custom."

"She with that wagon with the four kids?"

"Yeah."

"Say where they're headed?"

"Demonbanes, if you can believe it. They mean to push to Stormport." Jen's eyes widened. "I know, I know. I told her... well, the usual advice. Take the pass in daylight. She'll see Barnaba for a map."

"That pass changes its way," Jen pointed out.

"His maps will know."

"True." She seemed to think for a moment, and then tilted her head. "They're from the east, then? Fleeing whatever?"

"She called it a cult as well. Said they tried to conscript her kids." Warren ground his thick molars for a moment, his powerful jaw muscles bunching and writhing. "*Kids*, Jen."

"Why here?"

"Why—oh, you mean instead of the southern route. Yeah, I asked that as well."

"And?"

"Fortune-teller."

Jen grimaced. "Been hearing that a bit too much, lately."

"Yeah."

"Something's lighting us up, and I don't know that I appreciate the attention."

"Agreed." The ogre shrugged. "But what can we do?"

"We can start to see to our defenses." The constable glanced around the square, took in the small knots of travelers doing business with the townfolk. "I'll speak with Leota."

"Warren!"

Warren's gaze darted past Jen, who turned at the call. Wilem was there, standing on the covered walkway in front of what had once been the dryads' cheese shop. "Come quickly!"

"What now?" Jen grumbled, setting off at a trot. Warren followed, his longer legs devouring the distance. "What is it, Wilem?"

"You have to see!" He was bouncing on his toes like an excited schoolboy, pointing to the door of the old cheese shop.

Jen and Warren peered inside. The old cheese shop was unrecognizable, transformed overnight into a cartwright's paradise. Neat stacks of lumber lined one wall, their fresh scent mingling with the rich, earthy smell of new leather. Rolls of thick canvas were piled high, and bins of iron parts gleamed. A small workbench stood ready, perfect for working on smaller pieces. The space was organized with meticulous care, each tool and material waiting to be used.

"Remarkable," Jen said, her voice filled with a mix of awe and skepticism.

Warren stared, his earlier fatigue replaced by wonder. "Did you do this, Wilem?"

The cartwright shook his head, eyes wide with excitement. "Not a bit of it. Since we decided to stay, Sam suggested we move in to the rooms above. So we did. We went to sleep last night, and down here was still that..." he searched for the right word, "lovely cheese smell. But empty. Woke up, and here it is! Like it was waiting for us."

"You'd decided to stay," Warren murmured.

Jen gave Warren a sharp look. "Gift?" she asked.

"Has to be," Warren replied. "Never seen one come on so fast, though."

"Cyntia's convinced," Wilem said, grinning. "She's already planning on a new sign for the place. Thinks we should call it 'The Wobbly Wheel.'"

"Sounds about right," Jen said with a chuckle.

Wilem beamed, the worry lines on his face softened by hope and gratitude. "I didn't think we'd feel so at home so quickly. Thought we'd be drifting for a while, after everything."

Jen's expression softened. "You're not the only ones. We've had more than a few stay."

"More than a few come and go, too," Warren said, remembering the dagger tucked away on its high shelf. "Speaking of which, I should get back to it."

Wilem watched them go, his heart lighter than it'd been in years. He looked around the shop again, scarcely believing it was real.

———

Warren found his mood lifting as he walked back to the smithy. The day was bright, the air clear, and the earlier tension seemed to melt away. He sighed with relief at a task completed, even if it was on the fouler side of the things he'd made. Maybe Mayd and her family would make it. Maybe the dagger would sit on its shelf, forgotten, for a week or two. Maybe—

"Warren?"

He blinked as Susan gave him a gentle smile. "Hey."

"Rough day?"

The ogre sighed, running a hand over his pate and down his face. "The roughest. Four out of ten. At best." His shoulders slumped. "But it's getting better. Is Darby all right?"

"He was a little hurt, but I explained." He expression turned a bit gray. "Not a good thing, then? Last night's dream?"

"No," Warren exhaled. "No, not at all. Innocent-looking, but it's foul. It's meant for something bad. For some*one* bad." He shook off the chill that had started creeping up his spine. "But on the good side, Wilem and Cyntia are staying. The cheese shop is now a cartwright's shop. Full of lumber, tools, everything."

Susan's eyebrows rose. "That *is* good news. It means..." She lowered her voice. "It means the icosahedron is complete, yes?"

Warren blinked again. "It does. And at just the right time. Jen was going to speak to Leota." He scanned the town square, but didn't see the rugged old constable. "Probably with her now."

"That sounds like trouble."

"That's what she's worried about. Too many people have taken the long way here, and say they were told by a fortune-teller to do so."

"Our little town becoming famous?"

"Unfortunately. And at the worst time, if it attracts whatever war-cult is building in the east."

"You mean if word gets out that we're some repository for magic artifacts."

"Exactly."

Susan considered, and laid a small, pale hand on Warren's thick forearm. "Can you... stop? For a while?"

The ogre shook his head slowly. "Not if the dreams keep coming, no. They... I can't, once they happen."

"I... know."

"And it won't just be me. Lucy's pots, Barnaba's maps, all the weird stuff Tyran's shop puts in front of people. Yesterday he sold a halter that lets a horse find the right direction in any kind of light or weather, no reins required."

"Goodness."

"It's not what we're doing or selling. We've always done that. It's just gotten to be *so many people*. How many are in town right now?"

Susan thought a minute. "Close to three dozen. Probably half will spend the night. Minnie's beside herself. That's why I've been going over and helping in the mornings."

"Well, that and your husband all but crushing you in your own bed," he sighed.

"Warren—"

"No, it's fine. I'm not in as dour a mood as that. Not truly. Six out of ten." He sighed again and looked up at the sky. "It's almost dinner. Would anyone mind if you and Darby and I kept to ourselves tonight?"

"I don't think they'd mind at all." Susan rubbed her husband's forearm for a moment. "You head in. Wash up, relax a bit. I'll find Darby, like as not he's in the stable yard. We'll get *him* washed up, and I know Dardrad and Cole have worked up some supper platters. I'll just abscond with one."

"You're a miracle," Warren sighed, pulling his wife into a gentle embrace.

"Oh, I know," she said easily, her voice muffled. "And you smell like burnt leather."

Warren grinned and squeezed her a bit tighter.

thirteen

. . .

THE FIRST DREAM had Warren's heart clenching in his chest.

Darby was there, standing in the middle of the town square. His ears had grown long and sharp, sticking out from his head like spades. His skin, Warren saw with a pang, was tinged a deep green. The boy looked happy, though. He was surrounded by what seemed to be children, but with each turn of the dream they became clearer; they were human. They taunted and jeered, the harsh words beginning to reach Warren even through the fog of sleep: "Ogreboy! Trollkid!" Darby's mouth moved, but Warren could hear nothing from him. His son's face turned slowly, and Warren saw tears in the boy's eyes.

The dream shifted, and Darby was older, taller, his limbs long and gangly, his frame massive even though it didn't yet carry bulk. The town square was empty, and Darby stood alone. His ears had grown longer still, his skin darker. His eyes, though, were the same. They searched the empty square for something, someone, and Warren experienced a despair that tore at him even in his sleep.

He tried to wake, but the dream clung fiercely. Darby was his own age now, a full-grown ogre, but still so young. He was miles away from town, on a lonely stretch of the trade road. A single figure was there with him, an old man who leaned on a staff. Warren thought it was Aran, but the dream was too insistent, too focused on Darby to let him see clearly.

Darby was alone again. He was as ogre as Warren now, as if the father had replaced the son. The dream pulled wide, and Warren could see the lake, the foothills, the town, their home. He could see everything, but Darby was alone. Alone.

Without warning, that dream ended and a new one began.

Warren found himself in the smithy, but it was different. Shadows hung on the walls, curling thickly in the corners like forgotten things. He moved to leave, but chains—heavy, dark, unyielding—bound him to the spot. A terrible urgency throbbed in his chest, telling him to make, to forge, to create, but when he looked around, everything was strange. He didn't know the names for the things he saw. A dull slab of iron, a black pit of coals, a heavy wooden bench littered with alien shapes. He tried to reach for his hammer, but couldn't even remember what it looked like.

He stood, helpless and dumb, while the pressure built inside him, a drumbeat pounding against his ribs. It was like a Forge Dream's insistence, but more relentless, more demanding. He strained against the chains, but they held fast, mocking his strength. Time stretched, a thin wire pulled tighter and tighter, and he was sure he'd burst from the force of it.

The dream dissolved into a thousand frantic images, swirling around him in a dizzying blur.

And then a third dream began.

This one had the fuzzy feel of a proper Forge Dream, but it started far sharper than he was used to. The dream swooped high and wide, a bird's-eye view of the trade road snaking between the foothills and the lake. Warren saw a train of carts and wagons, their outlines small and slow against the vast stretch of land. They moved like a procession of ants, laboring steadily forward, their progress plodding but determined. Warren's perspective shifted, narrowing in on the nearest cart, its burden heavy and its pace sluggish. As he watched, the cart hit a rut.

The wheel jostled violently, and a small iron pin somewhere near the cart's axel sheared away with a sharp, decisive snap. The wheel wobbled, threatening to come loose, and the entire cart shuddered as if it would collapse. Warren felt the familiar grip of the dream tighten around him, but instead of moving on, it looped back, replaying the same scene with an unsettling precision.

The pin sheared away again, the wheel lurched, the cart trembled. Over and over, the dream cycled through the same sequence, the same failure. But Warren didn't understand. He didn't know what the pin was, what it did, what it meant. The dream offered no answers, only its relentless repetition, a demand without explanation.

He tried to wrench himself awake, but the dream held him firm, insisting, insisting, insisting. Lurch. *Snap.* Wobble. *Snap.* Wobble. *Snap. Snap. Snap.*

Finally, Warren managed to rip himself out of it, his eyes flying open. He was lying rock-still, on his back, safe in his own bed. Susan sighed sleepily next to him as she eased from her own slumber. Early morning light streamed through the window. Down the hallway, Warren's sharp hearing picked up the soft sounds of Darby's gentle snores.

"Quiet night for once," Susan murmured. "No dreams?"

"Too many dreams," Warren muttered.

"You didn't move a muscle all night."

"Hrmph."

"One to ten?"

"Three." The ogre rolled out of bed. "I need to find Wilem."

———

"Sounds like a linchpin," Wilem mused. "Honestly, not much else on a cart that would shear. Here, look."

Warren had found the cartwright in the stable yard, staring contemplatively at his own cart. Now, the man leaned down and pointed to a thick metal pin that ran through the two pieces of wood that formed the cart's main steering mechanism. "Simpler carts won't have one, but they're harder to steer, especially in tight spots. See how the arms sort of rotate around the pin?"

"Mmm. You'd think they'd be stronger."

"Actually, no. They're made to shear if they're put under too much of the wrong kind of stress."

"*Made* to break?"

"Well, shear. But definitely. That way the steering arms themselves don't break. Easy enough to keep a few pins on hand as replacements, and once you're used to it, they're pretty easy to replace. Better that than having to fashion a new arm when you're a league away from anyplace." He tilted his head. "So you're to make a linchpin, this morning?"

"I think so." Warren shook his head, trying to clear his mind. "It was a busy night for dreams, but this one felt the most like... you know. A *proper* dream."

"Well, they're easy enough to fashion, although I've never done so myself. Here, look." He reached down, grunted a bit with effort, and then pulled the pin free. It was about the width of Warren's thumb, and the length of half his hand. "See here?" He pointed to two narrow areas near the middle of the pin. The metal had been scored, almost as if someone had taken a thin file and carved grooves into it. "Those are made to give way. If the arms bind, the pin snaps and you're safe. A few copper for a new pin, and you're back on the road."

Warren nodded. "Don't know if I've got time to make them so fine," he said, running a finger over the scored metal. "But I can have a half-dozen basic ones done by noon."

"Dad?" Warren turned to see Darby at the gate. "I thought we were going to work on pots."

"Change of plans," Warren said. He looked back to Wilem. "Could use your help, if you're willing."

"Sure. But you know I've never—"

"Good. C'mon, Darb."

Back at the smithy, a familiar urgency pressed at Warren. He ducked inside, his mind racing through the steps he'd need to take. The dream was clear now, its focus sharp and insistent. He set up a small forge on the workbench, a place to do the fiddly work of scoring the pins. As he moved, his anxiety eased, the purpose of the dream becoming more certain, more sure.

Wilem stepped in, his eyes scanning the cluttered space. "You really have a lot on your hands, don't you?"

"Pots and pans," Darby said as he followed. "Dad said we were going to make a bunch more."

"We will. But these first. I'll set you up with the molds, Darb."

"Okay," the boy said, though he didn't sound convinced. He set to work with the resolute energy of a child determined to prove himself, scooping sand with quick, practiced movements.

Warren turned to Wilem. "See this?" He pointed to a strip of metal he'd already begun scoring. "How deep?"

"Deeper," Wilem said. "And a bit longer."

Warren grunted, bending over the strip and running a thin blade down either side. The score marks appeared, bright against the dark metal. He worked quickly, methodically, the focus of the dream guiding his hands.

Wilem watched, a thoughtful expression on his face. "You know," he said slowly, "I've seen plenty of these when we were back east. But I don't think I've ever seen them cast like this."

Warren didn't look up. "Hmm?"

"The pins. Ours were always just… ordinary iron."

"Ah." Warren tilted his head, his eyes never leaving his work. "Yeah. Not these."

Darby glanced up from the molds, his curiosity getting the better of him. "They'll be like magic?"

Warren allowed himself a small smile. "Not magic, but close enough." He straightened, stretching his back. "Odd, though."

"Odd how?" Wilem asked.

"Whatever I see in the Forge Dream, I make from the ore Darby brings up from below." He nodded toward the trap door in the smithy's scarred wooden flooring. "I never know exactly how the ore will make the item special, but it always does. Sometimes I get a sense of it when whoever the customer is shows up and takes it. Like the pots and pans yesterday."

"What made them special?"

"She'll get more food out of them than she puts in. And it'll always be safe. Healthy."

"Fascinating. You know, I was cutting some lumber with my new saw yesterday."

"Oh?"

"Went through the wood like a hot knife through butter. Perfectly straight cuts. I barely had to pay attention, didn't even wind myself."

"Tools," the ogre said thoughtfully. "Makes sense. I'm betting your lumber will be stronger, too. Possibly lighter."

"It did seem like it."

"The shop's gifts. But... what would make a linchpin more special? It can't just be stronger, right? You *want* them to break, you said."

"Oh, I see your point. Maybe it'll shear more easily, though. That's it's job, after all. So maybe it'll do the job better?"

"Mmm. Maybe." Warren bent back over the strip of metal and resumed carving a score line into it. "This deep enough?"

Wilem considered. "Seems about right."

"Good. I'll do the pins the same way. Darb, get some of the ore."

"Got it, Dad." The boy pulled the trap door open and scurried down the ladder. He came back up a moment later with a small bag full of the dark silvery chunks, and a troubled expression on his face. "Hey, Dad?"

"Yeah?"

"The pile's getting smaller."

Warren blinked several times as his mind tried to grasp what his son had just said. "What?"

"It's always been the same size. No matter how much I take, it's always back to normal the next time I go down. But it's definitely smaller, now."

"That doesn't make sense." It was part of the smithy's gift that the ore replenished itself.

"Dunno, Dad."

"Is it a problem?" Wilem asked, his forehead creasing with concern.

"I... don't know," Warren answered slowly. He shook himself. "Two out of ten," he muttered. The stress and emotion of the night's dreams came back full force, and he shoved them out of his mind. "Let's just get the forge stoked up."

———

"What in the seven dwarven hells?" Warren cursed softly.

Not softly enough: "Rude," Dardrad grumbled. "Although true."

"Truly, I don't know what's gotten into it," Dooley said miserably.

Fully half of the town's enclosed square, from roof to roof, was covered in thick, sticky webbing.

"It was acting weird yesterday, but nothing like this," the menagerie owner added.

It was midafternoon, and Warren and Darby had finished a half-dozen of the scored linchpins when Warren called a halt for lunch. The few travelers who'd made it into town by that point in the day had all been seated in front of the pub, muttering darkly and casting fearful glances at the town's gates. Warren, fully preoccupied with the diminishing stock of special ore, anxious about his dreams, and jittery about who would eventually be coming for the dagger he'd made the day before, didn't pick up on the uneasy energy the travelers were giving off. Instead, he and Darby had stepped through the open gates and nearly gotten caught in the webbing there.

"How do we get *rid* of it?" Jen snapped. "Fire?"

"Won't burn," Dooley said, shaking his head. "Water will degrade it, but you'd need a lot of it. Usually starts to fall apart after a few days."

"A few *days?*" Jen grimaced.

"We can set up extra tables along the road," Lucy said. "Take our wares out there. So we're not out the business."

A soft rustling drew everyone's attention, and they turned to see the huge, red-bodied spider scurry up a section of web and onto the rooftops. It quickly vanished from sight.

"Dooley, just try and keep it from covering any more," Jen aid, clearly irritated. "Warn the kids to come all the way down to Dexter's before they step off the walkway."

"I'll do what I can," Dooley promised, hurrying toward his shop—now inaccessible from the square itself thanks to the webbing stretching from the grass to the top of the covered walkway—and making the *clicking* noises the spider used for language.

"Anyone seen Wil—oh, seven hells." Sam stopped at the sight of the webs.

"Yeah," Dardrad said flatly.

"The spider?" Sam asked.

"The spider," Jen confirmed. "Wilem's in his shop, I think. That bit's not covered up yet."

"Someone just rolled in with a busted cart wheel," Sam said.

"I'll get him!" Darby volunteered. Without waiting for a response, he dashed toward the cartwright's shop door.

"And Warren, there's a sketchy looking guy on horseback," Sam said. "Says he's looking for a blade."

A chill ran down Warren's spine. "Hard times circle 'round," he muttered, turning back toward the road. "Someone tell Darby to find something to eat. He's *not* to come to the smithy until I'm done."

"Dream?" Jen asked. "Should we be concerned?"

"Yes, and probably," Warren said. "I'm hoping he won't stay." He walked heavily toward the smithy. As he passed Knodalon, sitting on his bench, the old man gave him a long stare and a firm nod.

Somehow, the gesture made Warren even more edgy. *One out of ten and falling.* He rolled his shoulders, trying to loosen up the tense muscles, but they weren't having it.

The man on horseback couldn't have looked more normal and less threatening, and yet also couldn't have *been* more threatening, in some way Warren couldn't quite define.

He wore a dark cloak that hung heavily from his shoulders, its edges frayed and stained from miles of hard travel. Beneath it, his riding clothes were practical and worn, the fabric faded and patched in places. He had the look of a man who thought little about appearances. His boots were caked with mud, and his gloves looked as if they'd been through a dozen battles. An empty scabbard hung from his hip, its leather strap tied hastily to keep it from flapping as he rode.

The man carried himself with an air of cold, calculated purpose. He was lean and wiry, the kind of strength that spoke of endurance rather than brute force. As his eyes met Warren's, they were a piercing blue, sharp and predatory. They swept over the town like an eagle searching for prey, missing nothing, calculating everything. There was a chill to his gaze, an indifference that bordered on disdain.

A prickle of unease skittered down Warren's spine as the man dismounted, landing lightly on his feet. His movements were fluid, too smooth, a hunter's grace. He led his horse a few steps forward, and Warren noticed the deep red stain on the beast's flank. Blood, dried to a dark crust, looking as if it might belong to someone—or something—other than horse or rider.

"Smith?" the man asked, his voice curt and clipped.

Warren nodded. The man's eyes flicked to the smithy, then back to Warren.

"I need a blade," he said. "This one didn't hold." He gestured to the empty scabbard with a slight, dismissive motion.

Warren squinted, seeing the man in a new light. He didn't look like these other travelers. Not haggard and worn, not running from anything. In fact, he looked like he might be heading into the very trouble that was driving everyone else out.

"Broke it, did you?" Warren asked, his voice neutral.

"Aye," the man replied. "In an... altercation." There was a hint of amusement in his tone, as if the word was a private joke.

"What are you looking for?" Warren rumbled.

"Something quick. Sharp." The man's lips curled into a humorless smile. "Didn't expect to find a smithy out this way. But then, I've heard rumors."

Warren's eyes narrowed. "Rumors?"

"About this place." The man's voice was low, almost mocking. "I'm not the only one who's heard them."

"Not from around here," Warren said. "Most folks on the run from the east. You're the first I've seen coming from the other direction."

The man shrugged, his expression unreadable. "Opportunity," he said. "I tend to run *toward* where everyone else is running *from.*"

A cold knot settleed in Warren's stomach. He knew this type, and he didn't like it. The man was a vulture, feeding off chaos and war. The kind who found work as a mercenary, or worse.

"Do you have what I need?" the man asked.

Warren kept his voice steady. "Might have something in a dagger I could show you."

"Hmm." The man's eyes bore up into Warren's. "Let's have a look."

Warren turned to the smithy without another word. As he retrieved it from its resting place, the dagger laid heavier in his hand than its size and shape suggested. It was wrapped tightly, hidden from view, but he knew it wouldn't remain that way for long.

The man watched him approach, his eyes gleaming with interest. He took the package from Warren's outstretched hand and peeled back the cloth, his movements quick and sure. The dagger lay exposed, its dull silver surface catching the light in a way that made it seem alive, shifting. The man's expression remained impassive, but Warren saw the satisfaction in his eyes.

"Hmm," the man said, turning the blade over in his hands. He gripped it tightly, then loosely, as if testing its balance. He swung it once, twice, each motion a fluid extension of his arm. The dagger seemed to belong to him already. "This will do."

Warren's chest tensed, a mix of relief and something darker. "Gold," he said, as if the word weighed him down. "Ten pieces." An outrageous price for a dagger.

The man barely hesitated. "Done."

"You got that kind of coin on you?" Warren asked, surprised despite himself.

The man gave a short, humorless laugh. "I do." He looked back at the dagger. "What makes it special?" His voice was curious, almost playful.

"I have no idea," Warren replied truthfully.

The stranger looked at him, then down again at the dagger. "Hmm," he said again, a hint of satisfaction in his tone. He rewrapped the blade, securing it with a deft twist of the cloth. He reached into his jerkin and pulled out a small leather purse, opening it to count our ten shiny gold coins. Wordlessly, he handed them to Warren, who folded his enormous hand around them. The man turned and mounted his horse with an easy grace, the kind that came from years of living in the saddle. The horse stamped and snorted, eager to be on its way.

Warren watched as the man rode off through the east gate, his thoughts a tangled mess of unease and relief. He didn't know how long he stood there, staring at the empty road, until a voice broke through his haze.

"That one has a foul destiny ahead."

Warren turned and realized that Aran had been standing there the entire team, leaning against the stable yard fence. "Yeah."

"It pains you, doesn't it?"

Warren nodded silently.

"You keep doing it, though."

"I told you before. It's part of the obligation of this place. Every traveler, every adventurer, every quest—we serve all who come in—"

"Peace, yes, you mentioned." Every bit of Aran's former vagueness was gone now, his eyes sharp and clear, his expression thoughtful. "You're not a player in the play, you know."

"Huh?"

Aran waved one hand in a vague gesture. "You're backdrop. Not a player."

"Uh." *They're the players in it. Not us.* Sam's words, Warren remembered. Spoken—it seemed like moons ago. The rush of the past few days, the Forge Dreams, the customers, it all came settling heavily onto Warren's broad shoulders, and the ogre slumped. "Yeah." He looked more closely at the old man, but his expression was still calm. Focused. "So, ah, have you decided when you'll be moving on?" Warren asked.

"So anxious to be rid of me."

"No, it's just most people don't stay here long. They have... places to be."

"Quests to complete."

"Yeah."

"As it happens, I believe I'll be moving on tomorrow at first light."

"Ah."

"Be well, ogre."

"Yeah."

"Dad?"

Warren saw his son standing by the gates, his eyes wide with concern and his voice cautious. Hesitant. "You're not supposed to be here," Warren said, his voice gruffer than he intended.

Darby's expression shifted, a mix of hurt and determination. "I thought you were done. Mom said you might need help with the other... things."

Warren sighed, the weight of the past few days settling heavily on his shoulders. "We've got plenty to do, that's sure." He gestured toward the smithy, where the molds for the pots and pans still waited. "Let's get back to it. Did you get some lunch?"

Darby followed, his steps quick and eager. "Was that the guy from your dream?"

Warren's mind flashed to the stranger and the dagger, the terrible surety with which he'd wielded it. "It was meant for him, yeah. C'mon. We'll use normal iron for this batch. Doesn't take as long to melt down."

"Dardrad's got smoked elk slices."

"I'm not hungry."

fourteen

. . .

THE DREAM WAS unlike any Warren had ever had. It lacked any kind of action, not even the slow, creeping non-action of shadows lengthening against a wall of hanging pots and pans. It was just a gray, formless mist, with a shield floating in the middle.

The shield was round, its surface a dull, metallic gray. It hung there, unmarked, unadorned, a blank canvas waiting for a story. Warren could see it so clearly, floating alone in the mist. But it changed, and he saw it for what it was: plain, simple, and utterly resilient. It blurred, and another took its place.

This one was larger, more imposing. Its face was a deep, lustrous red, with thick iron bands crossing it in a bold "X" pattern. The metal strips held tight to the shield's surface, their edges riveted down with small silver studs. It was the kind of shield that commanded attention, that spoke of strength and fortitude. It held there for a long moment, then faded.

A new shield emerged. It was angular, almost triangular, tapering to a point at its bottom. Its surface was a rich, dark wood, polished to a gleaming finish. At its center was a single symbol, an unfamiliar rune carved deeply into the wood. The rune seemed to pulse with a quiet, steady energy, like a heartbeat. It was an enigmatic piece, full of mystery and promise. It, too, gave way to yet another.

This one was massive, a tower shield that covered nearly as much space as the first three combined. Its surface was covered in intricate, interlocking rings, each one a different shade of silvery metal. The rings caught the light as they overlapped, creating a shimmering, dazzling pattern that seemed to move and shift. It was a shield meant to dazzle, to confuse, to protect. It held its place in Warren's dream, and then it didn't.

Over and over, the shields cycled through, each taking its turn in the formless mist. Round and red, angular and wooden, massive and metallic. Each shield was distinct, each one a new demand, each one drifting away like a forgotten memory. They looped through Warren's sleeping mind, insistent and unrelenting, until he woke with a start.

The room was dark, and Warren lay still, letting his heart slow as he took in the quiet of their home. It was the middle of the night, and Susan slept peacefully beside him. The dream had been unlike any he'd ever had; it was the opposite of the dagger's nightmarish intensity, yet it was just as overwhelming. He felt the weight of it, the pressure, and knew he wouldn't find sleep again. Not with those shields haunting him. *Two out of ten. Maybe three.* His entire body was tense.

He rose quietly, his movements careful and deliberate. He stepped out into the cool night air, letting it wash over him, clear his mind. The town was silent, the only sounds the soft lapping of the lake against its shore and the gentle rustle of leaves in the foothills' breeze. Warren breathed deeply, trying to ease the tension that curled through him like a stubborn snake.

As the first light of dawn crept over the horizon, Warren made his way to the smithy. He didn't know which shield would be first, didn't know how he'd manage to make them all, but the urgency of the dream was pushing him forward. He would start with what he knew, what he'd seen most clearly.

But once he'd fired the forge, pumping its bellows until it glowed yellow-white, something strange happened.

He had no idea how to proceed.

He stared at the forge until the morning light spilled through the smithy's open doors, and the gentle sounds of the town waking drifted across the road. He could hear Trevor fetching travelers' horses, heard Sam propping open the door of the pub. Knodalon, he knew, would have already settled himself onto his bench.

And still, he had no idea how to start.

He glanced around the smithy, looking for inspiration.

He saw perfectly normal tools, some scraps from previous projects, the half-dozen linchpins sitting on a workbench. But nothing came to him. He could imagine how he'd begin working on a horseshoe, but when his mind went back to shields, it seemed to blank itself. He blinked a few times, trying to will the vision back into his head, to let it guide his hands. But nothing. He shook his head in disbelief, frustration building in his chest.

He thought of the round shield, how simple it should be. It was a trick the Forge Dream had never played on him before, showing him so much but leaving him with so little. He took a deep breath and stared at the empty forge.

"Warren?"

He turned to see Susan standing in the doorway, her hair loose and wild in the morning breeze. "Hey," he said, his voice a low rumble.

"I brought you some breakfast," she said softly, holding up a small basket. "Thought you might need it."

"Thanks," he replied, though he wasn't sure if he could eat. His stomach was as tangled as his mind.

Susan stepped closer, her eyes scanning the cluttered smithy. "You've been out here since before dawn."

"Yeah." He looked at her, his expression one of bewilderment. "Ever feel like you know exactly what needs doing, but have no idea how to do it?"

"Sounds like those dreams of yours are getting more creative," she said with a gentle smile.

"This one's different, though." He ran a hand through his hair, the gesture weary. "I've never had one like it. Never had one leave me so..." He trailed off, unsure how to finish the thought.

"Lost?" she offered.

"Yeah."

"Maybe you need to take a step back," Susan suggested. "Clear your head."

"I—"

"Warren." Sam stepped into the smithy. "Morning, Susan."

"Morning, Sam."

"What's up?" Warren asked. Then he frowned. Sam's expression was... confused. Concerned. Afraid? "What's the matter?"

"Do you think it'll be a busy day today?" she asked. But it wasn't in the way she'd normally ask it, the way all the townsfolk asked one another. Her brows were bunched and wrinkled.

Warren opened his mouth to reply, his mind simultaneously reaching for the information—a sense that the town always provided.

He came up empty.

"I don't know," he whispered.

"Minnie doesn't either," Sam said, her tone desperate.

"Warren?" Susan asked uncertainly. "Is something the matter?" She'd never had the busy-sense; it generally came only to the actual shop proprietors.

"Let's go see Makota," he said firmly. *She's always had the best sense for it,* he thought as he walked as quickly as he could without breaking into a jog. *Well, her and Minnie,* he added grimly.

Makota's shop was a flurry of activity. Flour dusted the air like snow, and the smell of yeast and sugar mingled with the slightly burnt scent of something forgotten in the oven. The usual order of the bakery was replaced with chaos, trays piled haphazardly, half-formed pastries waiting for their next step. Makota darted between them, her tail flicking with agitation as she tried to manage what seemed like a dozen tasks at once.

"Is it two dozen?" Kene asked frantically, his small hands struggling to wrap a bundle of sticky twists.

"Three!" Makota replied, her voice harried. "No, four! Wait, I don't know!"

Sora dashed past him, clinging to a tray of steaming buns. "Where do these go?" she shouted.

Makota paused, her eyes wild as they scanned the room. She seemed as lost as the rest of them. "I—just—" she stammered, then turned back to the dough she was kneading, her motions quick and distracted. Her usual grace was nowhere to be seen.

Warren, Susan, and Sam stood in the middle of the chaos, their presence barely registered in the frenzy. The shop was packed with townfolk, each of them wearing the same bewildered look.

Vamir hovered near the door, his brow furrowed as he watched the commotion. "This is... unusual," he said, the words heavy with understatement.

Lucy nodded, her arms crossed tightly over her chest. "I can't get a sense of it at all," she admitted.

"I've never seen us so off-balance," Prudence added, her voice tense.

Trevor and Darby were there as well, helping where they could—although it seemed to Warren they were just as puzzled as the rest.

"I'm sure it'll settle down," Makota said, but Warren could hear the uncertainty in her tone. Her hands moved mechanically as she shaped a new batch of bread, the rhythm as off-kilter as the morning.

"Here," Warren said, stepping forward and taking a tray from Sora. "Let us give you a hand."

"Thank you," Makota said, her relief palpable. "I don't know what's gotten into us." She glanced at Sam and Susan. "Any idea...?"

"None," Sam said.

"Not a clue," Susan added.

Makota's ears drooped slightly.

The shop rang with the sound of clattering pans, hurried footsteps, and murmured conversations. The townsfolk exchanged nervous glances, their unease growing as the morning stretched on with no clear answer. Warren felt the pressure of the shield-dreams still heavy on his mind, but this new uncertainty gnawed at him, the sense that something big was looming just out of sight.

"Let's not panic," Sam said, her voice calm and steady. But even she looked shaken.

"It can't be worse than last year," Trevor said, his voice trying for optimism but landing somewhere closer to doubt.

"Or maybe it can," Darby replied with a shrug.

Jen stepped in. "Does anyone—"

"No," several voices shot back in unison.

The constable's expression tightened. "Damn."

Warren blinked suddenly as something occurred to him. He stepped out of the shop, walking halfway into the grassy square until he could see out the gates.

Knodalon's bench was empty.

"Jen," he called.

The constable joined him, her eyes following his gaze, and he could feel her tensing when she saw the empty bench. "Leota," she said in a clipped, flat tone as she hurried across the square, Warren in town, to the witch's home.

Leota, never known for being an early riser, opened before Jen could even knock. "It's gone," she said flatly.

"Gone?" Warren asked.

"Gone. All of it. All the gifts. There's not even anything for me to channel my magic into. Nothing." She spoke quickly, and an involuntary panic rose in Warren's mind.

"Damn," Jen said softly. She turned and began marching toward the gates.

———

"Knodalon's fine," Jen began, her posture even more tense and her voice tight. "He just doesn't want to come out of the storehouse right now. He won't say why."

The proprietors of the town had all gathered in the pub, which Sam had hastily closed up.

"It has to be related," Dardrad grumbled.

"Probably. We've confirmed that none of us has any sense for how busy it'll be today. Most of the overnight travelers have left or are about to, and it'll be a while before the day's business rolls in. So we have some time to... I don't know."

"Leota says the gifts are all gone," Sam added, her own expression worried and her posture wary. She reminded Warren of a fighter about to go into battle.

"That's going to be a problem for Cole and I," Dardrad said. "Food will spoil quickly."

"Knodalon says the storehouse will still keep things fresh," Jen said. "I don't know how. But you should start moving your stores there. Calder, your stores have always technically been in the storehouse, so they should be fine. But don't bring back more than you can fit in your section."

"Aye." The old fisherman's expression was grim.

"Dooley, I'm assuming you can't do anything with the damn spider," Jen said.

"I can't even understand it anymore. But it's stopped building webs."

"And gone to skulking around the rooftops, I know," Jen spat. "Sorry. Damn thing is making me even more tense than I was."

"It's afraid of something. And..."

"Spit it out," Jen ordered.

"It's got a couple of friends." Dooley sounded miserable.

"What?" Sam yelped.

"They're keeping to the rooftops."

"What in the—"

"Not our biggest problem," Jen cut her off. Sam subsided, but her eyes kept flicking around the room, like someone who'd been backed into a corner and was looking for an opening.

"So what do we do?" Alred asked.

"We push through," Jen said firmly. "We're the only settlement in this part of the Mistrals, and people still need us. So we carry on as best we can."

The proprietors exchanged uneasy, anxious glances.

"Let's go. Explain things to your families. Simplify what you need to. Sam, close the pub early tonight."

"Why?"

"Because *my* gift is gone, too. We don't need any of the travelers getting drunk and starting fights."

"Oh. Right."

"Let's all meet here again after Sam closes up. Warren, could you—"

"I can't feel the forge at all," he said glumly. "You want me to lurk on the roadside?"

Jen nodded gratefully. "Just some kind of deterrent."

"No problem."

"Can Darby go back to helping with the horses?" Minnie asked. "Only because my Trevor will—"

"You'll need every hand," the ogre nodded. "Of course. I can help him."

"All right," Jen said, standing. "Let's go do what we do, gifts or no."

———

As the sun climbed into the sky, the townsfolk adapted.

Cole had deployed his kids to things the town's small farm had never before had to worry about: hunting for weeds, scanning for tiny pests, and even patrolling for larger pests like mice. He and his wife had begun ferrying perishables to the main lakeside storehouse.

Makota and her family had cut back and simplified their plans to just a couple of sweet-treat pastries and more basic breads. Given that their ovens were now cooking more slowly and less evenly, Makota herself was spending most of her time carefully monitoring the bakes that were underway.

Dardrad—grumbling all the while—had begun moving his own perishables to the storehouse. He'd emerged the first time pale and irritated, complaining that Knodalon was "lurking" amongst the shelves, muttering darkly about abstract topics like time.

Prudence and Lucy had both discovered how relatively lazy their shops had let them become. Lucy had refocused, spending almost twice as long to throw a single pot and complaining that she'd be able to produce much fewer pieces at this pace. Prudence had simply sighed and said she needed to get back to basics, and begun rooting through the paper patterns she'd brought with her when she moved to the town.

Vamir remarked that things wouldn't change much for him—his bookshop was still crowded, but his strange pet, Polyocular, was still able to help him find what someone was looking for. "If we don't have the book someone wants or needs," he said with a small shrug, "it is what it is."

Leota, with Alred's help, had positioned herself on a bench in front of the inn. "The town has no use for my magic now," she'd explained, clearly trying to reorient herself. "But I can do a bit out here to defuse tensions, should they arise." Warren stood on the opposite side of the road, in front of the stable yard, with his arms crossed, looking sternly at anyone who so much as raised their voice along the road. Jen mirrored him at the town's other road gate, giving the stink-eye and a grumpy welcome to every cart that pulled through. Fortunately, that was the western gate, and most everyone was exiting the town in that direction, not entering.

Although Warren was pretty sure her scowl wasn't much worse than his own.

Just as the sun passed its zenith, a single-horse cart rolled slowly through the eastern road gate. Warren knew at once that this was where his linchpins would go, for the cart had obviously been rigged to hold together after its original linchpin had sheared. "Wilem," he called.

The cartwright, who'd been sitting chatting quietly with Leota, looked up, caught sight of the cart, and nodded. He hurried across the road to the smithy and emerged with the linchpins in hand. "Might be we could help you," he said as the cart's driver slowed his horse to a stop. "I'm a cartwright."

"Sheared the pin a league back," the driver said, shaking his head sadly. "Damn ruts in the roads."

"There's been a lot more traffic than usual."

"And me not smart enough to carry a spare. How many can you sell me?"

"I've a half dozen for a silver, if you like."

"Sold."

"And free help getting the first one in," Wilem added.

"And sold again," the driver said thankfully. He climbed down and began helping Wilem pull apart the rigging they'd used in place of the missing pin.

Warren felt a pang of… was it regret? Those linchpins might be the last things he'd ever make using the special ore.

"Strange iron," the cart's driver commented as Wilem slipped a new pin into place.

"Common hereabouts," Wilem lied. "Bit softer. Should protect these arms better, is the theory."

"I'll take it. Any chance of rooms in that inn, there? I've a mind to stay the night. It's been a beast of a morning. If… you know. I'll trust you to tell me if it's a safe place or not."

"Safe as any can be," Wilem promised. "And I think Minnie's still got two rooms. Just yourself?"

"Aye."

"I'll help you unhitch your horse. Warren, what's the going rate?"

"Room, meals, and care for the horse, five coppers, I think," the ogre replied. The driver swallowed nervously at Warren's low rumble. "And we'll keep you safe as any being could," he added.

"Right enough, then," the man said. "C'mon, Brindle, let's get you out of those traces."

———

"Well, we made it," Jen said heavily.

"It wasn't that bad," Alred said with a shrug.

"Nothing in your shop is perishable," Dardrad growled.

"And the inn is the same amount of work whether people are having dreams or not," Minnie pointed out.

"The ones in tonight were fairly settled," Sam added. "But Jen, I think you were right about closing at sundown. Next time a minstrel comes through I'll just hire them until then."

"There weren't any ill-wishers," Leota said. "But there's a lot of stress. Nothing specific, though."

"Well, they're all fleein' this war cult," Minnie sighed. "Got a family of six crammed into one room, headed to live with some relations on the western shore of the lake."

"They left with almost nothing, too, poor things," Prudence said, shaking her head in sympathy. It was rare for her to put in an appearance at the pub, but the disappearance of the town's gifts had rattled everyone. She'd even left her toddler with one of Cole's kids. "Sold them a whole set of clothing for each of the kids." She looked around the room before adding, "For, of course. Linen isn't that dear."

"We've emptied out the farm storehouse and put everything into Knodalon's," Cole said. "I don't know what makes that any different from—"

"Damn old man creeping around in there scaring the daylights out of everyone," Dardrad grumbled. "But... it *is* somehow keeping everything fresh."

"I'll put out tomorrow," Calder said, his gravely voice even rougher than usual. "One day should see us fill our stocks."

"Fortunately we'd eaten down most of everything during the winter," Dardrad said, nodding agreement. "I've got room for three or four more highelks. Hunters usually start bringing them through about now."

"And we've moved everything salted or otherwise preserved into the farm storehouse," Alred said.

"It is worth pointing out," Dexter said in his dry, whispery tone, "that while my skills are unaffected, the shop has always sped healing and offered relief from pain."

"A point," Jen said. "Everyone needs to be extra-careful."

"I'm releasing all of the animals that haven't fully domesticated," Dooley said sadly. "I can't understand them anymore." He looked around the room. "I don't know how much I'll be able to contribute to—"

"Nonsense," Jen snapped. "We're family, here. We take care of each other, gifts or no. You can lend a hand to something else until... whatever happens next."

Dooley nodded his thanks.

"Sadly, my tools are worse than normal ones, now," Wilem said. "Warren, I was going to ask if I could have you take a look at them, especially the saws."

"I can put a new edge on them," Warren promised. "It'll be nice to have something to do, actually. And you can show me that rig you use for bending pieces into wheels."

"That rig will need some reinforcing as well," Wilem said.

"Again, it'll be nice to have something to do."

"Let's not be glum," Vamir said. "We may have less to offer our guests than before, but we've still plenty, as much or more than most towns, especially this far north. Take heart."

"Aye," Tyran rumbled. "Well said, elf."

"Anyone for another round?" Sam said, pulling herself off her stool and walking back behind the bar.

A chorus of affirmatives brought a smile to everyone's face.

fifteen

. . .

AFTER A SENNIGHT, the townsfolk silently but unanimously agreed to stop talking about "before" and "after." The town's gifts were gone forever, as far as anyone knew, and they might as well, in Makota's words, "Get on with it."

Now, a fortnight beyond that, they'd all more or less gotten used to the "new normal." After all, as Minnie had pointed out, most of their shops didn't do anything special for *them*, and if they no longer helped travelers find rare artifacts, have dreams about their destinies, or get a map that was somehow up to the very day in terms of accuracy... well, none of the townsfolk had any control over that.

It didn't stop Cole or Dardrad grumbling about the loss of the smaller and more convenient storehouse.

So while it was less convenient to have to store all their perishables in the lakeside storehouse, and while all the village kids were pressed into service round-robin style to help tend the little farm... well, that wasn't a worse life than any of them had known prior to coming here.

And so life went on.

"Hey."

Warren looked up to see Susan standing in the doorway of the smithy. "Hey, you."

"One to ten?"

"Oh, nine," the ogre replied with a tusk-filled grin. "One of the couples that came in last night were riding those little palfreys from down South. You know, the ones with the dainty little hooves?"

"Oh, I love them. I saw them prancing around the yard this morning."

"Well, they wanted to get them re-shod."

"Have you even ever made shoes that size?"

"No!" Warren said cheerfully, tapping his hammer on the shoe that he was forming on his anvil. "It's so much fun!"

Susan laughed—a bright, carefree laugh, one that Warren hadn't heard in some time. "Nobody wandering in asking for mysterious swords?"

"Oh, absolutely." Warren ran a critical eye over his work, and then set it aside. "But there's nothing I can do. I mean, if they just want a basic sword and don't mind waiting a couple of days, I can take a commission. But you know. Whatever fortune-teller was out there telling tales of magic and wonder in North Pointe Common Towne is behind on the news. I don't have anything in stock named 'Nailbiter' or whatever."

"Don't let Jen or Sam hear you mock their weapons."

"Perish the thought."

"Hey, did you notice the webbing this morning?"

"All but gone. Finally." The townsfolk had been forced to go out of their way to avoid the thick, sticky strands for nearly the full fortnight, much to Dooley's chagrin.

"And the spider's gone."

"Well. I can't say that I exactly miss it."

Susan chuckled. "Certainly not. And I noticed you've been sleeping more soundly."

"Like a rock. Hey, where's Darb?"

"It's his turn for farm duty today."

"Ah."

"It's almost lunchtime. Can you take a break?"

"I can indeed. What did you have in mind?"

"Calder's doing a fish fry. The morning's catch was a bit bigger than he's got left in storage space."

"Big ogre eat many fish," Warren grinned.

———

"That's it, then?" Warren asked, his voice both curious and impressed. "Doesn't look so hard."

Wilem chuckled, shaking his head. "This is just the rim. You'll see. And it's really about the soaking, to make the wood pliable. You can't just ogre it into a curve like this. You ready to give it a shot?"

"Sure," Warren replied, stepping closer. "What comes next?"

"Spokes," Wilem said, holding up a piece of wood shaped like a long, thin wedge. "These have to be just right. See this end? It's wider, and the other's tapered a bit. Give it a try. We'll need twelve."

Warren took the spoke, examining it closely before nodding. "I think I can manage that."

"This is where the fun begins," Wilem said. "Once you've got those cut, we'll set them in the hub—right here." He pointed to a wooden cylinder with holes drilled evenly around its edge. "They have to fit just so. Then we'll set them in the felloes and attach the rim."

"Felloes?" Warren asked, his brow furrowing.

"These," Wilem said, gesturing to the curved wooden pieces that would form a circle when joined. "Ready?"

Warren nodded, his large hands surprisingly nimble as he worked. "Never thought I'd be doing this by hand," he said. "Not with the way things used to be."

"Not so bad, is it?" Wilem grinned. "Once you've got the right tools."

"Speaking of which," Warren said, his eyes darting to the saw hanging on the wall, "you need me to touch that up for you?"

"Still sharp as a dwarf's tongue," Wilem replied. He showed Warren how to fit the spokes into the hub, carefully tapping each one into place. "Like this," he said. "See? Not too tight, not too loose."

Warren watched closely, then tried his hand at it. "Like this?" he asked, giving the spoke a gentle tap.

"Exactly," Wilem said. "Now, the felloes."

They worked together, the rhythm of their hands and tools echoing in the small shop. Warren experienced a strange sense of peace as they assembled the wheel, the simple, physical work a welcome change from the past months' chaos.

"Now for the rim," Wilem said, his voice tinged with satisfaction. "This is the part that used to give us fits."

"Why's that?"

"Getting it tight on the felloes. Had to soak the wood, heat the iron, and hope it didn't all come apart."

"And now?"

Wilem grinned. "Now it's easy," he said. "Relatively speaking. Experience matters."

They fit the rim over the wheel, securing it with careful taps and adjustments. Warren wiped his brow, feeling the pleasant ache of honest labor in his muscles.

"Not bad, for an ogre," Wilem said, stepping back to admire their work.

"Ha!"

"You know, Cynthia and I were discussing... moving on."

"What? When?"

"Oh, a few nights back. Don't worry, we aren't. It's just... well, it's been a bit bewildering, hasn't it?"

"Yeah, especially for you two."

"But she pointed out that... well, this is better than we were living back east. Friendlier folk, and we like putting our trade to use again."

"Well, good. But can I ask?" Warren hesitated and then plowed on. "Why tell me?"

"I get the feeling we're not the only ones thinking about it."

"Oh."

"You haven't? Seems your job has changed the most."

The ogre considered. "I suppose. Although I do enjoy just getting back to normal smithing. Honestly, it was... a lot, that last sennight or so. But... there's Darby."

Wilem frowned. "I don't—oh. The ears."

"And the skin. And he's getting big, really big, for his age. Half-breeds aren't welcome very many places."

"Sadly that's true."

"And honestly, with the pressure of the dreams off... I quite like making horseshoes."

"Seems like you should build up a stock of a few more basics. You've plenty of ore, don't you?"

"Plenty, and I plan to. *We* plan to—Darby loves helping. Pots and pans to start with. In fact, there's a set still cooling over there." He nodded to the workbench in the far corner.

"What else?"

"Depends. Might just wait and see what people ask for."

———

Darby waved to his parents as they set up tables near the lakeshore. "I already helped Cole with two loads," he said, panting slightly. "Think I can eat first?"

"Not if you want any room for the sweetbreads," Susan teased.

"I'll save room," Darby promised, his eyes wide as he watched Calder and Pavati set out tray after tray of fish. They'd set the fry up near the docks, where the afternoon breeze blew cool and fresh off the lake. It carried with it the mouth-watering scent of grilled filets.

"Catch more than you can chew?" Warren asked Calder, who nodded.

"Not more than you can, though," the old fisherman replied with a quiet laugh.

Pavati rolled her eyes as she set down another tray. "You'd think he'd never caught a fish before, the way he's going on about it."

"We've still got space for another two barrels in the storehouse," Calder admitted as he helped Pavati. "But thought we'd cook some up fresh."

"Good thought," Warren said. He watched as the first of the travelers made their way from the road. A sour-looking man who'd earlier asked for "anything pointy" joined the line, looking a bit more sullen when he saw it was nothing but fish. He took a plate anyway, and moved off to where a woman with four kids was already seated.

"Go on," Susan said to Darby. "Calder won't let you starve, will he?"

"Only if his dad eats it all first," the fisherman joked.

Darby rushed off to join the growing line.

"It's nice to see everyone relaxed," Susan said as she watched the townsfolk gather.

"Even Dooley looks like he's having a good time," Warren said, nodding toward the menagerie owner. Dooley stood with his wife, taking long pulls from a mug of chilled tea as he chatted with Dardrad and Sam.

"Think we'll have a lull here soon?" Susan asked. "For as long as that cult's banging around the east, I mean?"

"Hard to say. Doesn't seem to have settled yet."

"Pavati! Over here!" Galhani called, waving. "Save me some of that?"

"Get in line, you!" Pavati teased back.

"Not a chance! You finish up and come join us." Galhani was sitting with Makota and Jen, the three of them already busy on a basket of the Fellis family's latest batch of sweetbreads. She looked over at Jen as Pavati smiled and nodded.

"Galhani, this tea some of yours?"

"Yes. Sadly. It's all basic teas now. Nothing seems to have any special effects anymore."

"That chamomile last night was plenty relaxing."

"Oh, of course, yes, yes. All the usual effects are fine, I should have said. But I've put in a lot more of the black tea, took out some of the exotics."

"I've had to go back to basics a bit as well," Lucy sighed, using her fingers to pull a tender chunk of fish off her filet. "But I've gotten the large jugs down right, and people are still buying them."

Prudence nodded agreement. "I couldn't keep up with the orders, even if I had the patterns. Gotten my old hand back with the stitches."

"So how are you doing?" Susan asked Makota.

The Fellis shrugged. "Back to a normal pace, I think? First few days were really something. I haven't had to plan that hard since... well, since we decided to move here."

"That's good, at least." Lucy turned to Leota. "And you?"

The witch pursed her lips thoughtfully. "I think I'm fine, for now. And Vamir's given me a few ideas to keep me occupied. I might have some spells to help with the farm. But—"

"But we'll see," Jen finished.

"Exactly."

Leota leaned back against the dock railing, her face quiet and thoughtful. Her eyes followed Darby as he loaded his plate with fish and side dishes.

Warren rejoined them, stuffing a piece of bread into his mouth. "Can you believe how much fish?"

"I can believe how much you'll eat," Jen said. She gave him a speculative look. "How much longer do you think?"

"Before we get truly busy again?" Warren shrugged. "I thought we'd have more of a lull after the first few days of the temperatures going up. But there's no sign of it letting up. Maybe a few weeks, maybe a few months. Maybe even longer."

"Probably not that long."

"Probably not."

"But maybe."

"Two more ready, Warren!" Parvati called.

Dooley's voice rose over the gathering. "This is the best thing I've eaten since... well, since the last time we all had a fish fry!" A laugh rippled across the docks, and Warren leaned back, his long legs stretched out and Susan tucked comfortably under one arm. The sun sank toward the horizon, casting the lake in shades of pink and orange. The air was warm and easy, and Warren felt, for the first time in many months, something close to true contentment.

The smithy was quiet, the rhythmic clang of the day replaced by the soft rustle of evening. Dust spun lazily in the fading light, drifting like tiny sparks as Darby moved around the shop. He hummed to himself as he tidied up, the task almost meditative after the chaos of the last few weeks. He put tools back in their places, stacked cooling molds neatly on the workbench, and swept the floor with quick, efficient strokes.

The trap door in the corner caught his eye.

He hesitated for a moment, then set the broom aside and pulled the door open. The ore had been sitting heavy in his mind, a dull worry that he hadn't wanted to bring up again. He climbed down the ladder, his steps echoing in the small, dark space. The pile was smaller. Definitely smaller. "Dad?" he called, his voice echoing up through the floorboards.

"Yeah?" Warren's voice came back, muffled but warm.

"The ore—it's not back."

There was a pause before Warren replied, his tone thoughtful. "You think we should try using it?"

Darby scrambled back up, his expression a mix of hope and uncertainty. "Would it still work?"

"Not sure," Warren admitted. "It was always the town's gift, not mine. Never knew how it would turn out." He rubbed his chin, his fingers stained with a day's worth of honest labor. "It was a little weird to work with, even then."

"But we could try?"

Warren looked at his son, the eagerness in Darby's eyes reminding him of all the things he still wanted to teach. Things he could teach, now that the dreams weren't crowding his mind. "Yeah," he said, nodding slowly. "We could try."

They had two sets of pots and pans already, and enough horseshoes to fit out a whole town and then some. Warren was even thinking of making some basic armor and weapons, just to see how they turned out. He knew the work would take longer now, knew he'd have to do it the old-fashioned way, but he didn't mind. He was looking forward to it, even. "Want to learn how to make a sword?" he asked, his voice taking on a playful edge.

Darby's face lit up. "Really?"

"And armor. We might even try some new things. Alloys, maybe. Flexible and strong."

Darby's eyes went wide. "Like magic?"

"Like patience," Warren replied with a grin.

————

"Five, you say?" Warren mused, stroking his broad chin.

"We left in a hurry," the traveler said. He was a middle-aged man, going a bit gray around the temples, with wide shoulders and thick, almost ogreish arms. "I've got four more men with me, and all our wives and kids."

"Wow."

"We kept the wagons outside your gates. Didn't want to crowd things too much. And your inn," he added sadly, "doesn't seem big enough for us all."

"It's not," Warren agreed. "But if you've tents or even bedrolls, you're welcome to put folk up in the square. Just inside the town gates. Soft grass would be more comfortable."

"I might take you up on that. So what about the swords?"

"I can do them. You're okay with pretty basic?"

"Strong and, if possible, light, but yes."

"I can do that. It'll take... well, simple ones I can do maybe two a day if I keep at it."

"Then I'd take six."

"Silver apiece."

"Sold. When can you start?"

Warren glanced up. The sun had barely cleared the forest's top. "Well, since you got here so early, no time like the present. Hey Darb!" he called.

Darby, who'd been filling pails with water to take out to the travelers' horses, called back. "Yeah, Dad?"

"Come help me in the smithy." He turned back to the traveler. "It'll go quicker if he's helping. Mind caring for your own horses? How many do you have?"

"Nine."

Warren considered. "Add two silver for water and oats. Half if you're okay with hay."

"I'll take the oats, the poor beasts deserve it." The man pulled out a purse and counted out eight silvers. "Any chance for meals the whole time?"

"How many?"

"Eighteen."

"Minnie will have a fit," Warren chuckled. "But yes. Expect she'll charge you a couple coppers a head per day, but it'll get you three squares apiece. She runs the inn, pop in and tell her I sent you over."

"I will. And thank you."

"You're more than welcome."

———

The forge roared to life as Darby and Warren stoked the fire. The heat pulsed in waves, filling the smithy with a familiar, comforting glow. The half-formed sword blanks they'd spent the past few days making were lined up neatly, each one a promise of what was to come. The rough shapes would speed their work, allowing them to focus on refining and finishing rather than starting from scratch.

"Want to try the first one?" Warren asked, nodding toward the waiting blanks.

Darby grinned, his eyes alight with eagerness. "Yeah!"

"Let's see how fast we can get this batch done. I'll hammer, you watch the heat."

The boy nodded, busying himself with the bellows. The fire flared brighter, casting sharp shadows across the walls as Warren lifted the first blank and set it on the anvil. He worked with a swift, practiced rhythm, the hammer ringing out in time with Darby's steady stoking. The rough edges of the metal began to smooth, the shape growing more defined under Warren's skilled hands.

"Looking good!" Darby shouted over the noise, his voice full of excitement.

"Keep the heat steady," Warren replied, his focus intense. He turned the blade, working it from every angle. "We'll have these done in no time."

The sword took form quickly, the previous days' work making it easier than Warren had expected. The weight of the metal felt good in his hands, solid and sure. He moved with an ease born of years at the forge, and with each strike, the sword became more real, more itself.

Darby watched closely, absorbing every detail. "What about the hilt?" he asked, his curiosity boundless.

"We'll wrap it with leather," Warren said, examining the blade with a critical eye. "But we'll do all the blades first."

"Awesome!" Darby's enthusiasm was infectious.

Warren chuckled. They could do this all day, he thought. Maybe they would. The work was... *right*, settled, and he was glad to have Darby by his side.

They continued into the afternoon, the clang of metal a steady counterpoint to the crackle of the fire. The sun dipped lower, but the forge burned bright, a beacon of purpose and possibility. Warren knew they'd get the swords done in plenty of time, knew that even this flood of new arrivals wouldn't last forever. For now, though, he didn't mind. Not at all.

"Let's get this one cooled," he said, gesturing toward the pail of oil. Darby picked up the tongs and lifted the glowing blade, his movements careful and precise. He lowered it into the pail, and the metal hissed.

"Why oil?" Darby asked. "You said sometimes you can use water."

"Water's cheaper, obviously. And faster. Oil takes longer, but you get a better temper."

Once the sizzling had died and the oil stopped bubbling, Darby asked, "That good?"

"Perfect," Warren said, setting the next blank on the anvil. He enjoyed the old spark of creativity and craftsmanship, the joy of making something with his own two hands. The time without the dreams had given him a new appreciation for the work, a new determination to make it his own.

They fell into a rhythm, the forge a world unto itself.

This is okay, Warren thought with satisfaction.

sixteen

. . .

AS THE SUN rose toward midday, three covered wagons rolled through the East road gate, their wheels groaning like wounded animals. The canvas tops were shredded, the wood splintered and scored with deep gouges. From the driver's seat of the first wagon, a woman clutched her arm, her sleeve soaked in dark red. A child's head peered out, eyes wide and scared, hair matted with dirt and tears.

The second wagon trundled behind, one wheel wobbling dangerously. A man held the reins with shaking hands, his face ashen and smeared with sweat. Beside him, a girl held a cloth to her leg, grimacing with each jolt. The last wagon lagged, pulled by a pair of exhausted horses with visible cuts on their flanks. The animals stumbled, dragging their heads low.

As the wagons came to a stop in front of the stable yard, Warren stepped out of the smithy, his expression filled with concern. "What happened?" he called. "Are you alright?"

"T-terrible creatures," the woman in the first wagon stammered, her voice brittle with fear. "They came out of nowhere. We barely escaped."

Warren hurried over as Sam and Minnie stepped out of their establishments. "Creatures, you say?" He surveyed the damage with a blacksmith's eye, noting the ragged slashes across the wood and canvas. "What did they look like?"

"Big," said the man from the second wagon, his voice trembling. "Lizards, but not like any I've seen before. And fast—too fast."

"Red eyes," the girl added, her voice a small squeak. "Sharp teeth."

Nodded slowly, Warren seemed as if he'd already known the answer. "Skraelings," he said, the word heavy. "From up in the Mistrals. They must be moving down from the high ground."

The townsfolk exchanged nervous glances. Skraelings were known for their ferocity and their hunger.

"Dexter," Sam snapped.

"Everyone!" Warren bellowed. Town warning bells were unnecessary when you had an ogre.

Jen, her sense for danger no less diminished by the loss of the town's gifts, was already hurrying over, Tyran and his wife just steps behind her. Calder and his family spilled out of the town gates, Alred hot on their heels. Suddenly, Dexter was there, as if he'd just been hiding behind Sam. "Get them down," he said in his quiet, dry tone.

Hands reached up to help the woman down from the wagon, and she winced as her feet hit the ground. The child inched closer to her, clutching at her skirts. Susan appeared with a wooden bucket sloshing with water, her face tight with concern.

"Bring them this way," she called, motioning toward the inn. "We'll see to your wounds." Minnie had already thrown the door open. Fortunately, the town had all but emptied out that morning as travelers set out on their way. Warren had delivered the six swords before sunup.

The injured travelers stumbled forward, guided by gentle hands. Warren watched them go.

"We can't stay here," the man said, his voice barely a whisper. "Not if those things are..."

"You're safe now," Warren assured him, though the doubt lingered in the air like smoke. The townsfolk would do their best to deal with the threat. They always did. "Jen," he said quietly.

"The gates?" she murmured, intuiting his next words.

The ogre nodded. "If they're skraelings..."

"I'll speak to Leota. But... agreed."

Inside the inn, Dexter worked with an intensity that bordered on ferocity, his lean frame darting between patients sprawled on the floor and benches. Without the town's gifts, his bandages were rudimentary, his methods exhausting. He bound the woman's arm with strips of cloth, tying them off with sharp efficiency. He checked for signs of venom, his fingers moving quickly, precisely, but his mouth set in a thin line of frustration.

The man from the wagon leaned back in his chair, grimacing as Dexter examined a gash across his chest. "Will it..." he began, but his voice faltered.

"Not infected," Dexter said briskly. "Yet." He grabbed another length of cloth.

Galhani burst through the door, her arms laden with jars and a kettle. Her brow was furrowed with urgency and irritation. She set her supplies down with a clatter and began pouring steaming liquid into chipped mugs. "Here," she said, her voice bright but strained. "Drink this. It'll help."

The girl took a mug, her eyes wide, uncertain. She sniffed at the tea. "It smells..."

"Different, I know," Galhani interrupted, the words tumbling out. "But it's good. You'll see."

Dexter moved to the girl's side, wrapping her leg in a makeshift splint. He didn't look up, but his silence spoke volumes. Galhani glanced at him, her expression mirroring his: a blend of determination and discontent. They worked in tandem, as they always had, but something was missing, something they refused to name.

The child huddled against the woman, sipping cautiously at the mug. "A little sweet, isn't it?" Galhani asked with forced cheer. The child nodded, and Galhani managed a quick, tight smile.

Dexter finished with the girl and turned to the others, his mind methodically ticking through possibilities. He felt the absence of their former abilities like a weight in his hands, but he pushed it aside, focusing on what he could do now. They all did.

"Thank you," the man said, his voice a hoarse rasp.

"Rest," Dexter replied, already moving to the next patient, his eyes scanning for any sign they might have missed. "We'll get you healed up. All of you."

The travelers settled into a weary silence, the woman's hand clutching the child's, the man resting his head against the wall. Galhani moved among them, refilling mugs and offering words of encouragement, her own frustration simmering beneath her quick movements.

Outside, the town buzzed with activity. Warren, Sam, and Jen conferred near the gates, their expressions grim.

"Someone needs to help the horses, Dad," Darby said quietly.

"Damnation," Warren growled. "Thank you, Darb. Go get Dooley."

The menagerie owner was already hustling toward them, still pulling a vest on over his rumpled shirt. "I heard you bellow, Warren, what's—oh, gods above."

"Skraelings," Warren said.

Dooley's eyes darted over the horses as he worked his way from cart to cart. "They're scratched, but not hurt. No sign of venom, the cuts would already show it. Darb, help me get them unhitched and in the yard. Is Trevor...?"

"Helping with the travelers. In the inn," Warren said. "I'll help."

Quickly, they unhitched the horses and led them slowly into the yard. Darby filled a trough with water, and the grateful animals began to drink deeply.

"They're exhausted," Dooley noted. "Must have run them all the way here."

"Damn luck the carts didn't fall apart on the way." Wilem and his wife wandered over. "Warren, when you're done here we can start making some repairs. Just leave them in the road."

"Warren!" Jen called as she and Sam finished conferring. "Leota thinks she can keep a go-away-you going for a while. Should deter critters from coming in. I'd hate to have to lose the gates and—"

"Lock out anyone else who needs us," Warren agreed. "Yeah. I'll be out here working on the carts. I'll keep an eye toward the gate."

"I'm going to wander down the road a bit and take stock," Jen said. At Warren's frown, she added, "I'll have my sword."

"And me," Sam put in, rolling her eyes. "And *my* sword."

Warren relaxed a bit. The two old mercenaries were more than capable of taking care of themselves, especially when they had each other's back. "Holler if you need me."

"We will."

———

The sun tipped over its zenith, and Wilem and Warren wrestled the first wagon's broken wheel off its axle. Warren hefted the damaged wheel into the street, and his ears pricked up at the sound of the chirgeon and the herbalist still bickering inside. "Give them a mark to rest and—" Dexter's voice was sharp with tiredness. "A mark? They need —" Galhani's voice was still bright, but it had an edge to it. "I know what they need," Dexter replied. The door to the inn flew open. Galhani followed the chirgeon out, her tiny hands on her hips. "You always do," she said with exasperated fondness.

"Anything serious?" Darby asked as he rubbed a brush over the cuts on the horses' flanks.

"No sign of venom," Galhani sighed. "I'm beginning to think Dooley and Trevor know what they're doing. Even without our help."

Darby laughed, and the herbalist joined in, her cheerfulness returning now that the immediate danger had passed.

"Maybe you can help with the horses," Darby said. "They're fed and watered, just need a bit of salve."

"Let's see what we can do," Galhani said, and she followed Darby to the stable yard. "I've foxglove balm if nothing else."

Dexter lingered for a moment, casting a glance at the carts and the road. His expression darkened with thoughtfulness, and then he shook his head and went back inside.

"Need a hand, Warren?" Galhani called.

"Go help Darb," Warren said. "We can handle this."

Wilem grunted his agreement as Warren lifted the front of the first wagon high enough to slip a block underneath.

Leota stood outside the pub, her eyes closed in concentration. Her long hair whipped about her face, but there was no breeze. "You think she can really keep them away?" Wilem asked. He and Warren pried the last wagon's sideboard back into place.

"She can," Warren said. "For a while."

They worked in silence for a few minutes, then Leota opened her eyes. "Warren?" she called.

"Yeah? What do you need?"

"Nothing," she said. "Just letting you know I'm still here. I'll keep watch."

The ogre smiled. "Thanks. We'll get these repaired and be ready to pull them inside if we have to."

Wilem hammered a nail into the wood with a satisfying thwack and stepped back with a nod. "They look rough, but they'll hold," he said. "No sense making them pretty at this point."

"Let's finish up this one and start on the next," Warren said. He glanced toward the inn, then called over his shoulder to the pub. "Leota?"

"Yes?"

"Get some rest when you need it. We'll take turns keeping watch."

"Will do," Leota said. She sat down cross-legged in front of the door and closed her eyes again. "We should speak tonight. Everyone."

———

Inside the pub, the townsfolk crowded around a long, splintered table. Sam leaned against the wall, her arms crossed, eyes scanning the room. Leota sat nearby, pale but composed, still catching her breath. Calder and Alred huddled together, their brows furrowed with concern, while Tyran and his wife whispered urgently to one another.

"The gates," Jen announced, striding into the room. "We need to talk about how we're handling them."

"Close the road," Calder said. "Keep the critters out before they get near."

"And the travelers? What about them?" Alred asked.

"Jen and Sam can keep watch," Tyran's wife suggested. "Warn us if anything's coming. We can always open the gates."

"Easy for you to say," Warren muttered. The gates were heavy and not often used, and they protested being moved.

"Or," Galhani chimed in. "Another plan. Keep the town gates closed and the rest open."

"It's a damned risk," Tyran said. "Speaking as someone who's outside the town gates."

"Then we take the risk," Susan replied, her face grim. "Isn't that the job? The pact?"

"The pact came with gifts," Dardrad muttered. "Protections."

"But it's still the right thing to do. It's a chance we take," Warren said from near the doorway, his voice heavy. "If it means helping folks like the ones today, it's a chance we take."

"Agreed," Jen said. "And if they get this far, we'll have warning. Leota?"

"Still working," Leota said quietly. "But not forever."

"Dexter," Warren called, glancing toward the inn.

The chirgeon appeared as if summoned, his expression tight, his movements precise as he stepped through the pub's rear door, which connected it to the inn. "They're resting," he said. "What's left to decide?"

"Whether we're closing the town," Sam said. "Or the road as well."

Dexter hesitated. "They were grateful. The travelers. For help."

"Then we do what we can," Warren said. "Like we always have."

"Even without the gifts?" Tyran asked, a challenge in his voice.

"Even without," Warren replied, his gaze steady.

"Damn it," Sam said. "Since when do we close our doors to people who need us?"

Calder sighed, his shoulders slumping. "We don't."

"Then it's settled," Jen said. "We keep the road open. And stay ready for anything."

A murmur of reluctant agreement spread through the room. "But the town gates?" Lucy asked.

"It'll be hard on business," Sam warned.

Lucy snorted. "Business hasn't been all that. And we can set up tables along the road. But at least we'll have someplace safe to retreat to."

Jen cast her eyes around the room and, seeing no objections, nodded. "Agreed, then. We close the town gates. Urge people to keep moving if they can. Help those who can't. Dooley, any idea why skraelings would be down this far? Don't they hate the warmth?"

Dooley nodded slowly. "They do. Orcs will upset them, sometimes, send them scurrying. Given time, they'll climb back into the mountains."

"How much time?"

He shrugged. "It could be a while. And..." he trailed off uncertainly.

"And what?" Sam asked.

"Well. It's just rumors. It's said that skraelings..." Again, he trailed off, looking uncomfortable.

"It's said," Vamir took over, his tone calm and even, "that skraeling are attracted to misery. To desperation. In some tales, they're harbingers of it, in others they survive on it."

"Certainly been enough of that recently," Makota said darkly.

"They're out there," Leota said distantly, almost dreamily, her eyes closed. "I can sense them. They're not interested in us, yet. There's more... they're turned east."

"Can you tell how many?" Jen asked. Her tone made Warren frown.

"Mmm... no more than two?"

"A breeding pair," Vamir said heavily.

"Meaning what?" Sam asked.

The elf shook his head sadly. "In the tales that have them living off desperation and misery, a breeding pair will consume all they can before returning to the mountaintops to lay their eggs. But in the meantime, they can be especially... vicious."

"Jen..." Sam said, her tone filled with caution.

"What are you thinking?" Susan asked.

"Being proactive," the old constable said evenly.

"Closing the gates," Lucy said, nodding slowly.

"I object," Warren said suddenly. He blinked, as if surprised to have those words coming from his mouth.

"Me too," Sam sighed. Jen's expression grew dark. "No, don't look at me like that. First of all, we can't just shut off the trade road. The town square, sure, but not the whole—"

"We take turns guarding," Jen growled. "We open the gates when people come."

"Yeah, but that isn't what we're *for*," Warren objected.

"Warren—" Susan started, but the ogre gave a small shake of his head.

"That was when there was a *pact*," Makota pointed out gently. "When the town's gifts helped—"

"Doesn't matter," Warren said stubbornly. "It's still the right thing to do."

"I agree," Sam said softly. "People don't need us less just because the pub doesn't tell them their destiny, or Galhani's herbs can't cure their headache."

"I can still do that," the gnome protested, although there was a teasing twinkle in her eye.

"You mean going after them," Alred said.

Sam nodded. "If they're close enough for Leota to sense..."

"A half-day's walk. No more. Likely less," the witch said confidently.

"I'm going with you," Warren insisted.

"Damn right you are," Jen agreed.

"And I," Dardrad said.

"When do we go?" Sam sighed.

"They'll be at their slowest around now," Dooley said.

"Then we'll set out tomorrow," Jen said firmly. "If Leota can still sense them. We'll aim to intercept them around this time of day."

"And until then?" Galhani asked.

"We close the town gates, as agreed. We set guards on the watch towers. We give Leota a rest," Jen added, giving the witch a firm poke in the ribs.

Leota smiled, but kept her eyes closed.

"Come on," the constable said, standing. "Let's get things done."

seventeen

. . .

WARREN'S heavy strides kicked up tiny pebbles as he and his companions moved along the trade road. The late-morning sun beat warm on his skin, and the world was eerily still. Despite having traveled the wide dirt track countless times, he wasn't used to the emptiness. The others were quiet, senses straining. Dardrad's hand never left his battle-axe. Jen's watchful eyes flicked between the treeline and their group. Sam held her sword at the ready. Even the lake was silent as they passed. Warren, unarmed, simply clenched and unclenched his huge hands.

The lake shimmered blue-gray to his right. His thoughts were wandering—always a bad sign. His attention snapped back to the road and his companions, the only sound that of their soft footfalls on the packed dirt.

The tension must have shown. Jen's voice broke the silence. "You're looking grimmer than usual, Warren." She flashed a tight smile, one hand adjusting the wide-brimmed hat she'd donned against the sun.

"It's been so busy and now it's so quiet."

"Hmm. It'll probably pick up."

"Probably." Warren didn't feel the confidence that he was trying to project, and despite Jen's unaccustomed light tone, he felt on edge. The quiet unnerved him. The trade road had been so busy these past weeks, a steady stream of merchants, travelers, and would-be adventurers coming and going. For it to be this still and empty... it made Warren's green skin crawl. It was like the creatures they were after could sense them coming.

"Damp up ahead," Sam noted, indicating a thick grove of pines that hugged the road's left side, the beginnings of foothills in the distance. She shifted her grip on her sword. "Dooley said they'd stick to whatever cool they could find."

Warren shook his head. "Can't be that easy."

"It's enough to make you wonder what they're thinking, isn't it?" Sam mused. "Two steps ahead of us or two leagues behind?" She'd taken on a darker look with her light leather armor rather than her usual loose tunic. Her white hair, bold in a tight tail, caught the sun and shone brightly against it.

"My money's on a league ahead," Jen replied. "Or less. We're almost to where those travelers say they were attacked. Won't be long now."

"Surely they won't have stayed still."

Warren frowned. Sam was usually the optimistic one, but now Jen seemed the more confident of the two. The harsh emptiness of the road was pressing her down, just as it was the others.

The heat of the day began to grow heavy. Sam's hands moved easily along her sword's neatly wrapped hilt, as though she were still the same young mercenary she'd been when she'd first started at her trade. The sword's allegedly unbreakable edge caught the sun. It looked sharp enough to pierce the steel plating on an ore cart, and certainly stronger than the savage beasts they hunted.

"We should have brought more shields," Warren grumbled. "I have a couple of basic ones in the smithy. Stupid not to—"

Jen shook her head again, her deep eyes turning briefly from the pines to look at Warren. "Just a little nervous energy. We all have it, Warren. When this is over, I'll make sure that ale's waiting for you at the inn."

Ahead, the road continued in a slight curve that took it briefly closer to the trees. According to the travelers, this was where the two skraeling had attacked. The thick canopy stretched out like an enormous hand, a scattering of black shadows seeping out and merging into long fingers across the bright dirt track.

"Look at it this way," Jen said. "We know they're out here."

"Can't be far, Leota said," Sam echoed, her voice less buoyant but just as determined. "That counts for something, doesn't it?"

Warren was less certain, but if they had been as close as it seemed, Sam wouldn't have been holding her blade more tightly than before. Now Jen shook her arm slightly, and in an instant, writhing motion, her sword was in her hand. She looked knowingly at Warren. He returned her look with a tight smile.

A cloud passed over Warren's mind, shading his thoughts as deeply as the black shadows in front of them. He kept pace with Sam and the others, willing his own nervous energy into a resolve as thick and heavy as his arms.

"Damn skraeling know we are coming," the stocky dwarf grunted. "Probably wondering why we're not scared off."

"Or wondering what ogre tastes like," Jen teased.

Warren realized that this is what Jen must have been like back when she was a merc heading to battle: all her gruffness gone in a display of casual ease, as if whatever was ahead couldn't possibly be beyond her fellows' capabilities. Sam had gone the opposite direction, from the affable pub-owner to an alert warrior who was forcing herself to seem relaxed.

Funny how opposite the two were, yet at the same time so much alike.

"Anyone bother to ask if skraeling is good eating?" the dwarf grumbled.

The massive ogre chuckled. He'd never suspected the dwarf had such a dark sense or humor. "Ogre eat lizard," he murmured, a smile playing across his expression.

Something rustled in the undergrowth.

Shadows blurred. Scaled hides glinted, and the skraeling were upon them. The lead beast was nearly twice the size of its companion, claws clicking against stones as they skittered sideways into the road.

Then they leapt.

Dardrad braced against his shield. Warren reached for a fanged maw, but Sam was faster. Her wild swing nicked the first beast, sending it twisting sideways and Warren's fist shuddering into its side. Another pair of claws slashed in, razor sharp, and he staggered with a rough grunt.

The second skraeling let out a rattling hiss as it flanked them, thick tail snapping like whipcord. "Stay loose," Jen called. "One big, one fast. Pick your size and keep to it!"

Dardrad grunted in reply, Warren and Sam too busy for even that. The smaller skraeling crouched, hind legs taut. Dardrad got his shield up again just as it sprang, a discordant clang ringing out from steel against scale.

Sam took her chance and dashed toward the pines, the larger beast turning on her in time to meet a wild cut from her sword. Jen had called it right: one big, one fast. The first of them was out for blood, and the second was almost faster than they could track. Jen was with Warren now, edging closer to Sam's side of the road and calling the others along. Dardrad and Warren closed on the big one, the dwarf with his battle-axe at the ready. The lizard-like beast reared back, the sharp edge of its tail slicing air like a knife.

A splintering crack from Dardrad's shield; a spray of pine-scented sweat from Sam's gloves; coppery droplets misted the air as the smaller one wheeled around. Warren caught the flash of red eyes and white hide, and a surge of satisfaction as his fist swung forward. He was too slow, though, and the beast slipped past.

The second skraeling ducked behind the curve of the trees, then shot back with such speed and strength that Warren barely had time to react. He swung a fist the size of a small boulder toward its snarling mouth, again missing and feeling the rush of wind as its jagged claws raked his shoulder.

Refusing to let the fighters divide it from its mate, the larger skraeling darted in as Warren reeled back, pain lancing through his side. It moved with brutal speed, not as slow or as dumb as Jen had guessed. Warren regained his footing, and the air shook with his thunderous roar. "On me!"

He reached again, getting a grip around the thing's thick neck and ignoring the gnashing fangs and bloodied claws as Sam ducked in with him. The thing twisted, caught a wicked stroke from her blade, and let out a shrill cry. They'd hit the creature before it could dodge this time. Just one hit, but a good one. Coppery ichor spewed onto the dirt road.

Warren grinned as the thing bolted back toward the trees, expecting Dardrad and Jen to set off after it. Instead, they drew further back. Were they retreating?

He didn't care. One strike was one more than last time, and it gave him the jolt of energy he needed. "Over here!" he shouted, the words booming out toward Dardrad and Jen. "Come on! Before it gets away!" His own blood pumped hot and loud in his ears, and he gave way—*just a bit*, he thought—to the primeval thrill of the hunt. He was an ogre: apex predator of the Forbidden Continent, and no lizard-beast was going to stop him.

Jen shook her head and pointed toward the road, her eyes locked on the smaller beast. "Stay on the road!" she yelled. "It's not letting us go, but don't give it its ground!"

Heat burned in Warren's chest. Were they following the original plan, or making up a new one? Then he realized: The first creature wasn't running—it had circled back and were still closer than he'd thought. The pain in his side was already ebbing, though, and so he followed the larger skraeling's dark outline as it shifted through the dense trees, keeping his feet to the edge of the road and his eyes just beyond it.

Now Sam sprinted ahead of him, toward the next curve in the road. "One more turn, and then it's ours," she called, sounding like she hoped the words were more true than false. "Ready, Warren?"

Warren was never not ready.

Another tight loop of the road, closer to the lake now, and they saw the black, curling shadow of the skraeling they'd struck. It was slower than before, its long tail a heavy whip at its back as it darted back and forth. Warren's iron-hard fist had marked its side. He let out a growl, trying to draw it close.

The two monsters dashed forward as one, the smaller one rushing past Jen and leaping over Dardrad to attack Warren and Sam from behind as its made flashed toward them from ahead.

Dardrad's shield caught it on its scaly underbelly, sending it off-course, but it recovered quickly, dancing sideways as it landed and rushing forward again.

A flash of teeth.

Warren surged forward, fists at the ready, but the big skraeling darted around him, aiming for his more vulnerable companions.

Jen's sword barely deflected a deep slash as she called Warren back, a sharp cry escaping her lips.

Sam fell back, turning with her sword up to match the fast skraeling's pace. Jen joined her, Warren only now catching up as the two skraeling began circling them. Dardrad rush in, swinging his battle-axe to one side and scoring a strong hit on the larger beast's tail.

"We keep this pace," Jen said, "then wear them down. We keep this pace, then we have them."

"Wear *them* down," Sam said through gritted teeth. "Got it."

Jen's gruff voice and Warren's thick muscles were almost enough to make the hope come true.

The bigger skraeling doubled back on them again, slower now, the deep wound from Warren's blow staining its hide with something blacker than blood. The white of it all turned almost gray. Its hooked tail still flicked forward and back, but with less force now and more effort.

"You hit it harder than I thought," Jen said, still panting. "I think you must have broke something."

The companions moved to flank it, Sam keeping a close eye on its smaller mate, which was still crouched low and hissing, bright ichor staining the ground beneath its tail. Dardrad, closest to the larger creature, jumped ahead of them all. Warren heard him bark something in dwarfish and guessed the sound was a challenge more than anything.

Dardrad was quick for such a stubby fellow.

Not quick enough for the razor-edged claws of the second skraeling, though. It sprang, almost instantly this time, slicing past Warren, its daggerlike claws cutting a huge gash along one of Dardrad's stocky legs. Warren thought it had knocked him clean off his feet.

But the dwarf was already back on them and clearly having none of it.

The smaller creature snapped and slashed with vicious speed. It focused on Dardrad, coiling its body like a lethal spring and nearly missing the chance to lunge in once more.

Before it could strike, Dardrad gripped his shield with both hands and swung it wide. The force of the blow caught the it, sending it tumbling back toward the road. It shook its head, recovering too fast. Warren took Dardrad's side, and they pressed their advance on the stunned skraeling.

The huge ogre caught hold of one thrashing limb as it stumbled, but not for long. It slashed with its razor claws, fangs snapping inches from Warren's neck, and he fell back with a loud crack as he hit the ground.

"One down!" Sam called. She'd stayed with Jen, the two of them edging in against the first skraeling—they'd gotten another strong hit, this time across the things throat, and it was thrashing madly in the road. Not *down*, but not in it for the moment.

The second one, maddened by its mate's injury, leapt again, its back arched, its hide streaked with a wound that matched Sam's sword almost exactly.

Jen pulled Dardrad aside just as the larger skraeling stopped thrashing and refocused on them. She, the dwarf, and Sam turned to it, weapons at the ready—leaving the smaller beast to the ogre.

Warren lumbered to his feet and stepped toward the creature. His huge hands closed like iron on the smaller creature's limbs. It thrashed in his grip, talons gouging into the thick skin on his forearms. Each blow sent numbing shivers through his massive arms, but each strike held less strength than the one before. It tried to twist its fanged head toward his throat, but Warren swung it back and held firm. With the others against the injured skraeling, they would have to give him this time, and enough time, and he'd make sure the favor was returned. He'd see them all in one piece back in town, drinking ale and laughing about two dead ahead.

A grating crack echoed across the hills, then another and another, until the same dull crack resounded in Warren's thoughts.

The smaller skraeling fell limp in Warren's hands, and he let it drop to the ground.

Time stood still.

The larger skraeling, hot ichor still pulsing from its throat, paused for the briefest moment, considering its options. Sam and Jen were closing from its left and right, swords at the ready. Dardrad advanced between them, his battle-axe poised to swing. Already, Warren was turning from the dead, twitching body of its mate, his chest covered in gore.

It decided to run.

With a speed Warren wouldn't have credited to a wounded monster, it turned and darted into the forest. It made no attempt at stealth or cunning now, and simply *bolted*, its sinuous body twisting between trees until, in just a breath, it was gone.

"We chase it," Warren grunted, stumping forward.

"We don't," Jen ordered, laying a hand on one of the ogre's bloodied forearms.

"It won't last the night," Sam agreed. "There are plenty of animals in the foothills who can take it, now."

"And you need to get that arm looked at," Dardrad said gruffly.

"Hmph," Warren grunted. But his hot blood was already cooling, the predatory urge in his chest becoming less urgent.

"Come on," Jen said, turning wearily toward home. "We owe you that ale, I think."

———

"I do feel bad for them," Dooley said, taking a sip of his ale.

"Mmm," Vamir murmured as he took a swallow of wine. "I, less so."

"Truly?"

"I spent the day reading about them. What's known about the skraeling, at least. Not just the stories."

"And?" Warren asked. His upper lip was generously coated in foam from his ale.

"They rarely venture down from the cold heights they prefer," the elf said. "And when they do... they do not return. I may have been incorrect earlier, about them devouring everything and returning to the mountains to lay eggs. There are few accounts, but all of them agree that the stories are wrong: whatever lures a skraeling, especially a mating pair, down from the peaks... once they are down, they stay. They'll seek out caves, ponds, anything that's cool. But they won't leave."

"Gods," Jen muttered.

"Two of them can take out a village," Vamir said softly.

Sam's eyebrows shot up. "A *village?*"

"You had an ogre with you," Warren grinned. "That's like half a village."

"Of appetite," Cole teased. But then he grew sober. "You three got lucky."

"Luck," Dardrad snorted dismissively. "Dwarves don't believe in luck. We make our *own* luck."

"All without the town's gifts," Sam put in, raising an eyebrow at Jen.

"Fine, fine. We're fine on our own," the constable grumbled.

"And tomorrow is a new day," Warren said with satisfaction. He smiled at Susan, who smiled back. "And everything is as good as it needs to be."

"I still wish I had a sense for tomorrow's custom," Minnie sighed. "But I suppose it's nothing any innkeeper hasn't had to worry about."

The townsfolk raised their mugs, thumping them gently against each other in a toast to the next day.

eighteen

. . .

"I SUPPOSED IF I'D KNOWN," Minnie sighed heavily, "I'd have stayed in bed with the doors locked."

More than a moon had passed since the skraelings had been dealt with, and every day seemed to grow busier than the last. The townsfolk were, to a person, exhausted.

Each day, travelers started rolling through town shortly after the first light of dawn. Those were the ones who'd camped along the roadside and rose before first light; they would often stop to take on whatever provisions the town had to offer, but were always eager to be on their way. Their expressions were tight but determined.

"Fire cult," one middle-aged woman had told Sam, shaking her head in frustration. "Install their leaders, build an altar to their god, or they begin setting the town alight."

"Is that what happened to you?" Sam asked softly.

The woman snorted as she hefted a thick package of cured pork onto her shoulder. "We're not so slow. They were still two towns away when most of decided to leave." She turned toward her wagon, where her husband was already loading a small barrel of salted fish.

And so the day proceeded.

The most timid of the trees had already begun their transformation, with their leaves turning into shades of pale gold and gentle yellow that stood out like delicate brushstrokes against the canvas of the foothills behind the town. The once uniform green was now interspersed with these soft hues, creating a subtle yet captivating tapestry that hinted at the arrival of autumn.

And still the travelers came.

"Didn't it slow down this time last year?" Sam asked.

Minnie sighed. "Almost always, by now. Down to a few a week."

"You wonder if there's any left, out East."

"You wonder where they're going to put them all, in the West."

A snort from behind them announced Jen's arrival. "Goblin territory," she growled. "It'll look easy enough at first, but come winter when those little devils are hungry, these folks will have a whole new kind of problem on their hands."

The three women fell silent, watching the slow, methodical procession of carts, wagons, and horses plod through the town.

Hours later, the sun just past its highest point in the sky, the traffic still showed no signs of stopping or even abating: Wagon after wagon rolled by, each carrying a load of solemn, grim-faced travelers. Their expressions were set in determined lines, and many offered only a tight, curt nod to the townsfolk who stood watching from the sidelines. This time of day, the travelers could expect to make it several marks further down the road, although they'd find nothing more than small settlements of two or three families apiece. Only a few would stop to briefly purchase some supplies, small pieces of equipment, or articles of sturdy, warm clothing.

"Won't be long now," Minnie said at last. "I'll check that Trevor's gotten the last rooms cleaned out."

"Yeah," Sam said heavily. "I think I need to get another keg of sale into position." The evening's custom would begin arriving soon, these travelers grateful for a roof over their heads or at least a protected lawn on which to sleep. A representative from each family would gather in the Broken Claw that night, exchanging tales from the road, memories of what they'd left behind, and what hope they could muster for the future.

Sam found it incredibly depressing.

"I'll give you a hand," Warren said, following Sam into the tavern. "The afternoon trade never wants anything from me." The overnighters, at least, would often buy a horseshoe or two, he'd found.

He helped Sam get a full keg into position on the large rack that ran alongside the tavern's side wall, and then stepped back outside to traveler-watch.

The wagons continued to move steadily through, the horses trotting at a measured pace designed to endure the long haul of the day. Unusually for this time of day, a few travelers steered their horses to the side of the dusty road, dismounting with a purpose, their boots crunching softly against the gravel as they took a momentary respite from the relentless journey.

These ones stepped into the Broken Claw, and shared their stories of what had happened.

"That Lord Welting, as he called himself, he was bad enough," one man said, shaking his head at Warren as Wilem examined a damaged wheel on his wagon."But at least when he took over a town, he moved to end the fighting quickly. Once you bent the knee, he'd appoint someone to run the town and move on to the next. But then *she* came through."

"Prophet of some fire god, she said," another woman told Sam as she gratefully accepted a pint of cold ale. "Torendam, the village down the way from us, was told they had to rededicate their church to her god, or she'd burn it down. They refused—and she did."

After hearing a few of those stories, Warren had grumpily left the travelers to Sam, Minnie, and the others on the trade road and retreated into the forge. He left the large doors wide open so he could keep an eye on things, but otherwise focused on making horseshoes, pots, pans, and small knives. When he wasn't tending to a traveler's weary horse, Darby would join him.

A smith's hammer at work was all muscle memory, a rhythm Warren had practiced for years. The hammer rose and fell with the same deliberate cadence as the hooves passing out on the road, and the hot iron on his anvil sang its own sharp notes, ringing counterpoint to the dull thud of wheels over ruts. The repetitive clink of his work was a comfort, a wall against the building unease outside.

He glanced up periodically from the day's work—a set of pan handles, promised to Minnie and now needed more than ever with the unabated daily influx of guests—and watched the way people flowed through the town like a stream. Movement and purpose everywhere, a kind of nervous energy that infected even the stone facades of the buildings. North Pointe had always been a place to pass through, but these past sennights had felt as if the whole world was trying to pass through at once before it was too late.

Darby, perched on the lower step of the bellows with a pair of tongs nearly as long as his arm, watched his father with a seriousness that bordered on comic. He had inherited some of Warren's size but not yet much of his patience, and every few minutes he'd be distracted by the commotion outside. The boy's eyes flicked to the open doors, where the cross-currents of travelers and townsfolk surged and parted, then back to the flickering mouth of the forge.

"Don't think I didn't see you drop that," Warren muttered, not looking up as he hammered out a square taper.

Darby reddened, fumbling for the iron rod that had slipped from his grip. "Sorry. That man outside—the one with the big hat—he looked like he was about to punch Wilem."

Warren eyes the angry traveler. "Wilem's fine," Warren replied. "And hats don't make fists hurt more." He rolled his shoulder, straightening, and nodded toward the bellows. "Two pulls. Steady, not frantic."

Darby obliged, and the forge fire brightened, throwing their two shadows high up the wall. Warren liked the way the heat made the world smaller, the way it chased out every other concern. Even as the stories stacking up outside pressed in, he could imagine, for a moment, that his only job was to make one thing at a time until the world calmed itself.

But there was too much noise. Even with the anvil's ringing, Warren could hear the murmur of the crowd at the Broken Claw. Sam's voice, loud and distinct, carried all the way across the square, somehow managing to cut through the din with a practiced authority. He could picture her at the bar, one finger pointed at some battered traveler, brow arched as she dispensed both advice and insult with equal generosity. It was the only way to break the tension; let everyone pretend, for a few minutes, that they were just passing through a normal day.

"Darby," Warren said, "take these out back to the cooling trough, would you?" He slid the lined-up handles onto a battered tray. "Careful—don't trip on the sacks, and don't stop to listen to stories."

"Dad, why are there so many people today?"

Warren sighed, laid his tools on the workbench, and stretched his back. "I know. It seems like the whole of the East is emptying out, doesn't it?"

"They all look afraid."

"They've left their homes behind." He sighed again. "Okay. Let's go see what Sam's picked up. We'll put these in the trough first." He let his son carefully carry the tray out and slide the handles into the cool water of the trough, and then led the boy across the road.

Sam must have seen him coming through the pub's open door, because she met him on the walkway out front. "Taking a break?"

"Darby's having trouble focusing," he said, ruffling the boy's hair to take any sting from his words. "Truth be told, I am too. Never seen such a procession."

"It's bad news," Sam said, shaking her head. "Seems like all the smaller villages around Smallhaven are losing people left and right, and I've even spoken to a few from Stronghold."

"Something about a fire god?"

Sam frowned. "That's the odd thing—I'm getting a few different stories. From the people who claim to have seen something in person, yeah, it's someone claiming to be a prophet of a fire god. But some-times it's a man, sometimes it's a woman."

Warren's expression mirrored Sam's. "If they've *seen* someone, you'd think their stories would line up."

"Unless there are multiple fire god prophets running around."

"What else?"

"Again, best I can put together is that the rosefruit towns have been going through there usual every-few-generations upheavals. Most folks seem fine with that. Used to it, and all. But more than a few of the younger, stronger warlords have been trying to bring multiple towns together—want-to-be emperors and the like. And *that's* been more disruptive than anyone can stomach. And then you start hearing about this fire god. Seems to always crop up in the towns that have already been through the most chaos and fighting—and seems to always be the one to put an end to it."

"But not nicely."

"To say the least. Although nobody *I've* spoken to has come from a village that was burned to the ground, it seems they've all *heard* of one that was." She peered at Warren, who'd suddenly tilted his head back. "What?"

"You don't hear that clicking?"

"Your ears are twice the size of mine at least."

Warren shorted. "It's those spiders. They're still skulking about the rooftops."

Sam shuddered and Darby took a quick step closer to the pub's open door. "So long as they stay on the rooftops, I suppose," she muttered. "Hey, Wilem's trying to get your attention."

Warren turned to see Wilem's waving easily. The ogre's shoulders relaxed just a bit: a more frantic wave would have indicated a problem, a subtler wave, from waist height, would have indicated a *big* problem. He stepped off the raised walkway and into the hard-packed trade road. "How can I help?" he asked.

Wilem was standing next to a cart that had pulled just enough off the road so as to not block traffic. A younger man and woman, clearly the cart's owners, seemed to grow apprehensive as Warren approached.

"Sorry," he said, giving them a closed-lips smile. "I meant to say, 'Friendly ogre help travelers.'"

The man's lips twitched into an uncertain smile.

"Warren's a friend, and our blacksmith," Wilem explained. "Warren, I just need to replace a couple of pins on their cart's linkage." He held out one hand, displaying the two metal pins. "Fortunately," he added in an aside to the young couple, "Warren here's been making these pins on a daily basis. You're not the only folks to have this trouble, especially with a cart that's seen as much usage as this one."

"I've never seen a road so rutted," the young man admitted.

"Been more traffic than anyone can remember," Warren said. "It'll take the winter snows and spring melt to even things back out, I expect."

"But we'll be able to get you on your way in a moment," Wilem said. "Warren?"

"Need me to lift up the front end?"

"Please."

"No problem."

Warren squatted at the cart's tongue, placed one massive hand underneath, and with only a faint grunt lifted the front end a full handspan off the ground. Wilem, nimble despite his age, ducked beneath. The cart's owners gave each other a quick glance—half wary, half impressed—and then watched as Wilem set to work with practiced efficiency.

The ogre's arms barely trembled. "Don't worry," he said over the creak of the timber, "I've held up heavier—though usually it's a cow that doesn't want its hooves trimmed, not a cart that does." He flashed the couple a tusky grin, then called down to Wilem, "You need me to keep it still?"

"Steady as you can. This one's a bit warped." Wilem's voice was muffled beneath the cart. "You all headed very far?"

"We're hoping to get as close to the coast as we can," the young woman replied. She was wrapped in a wool shawl that looked better suited to summer than the chill that was beginning to creep into the air as the sun tipped toward the horizon. "We've family near the port at Lanter's End."

Warren considered. "That's a fair ways, and the road doesn't get much friendlier. They're saying the mountain pass might close early this year."

The man's face—pale and dotted with old acne scars—twisted briefly in dismay before settling into resignation. "We'll take what we can get. Nothing left for us back home."

"Where's that?" Warren asked.

"Just outside Fortenvale," the woman said quietly, as if the words might summon something grim from the past. She raised her chin anyway. "They took the town quick. Not much warning. Our church elder said we could ride it out, but then the rumors started. About the fires. The strangers in masks." Her voice faltered, but she pressed on. "We left that night. Only turned back once. After that, we never stopped moving."

Warren held the cart a little higher, making room as Wilem hammered one pin free and tapped the fresh one in. "We've been hearing similar tales."

The man nodded. "We tried to keep our heads down. No one cared until the next town over was gone. Next thing, there's torches and shouting and strangers claiming they could fix everything, if you just did what they said." He glanced at Warren, uncertain. "You haven't had trouble, here?"

"Not so far," Warren said. "Town's a bit less... grand than Fortenvale, and the folks here like to keep their own business, I guess. And we're pretty far away." He smiled faintly again, more to set them at ease than anything. "But we're keeping watch. That's why we're making so many pins and hinges. Never thought I'd wear out the anvil before my own knuckles, but here we are."

Wilem's head popped out from under the cart, his hair wild with dust. "That's one," he said, voice triumphant. "Other side, please." Warren obliged, shifting his grip and leaning his bulk into the wooden tongue, lifting the battered cart with the same casual ease he'd reserve for a sack of flour. Wilem crawled across, his knees creaking in sympathy with the timber, and repeated the operation. The old man's fingers were a blur—twist, pull, align, tap, hammer—before he declared it done with a grunt of exhausted satisfaction.

"Ready for another ten-league stretch, at least," Wilem said, brushing his palms together. "You'll want to keep an eye on the shoes, though—your horse is favoring his left hind. If you've time, Warren can look at it when he's free."

The couple exchanged another private look, the kind Warren often saw from people who'd been through too much together: a silent calculus of risk, time, and trust. The man nodded, relenting. "We'll take you up on that, if you can spare a minute."

"Of course," Warren said, easing the cart nose to the ground. The horse—a plain bay, sturdy and rangy, with a streak of white down its nose—stood hitched to the post, watching the proceedings with the patience of a creature that'd long ago resigned itself to the whims of humans. It did, however, lift its ears at Warren's approach, and caught his scent eagerly.

"Don't bite," Warren said, ducking beneath the horse's barrel chest. "I'm here to help." He ran his large, calloused hand down the horse's flank, then gently lifted the offending hoof. He whistled softly at the split in the old shoe, and shook his head. "You've been carrying too much, friend," he murmured, "but we'll get you sorted."

Darby reappeared at his side, an apron now slung haphazardly over his tunic and a hammer in each fist. He held them out solemnly. "You might need these."

Warren grinned and selected the lighter hammer, then set to work. His movements were gentle, surprisingly so for a creature of his size—he eased the shoe free, set the new one from his day's batch, and hammered it in place in three swift, sure taps. The horse didn't so much as flinch, though it did cock its head toward Darby, who fed it a wizened apple from the bucket beside the post.

"There," Warren said, giving the animal's shoulder a reassuring pat. "She'll serve you well the rest of the way, unless you pick up a goblin along the route."

"They'd have to catch us first," the man said, some of the tension draining from his shoulders.

"Best way is not to stop in the woods, if you can help it," Wilem advised. "You look like you could handle yourself, but they go for the easy targets. You'll want to keep together with the other carts when you get past the lake and into the lowlands. That's where the raiders like to try their luck."

"We'll remember," said the woman, clutching her shawl tighter. Now that she wasn't focused on the repair, Warren noticed she was younger than he'd guessed—her eyes were bright and raw, and she and her companion stood close enough to pass for siblings. "Thank you," she said, and Warren couldn't tell if she meant for the horse, the cart, or the warning. It was all the same either way.

Wilem dusted his hands. "If you're stopping overnight, you'll find better company here than down the road. Otherwise, there's a decent stretch of clear ground near the causeway bridge that should be safe enough for a night's rest."

The young man nodded. "Thank you," he said, the words a little stiff but genuine, and together they guided their patched-up cart back into the flow of travelers.

Warren watched as the couple worked their way into the procession. He waited until the cart had disappeared from view before exhaling the breath he'd been holding. Around him, the ordinary bustle of the road seemed to return to its usual tempo.

He glanced at his son, who was stroking another horse's nose with quiet, intent focus. "You have to watch for the soft spots," Warren said. "On a cart, or a person."

Darby looked up, eyes wide. "Do people have soft spots, too?"

"Oh, plenty," Warren said, with a crooked smile. "Most are just better at hiding them than a cracked wheel or a bent shoe. But in the end, everyone's got one."

Darby considered this as they made their way back toward the forge, his little jaw working the thought over. Warren liked that—liked the idea that Darby would be the kind of person to weigh things carefully, not just hammer away at them.

It took only moments to settle back into the day's rhythm: hot iron, cool water, the ever-present rise and fall of voices outside.

He was setting out a new stack of nails when, behind him, a familiar set of footfalls scuffed the dirt. He didn't turn right away; he'd know Susan's step anywhere, light but deliberate, the way she always managed to make herself heard even when she was trying not to.

She ducked inside, hair pulled back tight and her apron flecked with flour. She looked around the workshop with the frank appraisal of someone who'd lived half her life among its clutter and noise. "You're running low on those," she said, nodding at the dwindling pile of horseshoe blanks beside the anvil.

"I am," Warren said, "but I've got it under control." He set his hammer down and wiped his palms on his apron, then, because he knew she wanted him to, met her gaze. "You need something?"

"I thought I'd check how you were holding up," Susan said, rolling her weight from heel to toe. "You haven't come up for a proper meal since breakfast."

Darby, sensing this was a conversation for grown-ups, slipped out the back door, calling over his shoulder that the pan handles were probably cool enough by now.

Warren gave her a sheepish half-smile. "I'm fine. It's just busy. Everyone needs something."

"So how *are* you?" Her eyes cut through his own and into his soul.

"Solid eight," he assured her. "You?"

She relaxed a bit. "I'm good. Really good. We have a safe home—safe as anything these days, I suppose. Darby's loved. And..." She trailed off, biting her lower lip.

"Your glad the dreams are gone."

She nodded quickly. "Very. Not that the town's gifts aren't missed, but..."

"There's less pressure."

"This is *normal*, Warren."

"I know. I don't mind it either. I *like* making horseshoes. And pins. Even knives—if they're the plain ones I make now."

There was a quick, small ruckus outside, and Susan turned as the two of them assessed the situation. Several travelers had stopped and were pointing to the rooftops. "Dooley's damn spiders," Warren muttered.

Susan shivered slightly. "He says there's at least a half-dozen of them now."

"Keeping to the rooftops?"

"And the foothills."

"Good enough, I guess."

"There he is now," Susan pointed. And sure enough, as the crowd finally broke up and moved on, they left behind the diminutive menagerie-keeper.

"Dooley," Warren said—softly for an ogre, but his booming voice carried well across the trade road—"how goes it?"

Dooley was in a mood. Not his usual chipper self, whistling at the corners of every sentence and twinkling at the world like it was all a wonderful pageant of possibility. Today, he glowered at the stones of the buildings as though they were personally responsible for the disappointment of the morning: two broken cages, three missing ferrets, and a pair of skittering red shadows that had stalked him all the way from the green to the edge of the trade road.

He crossed the road and paused at the foot of the smithy's porch, studying the roofline of the tavern and inn with narrowed eyes. "Somewhere up there, one of them is watching."

Warren waited, arms folded, giving Dooley the patient silence he sometimes required to shift from animal to human concerns.=

"Those things," Dooley began, not even bothering with a greeting. "They're ruining me. You know that? The new arrivals, not even a moon since the last batch of eggs cracked, and already they've scared off every hedgehog, marmot, and possigla in the lower Mistrals. Nothing left for me to catch. Nothing left for anyone to see. Not a single paying customer since last week." He looked as if he was about to spit, but remembered himself and instead rapped a nervous rhythm on his cane.

Susan, ever the diplomat, said, "Maybe they'll move on soon?"

"They're smart," Dooley muttered. "Too smart. They're not wandering. They're watching. And I don't know what for." He pointed upward, and Warren followed his finger to a scarlet sphere tucked against a chimney pot, legs clamped over the bricks like a monstrous clamp. "Look at that—she's not hiding. She wants us to know she's there."

Warren squinted. He could just make out the gleam of the spider's eyes, a cluster of glistening black set within the angry red of its body. "Maybe she's sick of rats and wants a real meal."

"Not funny," Dooley huffed. "And that's the thing, they're not *threatening* anyone. Oh, they've made it into my shop and broken some cages, but they probably thing they're doing a good deed."

"Have you tried baiting them elsewhere?" Warren asked.

Dooley looked at him like he'd sprouted a second head. "What, you mean lead them to the next town? That's someone else's problem?"

"Not what I meant. I just thought—maybe if they're after something specific, you could give it to them out of town grounds. Get them to chase a trail."

Dooley snorted. "They're not that stupid. They know exactly where the food is." He shook his head and began clomping back toward the road. "No scaring them off. No luring them away. We'll just have to deal with them."

"I feel bad for him," Susan said in a low voice. "It must be frustrating to not be able to understand them anymore."

"Aye," Warren said. "He's right, though. This isn't in character for them at all. He cast his gaze down the road, toward the town's western gate. "How's everyone else doing?"

"Good enough," Susan said. "Everyone's gotten used to bringing wares out to the road. Those tables Wilem through together have been helpful. More people are stopping, at least, when they see what's available."

Lucy's table was probably the brightest spot on the whole trade road, if not for the garish blue of her pottery then for her voice, which rang out every time she laughed or, as now, haggled with a pair of tired travelers. She'd set up a display of mugs and bowls on a plank balanced over two stumps, and was presently holding up a squat, lidded jar as she extolled its virtues to a red-nosed man and his partner.

"See, with this lid, you can actually keep your tea hot," she said, peering meaningfully over her glasses. "Or your soup, if you eat soup for breakfast like some people who shall not be named." She gave the woman a pointed look, and the woman grinned, her cheeks pink from the wind.

"Can it also keep broth from leaking out?" asked the man, who, from the way he cradled his left arm, had seen better days. "Our last crock shattered the first time we went over a rut."

Lucy gave the jar a tap with her knuckle. "Hear that? Solid. I fired this batch extra long, and I'd bet my good eye it'll last the rest of your journey, even if you run over a goblin." She held it out for inspection, and the woman ran her fingers along the glaze, which shone in the late afternoon like a slice of the lake on a clear day.

"How much?" she asked, and Lucy named her price, but before she could start her ritual of feigned debate, the woman nodded. "Done."

Lucy, momentarily stunned by the lack of resistance, recovered quickly and wrapped the jar in a scrap of old cloth, then handed it over with a flourish. "You get two mugs with that, no charge," she said, pressing them into the woman's free hand. "Can't have a drink without a friend."

Not to be outdone, Prudence had laid claim to the next table over, where she'd arranged her cloaks, shawls, and gloves with military precision. She kept her hands folded, a faint look of disapproval on her face as she watched passersby, but when a customer paused—especially one who looked like they might freeze to death before the first snow—she switched effortlessly into a softer, conspiratorial tone.

Today, a young boy with tufts of yellow hair stood shivering at the edge of her display. His mother, deep in conversation over a battered pack with the old cobbler, seemed oblivious to her son's predicament.

Prudence slid from behind the table and lifted a small, navy blue cloak from her rack. "Try this on," she said, draping it over the boy's shoulders. The hood fit perfectly, and the wool looked almost comically warm compared to his thin tunic.

"It's heavy," the boy complained.

"That's how you know it's good," Prudence replied. "Come here." She crouched down, adjusting the clasp at his neck and smoothing the fabric. "See? Fits like it was made for you." She gave him a look that brooked no argument, and he nodded, fingers already burrowing into the deep pockets.

His mother finished her transaction and broke away from the potter, turning with an apology already forming. But Prudence intercepted her with a folded smile and a quick, practiced exchange. "It suits him," said the mother, running her hand over the thick cloth. She hesitated, voice low: "I haven't much left."

"We can barter," Prudence replied, quiet enough that only the mother heard. "Your boy said you bake. I might need a few loaves, once you're settled."

The woman's jaw worked with gratitude and something like

embarrassment, but she nodded, and the boy, already swaggering in his new cloak, tugged at her sleeve by way of thanks.

Warren lingered, watching this small theater, then ducked his head to murmur to Susan. "Be right back." She nodded, stepped outside, and leaned back against the smithy's stone walls, watching the slow, even flow of wagons through the town.

Warren stepped to the edge of the road, nodding politely at an alarmed-looking couple seated high on the bench of a covered wagon. He had seen more commerce in the last week than in the whole of the previous year. Even the little things mattered, he thought—pots, cloaks, pins, bread—kept people moving, kept hope from drying to dust.

He was about to turn back to the forge when he noticed someone standing a few paces from Lucy's display, still and out of place. At first glance it looked like a scarecrow propped against the stone wall—thin as a reed, with a hat pulled low and clothes that hung off his frame like laundry on a cold line. But as Warren looked closer, he recognized the man as one of the travelers who'd taken up residence at the edge of town: the ones who never seemed to join the gatherings, who always kept to themselves.

This one's eyes flicked up and caught Warren's, and in that instant, Warren felt something pass between them. Not threat, exactly, but a question, as if the stranger were sizing up the town, weighing its defenses, its customs, its people. The man nodded just once, then turned away and was gone, blending into the slush of wagons and foot traffic heading toward the lake road.

Warren didn't like it. He watched where the man disappeared, waiting to see if he doubled back, but the shape never returned. He made a mental note to mention it to Jen, who had a nose for trouble and a memory that rarely missed.

He didn't get the chance right away. As he stepped onto the porch of the Broken Claw, Sam was already there, arms crossed and watching the same stretch of road. "See that?" she said, not looking at him.

"I did."

"He's been here two days. Never bought a thing, never spoke to anyone."

Warren considered. "Maybe he's just passing through."

Sam shook her head. "Maybe. But I'll have Jen keep an eye out."

She turned, and the lines on her face looked deeper than they had that morning. "You ready for the evening rush?" she asked, changing the subject.

Warren rolled his eyes, but there was no bite in it. "As ever."

"Heard you patched up three carts and two horses before lunch," Sam said. "You're going soft." She grinned, but it faded quickly. "I'm glad you're here, Warren. I don't know how we'd..."

"We're happy, Sam. You know what Susan said earlier?"

Sam shook her head.

"This is normal. And she's right. We've got it good. I think... I know we don't talk about it. *Them*, I mean. But... this *is* normal. I feel like we all still think we lost something."

The former mercenary nodded slowly. "You're not wrong. And I guess I didn't even have as long to get used to it as all of you."

"So you're still happy here?"

"I am."

"Good."

"Think it'll be busy tonight?"

Warren eyed the road and grunted. "I'll sit the door, just in case. And get Darby to come help run orders and wash mugs."

Sam chuckled. "Very *normal*. I'll take it."

nineteen

· · ·

WARREN ROSE from bed when the first of the town's bells began their morning disagreement—an argument about whether today's sunrise was especially early or late, as if the sun would care one way or the other. He could have slept straight through it, but the faint clamor of bickering bells set off a sharper clamor in his head. Sometimes, when he'd spent a whole night forging, he woke up with the sound of his own hammering still echoing in his ears. Sometimes he woke up wanting to split something's skull with a hammer. There were probably words for that, if you asked a healer or a holy one. Warren just called it "Today."

He paused, as always, to watch Susan sleep. His wife didn't snore so much as purr, a noise low in her throat that vibrated the bed frame. Her arms sprawled across both their pillows, fingers curled like she was grasping something in a dream. She was, Warren decided, the most beautiful person in the world, even after all these years, and even when she drooled. Especially when she drooled.

Downstairs, Darby had already made a mess of breakfast—there was a pan of burned eggs, four unbroken shells perched elegantly on the rim of the mixing bowl, and a sort of mushroom goo boiling over onto the stovetop. It was probably a recipe he'd learned from Sam, who believed if you could chew it, you could cook it. Warren scraped the pan and left it for the cats to clean, then nudged open the back door.

The morning had a heavy, iron smell. A thick mist still clung to the ground between the smithy and the trade road, dulling the colors of the inn's banner and the flags on the green. There were three or four wagons already staged outside the west gate, piled with luggage and supplies, their owners nervously pacing, waiting for their families to climb aboard so they could be off. Somewhere, a burro brayed as if the world's end could be delayed a few more hours if only everyone would stop making such a damn racket.

Warren grabbed his heavy apron and a half-eaten loaf from the night before. On the way to the smithy, he nodded at the overnighters clustered around the Broken Claw's porch. Sam herself was perched on a barrel, hair still wet from a recent wash, arguing with two travelers about the best way to skirt the passes.

"I'm not kidding," Sam was saying. "The mudslide at Bearclaw Switch will eat your entire left wheel. You won't even know it's gone until you try to brake for dinner."

The smaller of the two travelers—both bundled in dark cloaks—held up a hand. "We're not unfamiliar with mud, Miss," she said, with the careful condescension of the over-educated. "We spent six months on the flats of Tarsis."

"Unless you also spent six months up to your armpits in snowmelt, I'd recommend you listen to the locals." Sam's face didn't have a lot of range—she'd lost part of her upper lip to an now-dead foe—but she scowled with the full weight of a person who'd seen every mistake made at least twice.

Warren stepped around the argument, grinning, and crossed to the smithy. He set his bread on the workbench, looked around for the better tongs, and grumbled when he remembered he'd left them soaking in a pail the night before. Then he crossed back, right through the argument.

"You're up early," Sam said, barely missing a beat. "Dreaming about swords again?"

"Dreaming about breakfast," Warren said. "What's the rush with these?"

"Merchants, I think. Or smugglers. Smell like sandalwood and onions." Sam glanced sidelong at the two, who were now pointedly ignoring both of them. "Not the chatty kind. I'd bet all three heads they'll be the first to bail if the road turns ugly."

Warren sniffed the air. The travelers really did smell of onions, which meant one or both of them had spent time hiding out in a storehouse. He shrugged. "Suppose we all do what we must." He looked down the road. "Think there's trouble coming?"

"I always think that." Sam shrugged. Then her expression grew pensive. "But today there's more, isn't there? Something in the air."

"Yeah." Warren left her to her watching and went back to his forge. The workbench was cold, and a sword-in-progress lay across it. He stared at it for a moment, relieved that it was *just* a sword, not someone's destiny. This particular sword was taking him longer than usual, though, and he decided to blame the uneasy atmosphere that had settled over the town in the last few days.

He hammered the blade until the sound was more comforting than aggravating, then set it aside and started on the mundane work: horseshoes, then a few new nails for the gate, then the fixings for a child's fishing spear. By the time he finished, the morning had brightened and half the overnighters had already vanished, their rooms already being cleaned by Minnie and her erstwhile son.

The morning traffic—mostly small parties or solitary wanderers—didn't stay in the town long. They passed through like water through a sieve, pausing only to buy a loaf or a bundle of dry rushes before setting out again. A few stopped at Warren's for repairs, but most had come prepared. That was the first sign of change: fewer people showing up needing a patch job or a makeshift shield. They were starting out wary, expecting trouble.

Around noon, Warren watched as a pair of old men in matching brown cloaks unloaded a trunk from their wagon and lugged it to the lakeshore. They worked in perfect silence, faces locked in identical frowns, and opened the trunk together, as if expecting a demon or a banshee to leap out. Instead, a battered rowboat unfolded from the inside, like a flower blooming sideways, and the men set about prepping it for the lake. They worked with grim determination, barely glancing back at the road or at the town.

Warren watched them for a while, then went back to his own business, only to realize he had nothing to do. There hadn't been a single order for replacement cart axles, no desperate calls for arrowhead repairs, not even a missing horseshoe. The only work was the annoyingly normal sword, and even that felt less urgent with the slow, grim parade of travelers streaming past.

He leaned against the smithy's doorframe, chewing on a bit of cold bread, and tried to puzzle it out. Most years, the end of autumn brought a mad scramble of last-minute travelers—people racing to get through the passes before snow made the roads impassable. There'd be a frenzy of trade, a few brawls, sometimes a whole family looking to buy out half the dry goods in the market. This year, though, nobody was panicking. They were moving fast, but not in a hurry—more like they were obeying some unspoken rule, like a whole flock of birds veering away from a hawk in perfect, frightened sync.

Susan padded across the square with Darby trailing behind, his mouth stained with a bruise-colored jam. She waved at Warren and came to lean against the fence, her arms crossed.

"Quiet day," she said. "You lose your touch?"

"Lost it years ago," Warren said. "I'm retired now."

"Tell that to your arms." She pinched his bicep and snorted when he pretended not to feel it. "Have you noticed anything strange about the travelers?"

"They're getting smaller and faster," Darby offered. "Like the people are shrinking."

Susan tousled the boy's hair. "Not just that. There's a cold in the air, and I don't think it's the weather."

Warren looked at the sky, then at the town's two gates. Both were open, but the traffic was mostly one-way: out. "Jen says it's the madness in the east. Fires. Bandits for certain."

Darby made a face. "Do bandits eat people?"

"Only if they run out of goats," Warren said. "And I hear they're low on goats."

Susan's laugh was brief but bright. "You're a terrible liar."

"I'm a father. It's my job."

They stood for a while, watching the road. A party of four came up the road, each with a pack slung high on their shoulders and their hands never far from their belts. Warren recognized two of them from three days prior—young, loud, and eager to swap stories. Today they looked straight ahead, eyes rimmed with red, their boots covered in mud up to the knees. He didn't even bother calling to them.

The noon bell clanged, half a beat off, and the town's rhythm changed. People moved faster, like the shadow of something big and hungry had finally crested the hills. There were more animals being led through the gates, more goods packed onto carts, more children corralled by their parents with an anxious urgency that never looked right on the face of a mother or father.

Warren didn't have to ask Susan if she saw it. The fear was a smell, a taste, a sound. Even the crows that hung around the town's small compost heap were quieter than usual, as if waiting for something bigger to die.

He went back to the forge and forced himself to work. The sword didn't want to be a sword, but he hammered anyway, trying to beat it into sense. The sound echoed through the yard, up the stone walls and into the windows of the inn, where he caught Jen's silhouette—arms folded, chin raised, eyes fixed on the horizon.

The day wore on. A light rain started, just enough to soak the dirt and darken the slate roofs. The bells argued again at sunset, then gave up, and the town went nearly silent. The only sound was the restless wind, and the sharper, higher ringing of Warren's hammer as he finished his day's work. He stood on the porch as the sun dipped below the lake, watching the last few travelers scuttle out like mice from a burning barn. Susan joined him, her hands deep in her apron pockets.

"I think tomorrow will be worse," she said.

"Then tomorrow I'll bake bread," Warren replied. "Maybe I'll bake enough for the whole damn town."

She took his hand, squeezed it hard. "I'd like that." Then she laughed. "Makota will have some thoughts for you, though."

He chuckled. "Big ogre terrified of cat-lady."

In the darkness, the faint shape of the sword, finally finished, leaned against the wall, catching the last of the daylight and holding it for just a second longer than it had any right to.

Warren stared at it, and it stared right back.

———

It was barely dawn when the next piece of trouble trotted through the east gate.

Warren saw him coming while patching up a cracked cauldron for the inn. The morning sun barely had the strength to shine, but the man on the dun-colored horse caught what there was of it—his coat was scarlet, open at the chest to show a strip of leather bandolier, and he had the kind of mustache that tried to look aristocratic but ended up looking like a pair of wet rats clinging to his lip. The horse was big and glossy and not local, which meant it was stolen, and the saddle was weighted with more than just the rider's scrawny frame.

The stranger reined in right at the smithy, leapt from the saddle in one smooth show-offy motion, and kicked the dust off his boots. The boots were soft and black, curling up at the toe like a jester's, and probably worth more than most townsfolk's monthly wages.

Warren didn't bother straightening up. He wiped his hands on his apron and spat into the slop bucket. "Need a shoe?" he asked, not looking at the man.

The stranger's voice was thin, cheery, and nasally. "No, but I could use a drink. And a pair of good knives." He grinned, showing a mouth full of gold and gaps.

"We're not a bar," Warren said. "That's the Broken Claw, across the road."

"I know. Not my first time." The man sauntered into the smithy, poking at Warren's tools. "Knew if anyone could make what I needed, it'd be you." He picked up the recently finished sword from the bench, weighing it in one hand. "Ugly as sin. I like it."

Warren took it from him without a word, replaced it on the rack, and turned his attention to the man's hands. Knuckles rough as gravel, two fingers missing from the left, healed badly. The kind of hands that lived on the wrong end of a sword. "You in a hurry?" Warren asked.

The man grinned wider. "Not at all. Road's crowded today. Everyone's running from something, but I like to take my time." He winked, as if they were sharing some grand secret. "It's a highwayman's dream out there."

Warren nodded, as if he'd expected nothing else. "Knives?"

"Two. For now. Need them quick, but they have to look like nothing special. Good steel, won't break on a ribcage. Fit for a meal or a murder." He said this like he was ordering extra salt on his eggs.

"We serve all who come in peace," Warren said, voice flat. He felt sick just saying it, but rules were rules, and the rules had kept this town alive through harder times than these.

The man's eyes flickered, searching Warren's face for mockery. "I'm plenty peaceful. 'Til someone tries to rob me." He barked a laugh, full of his own joke. "Two knives, plain but sharp. How long?"

Warren sized him up again, measured the desperation behind the bravado. This man was the kind of animal that grew bolder when the world got sick. "I'll have 'em by the bell. Really just need to finish off one of them."

"Perfect," said the man, clapping his hands. "You're a legend, ogre. I heard all about you down in Kestleford. People say you once bit a man's head off for not paying full price."

Warren rolled his eyes. "They also say I sleep on a bed of horseshoes. I only bite heads off after sunset."

The man laughed again, then slithered out of the shop. Warren watched him through the open doorway as he strolled up to the inn, pausing only to admire his own reflection in a window.

Jen was waiting on the porch, leaning against a post with her arms folded and her eyes squinting into the morning glare. She didn't smile as the man approached, but she didn't reach for the sword on her wrist, either. That was the thing about Jen: you always knew where you stood, but you never knew how deep the water really was.

• • •

Warren set to work. He had one knife finished, and its twin fairly far along. He just needed to get the shape final and put an edge on the thing. He thought, briefly, about making the knives deliberately dull, but the town's creed nagged at him. Serve all who come in peace, stay in peace, and leave in peace. It was the logic of a person who'd never lived through a siege, but it was also the only reason the town still stood.

The knives were easy enough—short, balanced, with a half-moon pommel and a blade meant to slip between ribs like a whispered secret. He honed them until they gleamed, then wrapped the hilts in cheap cord and slotted them into a pair of plain leather sheaths.

By the time the bells struck, the highwayman was back. He walked straight into the smithy and snatched the knives up, weighing each one in his hands and testing the balance.

"Perfect," he said. "You really are a legend."

"Pay up," Warren said, holding out a hand the size of a shovel.

The man peeled two silver coins from a hidden pocket, then a third, and flipped them one by one into Warren's palm. "Keep the change," he said. "In case you ever need a favor on the road."

Warren closed his fist around the coins. "What I need is fewer people like you."

The man grinned, unfazed. "Don't we all, ogre." He tucked the knives into his coat, winked, and swaggered back into the daylight.

Warren followed him to the edge of the yard, arms crossed. He watched as the highwayman mounted up, tossed Jen a mock salute, and rode out the west gate, his crimson coat the last thing visible before the dip in the road.

Jen came over a minute later, her boots scraping against the damp gravel. "Did you get a good look at him?"

"Got a look at everything worth seeing," Warren replied. "You gonna let him through?"

She snorted. "What am I supposed to do, arrest him for future crimes?"

"If you did, the gaol would fill up before breakfast." Warren scowled. "I hate this. We're supposed to be neutral, but we just armed a bastard who's going to make trouble for every honest soul running from real danger."

Jen shrugged, eyes scanning the road. "If he'd started trouble here, he'd be dead. If you hadn't served him, he'd buy blades from someone else. At least now you know what he's carrying."

"I don't like it," Warren repeated. "Feels wrong."

"It is wrong. But it's also the only way this place survives."

They stood there, not saying anything, until the next wagon rolled into town, axles shrieking like they were about to snap.

Warren turned back to the forge, the taste of iron and bitterness thick in his mouth. He put the coins in the jar by the window—he'd melt them down later, make a new chime for the bell tower, something to drown out the sound of his own regret.

When Susan came by at noon, she found him hammering away at another bar of metal, shaping it into yet another sword—one meaner and crueler than the one before. She didn't say a word, just set down a fresh roll and patted his arm.

The air outside was cold and quiet, but inside Warren felt the old heat rising, familiar and dangerous.

There was more work to do, and the day was far from over.

———

Warren spent the next candle mark beating the new sword into something serviceable, letting each strike bleed off the anger that had pooled in his chest. The forge spat and hissed as he quenched the metal, releasing a stench of burnt bone and oil.

He was grinding the blade, sweat crawling down his neck, when Jen arrived. She didn't bother knocking—nobody did—but she waited at the threshold, watching him with that still, cop-eyed stare.

"Break something?" he said, not looking up.

"Just checking in." Jen stepped inside, boots leaving faint prints on the packed dirt. She leaned against the wall, folding her arms. "You looked ready to punch the moon when I left you."

"Was thinking about it." Warren didn't stop working. "Maybe the moon would put up a fight."

"Doubt it. Never met a celestial body that could stand up to you."

He let that hang in the air while he ran the whetstone up the blade. The black metal took an edge that shimmered weirdly in the forge-light, like water flowing uphill. "Why do we do it?" he finally said.

Jen raised an eyebrow. "Do what?"

"Serve people like that bastard. Sell them knives. Pretend we don't see what they are." He set the blade aside and turned to face her. "The old ways only worked because the gifts were strong. They're not anymore. The gifts are gone, so why hold to rules?"

Jen was silent for a long moment. She looked around the smithy, at the rack of repaired tools, the line of battered shields, the jar of silver coins by the window. "You remember the Crow Men?" she said, finally.

"Barely. I was a kid. But they came through." He scowled. "I remember hiding in the root cellar. I remember the screaming."

"They put forty men on the wall that day. Thirty-nine of them never made it down again." Jen's voice was flat. "Crow Men burned villages all the way up the valley, but they never took this town. Not because we had more swords or better shooters. Because we held the line. They came and just moved on."

Warren snorted. "That was a long time ago. And this place had its gifts."

"But it worked," Jen said. "Every time we picked a fight, we lost. Every time we stayed neutral—held to the creed—we survived. You want to make us a target, go ahead. But don't pretend there's a better option."

He turned her words over, letting the old pain surface. "What if the world's changed?"

"It always changes," Jen said. "That's why rules matter."

Warren grabbed a towel, wiped his face. "I just don't want to be the man who arms the monster that comes back to kill us."

Jen pushed off the wall, walked over, and jabbed him in the chest with a finger. "You won't be. You'll be the man who kept your word, even when it tasted like ash. And when the monster comes, you'll be ready."

He met her gaze. There was no softness in her face, only the steel of someone who'd seen enough evil to know it couldn't be reasoned with.

"Was there ever a time," he asked, "when you wanted to break the rules?"

Jen hesitated, then nodded once. "Every single day."

They stood in silence for a bit, the only sound the drip of condensation on the forge hood.

Jen looked down at the ugly new sword, then up at Warren. "Who's that for?"

He shrugged. "Don't know. It was just in the wrong place at the right time to get beat on. Maybe it's for me."

She grinned, sharp and brief. "If it is, you'll make a hell of a last stand."

Warren couldn't help but smile back, even though his hands still ached with anger. "Want to get a drink?"

"Later." Jen turned to go, then glanced over her shoulder. "For what it's worth, I don't like it either. But it keeps us alive."

She left, door swinging behind her, and Warren was alone with the sword and the silence.

"I know," the orge whispered.

He stared at the blade for a long time, tracing the twisted metal with his finger. If it was meant for him, he'd make sure it was the ugliest, meanest thing he ever forged.

Maybe that was the only way to hold the line.

———

The crowd thickened as the day stretched toward evening. North Pointe was a small place, but the main road now bristled with tables and push carts full of wares.

Warren wandered the road, making his usual rounds, nodding to his neighbors. After the morning's ugliness, he was in no mood to work, so he made himself useful in other ways—sharpening shears for the seamstress, hammering a loose wheel-spoke on the grocer's cart, untwisting a stubborn bolt for the cartwright.

Most people greeted him with the same friendly glances as always, but today their expressions were tense and guarded, with an edge of urgency. The travelers bargained harder, the mothers bought extra blankets, and everyone with sense in their skulls wore boots and heavy cloaks despite the sun. A few customers asked about sword oil, or if he could fix the rivets on a battered old shield. One even wanted to buy a crossbow, which Warren hadn't made in years, although he did have a serviceable one stashed in the back of the smithy.

"Going hunting?" he asked the would-be archer, a sallow-faced man from the hills who stank of bitterroot and dried fish.

"Not unless the meat walks on two legs," the man muttered, mouth twitching. "But best to be ready, yeah?"

"Yeah." Warren left it at that. The man took the crossbow and four mismatched bolts, paid in coin that clinked heavy and cold, and left without another word.

It wasn't just the customers who were on edge. Sam, always a strong, clear voice, kept her tone low and clipped, as if the town's walls had grown ears overnight. She pulled Warren aside in the middle of the day, her eyes sharp as a hawk's.

"Trouble in the air," she whispered. "Not just the usual. I've heard four different rumors in as many hours. One group says there's a whole army of bandits sweeping up from the south, another says the eastern road's crawling with white-walkers. Jen thinks the rumors are getting planted by someone, maybe to keep people moving, keep us unsettled."

"Or maybe there's just too many people and not enough hope," Warren said.

Sam barked a laugh, then caught herself and glanced at the crowd. "It's funny," she said. "Even when I was a merc, I never saw so many people scared to stand still. Like there's a fire behind every hill."

Warren looked at the people on the street. "Sometimes there is."

Sam changed the subject, steering him toward his stool, where she poured a double shot of ale into a mug. "On the house," she said, sliding it across the table. "For the world's largest blacksmith."

He took the mug, the bite of the drink making his sinuses flare. "You ever think about just closing up shop and running?" he asked.

Sam looked up at him, a strange, unreadable smile flickering across her scarred mouth. "Every day. But if I did, where would all these cowards buy their whiskey?" Then her expression softened. "But no. I don't. Like you said yesterday, this is *normal*. Maybe a little more tense than I'd like, but still."

He grinned, then finished the drink and thanked her. He made his way back through the crowd, picking up bits of conversation as he went. Most of it was pointless—petty complaints about prices, gossip about who had left without paying his tab—but underneath it all ran a current of real fear.

At Alred's dry goods table, Warren saw Susan with Darby, both arms full of sacks and bundles. Susan waved him over, her expression equal parts amusement and exasperation.

"We're restocking the cellar," she said, holding up a sack of dried peas. "Darby thinks we need enough to feed an army."

Darby, whose face was flushed from the cold and the effort of carrying things twice his size, shrugged. "I just don't want to eat mushrooms all winter."

"None of us do," Warren said, tousling his hair. "But your mother's right. We'll need more than that if things get ugly."

Susan's gaze flicked to the street, then back to Warren. "How ugly do you think it'll get?"

He thought about it, then shrugged. "Not sure. But I'd rather have too much than too little."

At the edge of town, Darby pointed up at the rooftops. "There's more of them today."

Warren followed his finger and saw what the boy meant. The spiders were out in numbers. They scurried along the slate shingles, hid behind the chimneys, and skulked behind the roof peaks. They never bothered anyone, and the town had long since decided to ignore them, but this was different. This was an infestation.

Susan frowned. "That's... a lot."

Darby grinned, showing off a missing tooth. "They're hunting something."

Warren watched as a spider the size of a small dog snatched a blue-bottle out of the air, wrapped it up, and disappeared back to the other slope of the roof.

"They know something we don't," he said, unsure of where that feeling came from.

They finished their day, carrying the food back to their town home and storing it in the cellar. Warren went back and worked the smithy for a while longer before closing up just as the evening's overnighters began rolling in and pulling their wagons off the road. He helped Darby unhitch the horses and get them fed and cared for. When all was settled, the two of them went home, where Susan had laid out a simple but substantial dinner for them. They spoke happily about the events of the day, recounting funny travelers or especially good nego-tiations they'd overheard. As the moon rose into the sky, they retired to their beds.

But as the lamps were turned low, Warren heard the spiders again, their claws ticking on the roof. He imagined them multiplying, swarming the town, building a fortress of silk above their heads. Maybe that was what it took to survive—a thick, tangled net between you and whatever waited in the dark.

He spent the night half-awake, listening to the rain and the whisper of legs above. Tomorrow, he told himself, he'd make more nails, or maybe fashion a few traps. Something to make the world a little less strange.

But for now, he watched the shadows on the ceiling, waiting for the spiders to finish their work.

———

It took less than a candlemark for word to spread that the two families bedding down at the Weary Head were from east and north of the lake —deep country, where people could go weeks without seeing a town guard, much less a constable. They'd arrived with the bare minimum of belongings: a pair of battered carts, one crippled donkey, three chil-dren between them and not a working set of boots among the lot. The four parents kept to the main room of the Broken Claw, huddled at a table near the stove, while the kids—two boys and a girl—hovered awkwardly at the edge of the bar, too nervous to ask for food.

Sam was in her element. She circled the pub, dropping mugs and bread loaves with the grace of someone who'd done it for two decades. The locals pretended not to listen but picked up every word. Warren came in just after dark, shook the dust from himself, and made a quiet circuit of the room, stopping at Sam's elbow behind the bar.

"They eaten yet?" he asked, eyeing the children.

"They're on their third bowl," Sam replied. "One more and I'll have to get Minnie to refill me."

He glanced at her face, reading the lines of exhaustion there. "What's their story?"

Sam shrugged. "Won't say. But the one fellow's hands are bandaged. Took a bad burn—smells like pitch."

Warren nodded. "Any sign of pursuit?"

"Not yet. But I'd wager the mother's got more scars under her dress than the man's got on his arms." Sam wiped down the bar, face unreadable. "They're afraid of fire, Warren. Like it's got a name and address."

He let that settle. "Did they see the spiders?"

Sam snorted. "Kid tried to catch one. Didn't seem to faze them."

Warren grinned, then took a seat at the end of the bar, where the talk always drifted first. He waited, listening as the night pressed in and the crowd did its best to act normal. Eventually, the two fathers— he learned one was called Marn, the other Julo—loosened enough to speak in half-formed sentences. Sam nudged things along, as she always did.

"Heard you came through the east wood," she said, topping off their mugs. "Road's been nasty. Still passable?"

Marn shook his head, jaw clenched. "They burned out the dead-falls. There's nothing left. Just ash and black snow."

Julo nodded, staring into his cup. "Saw a man hanging from an old oak. Pinned up like a scarecrow, only the crows wouldn't touch him."

The bar went quieter, if possible. Warren met Sam's eye, then looked back at the pair. "Who did it?"

The two men exchanged a glance. "They call her Christa," said

Julo, voice gone soft. "Christa Elledor, Prophet of Pyron. All dressed in red, with a voice like hot coals. She's got a following—some say a hundred strong, maybe more."

Sam sucked in a breath. "We'd heard tales of a fire cult."

"Worse than that." Marn rubbed his bandaged wrist. "They're not picky. First they went after gnomes, then half-breeds, then anyone who'd take a coin from such. Even humans, if you weren't the right sort. They call us traitors for trading with 'monsters.'" He spat the last word like a seed.

"They torch your place?" Warren asked.

Julo nodded. "We ran before they finished. Didn't even get a chance to bury the cat."

A lull followed, punctuated only by the clatter of cutlery and the pop of the stove. The three children devoured everything Sam put in front of them, eyes darting to the door whenever someone new came in. Warren felt his heart twist—he knew that look from old memories.

"Anyone following you?" Sam pressed, keeping her tone gentle.

"Not that we saw," Marn said. "But they don't need to follow. They know the roads, and they've got friends in every village, now."

Warren drummed his fingers on the counter. "What's their plan?"

Julo stared into his cup. "They want the lake. Everything around it. Say it's sacred, a place of 'cleansing.' Anyone not loyal to the fire god is marked for burning. I figure they'll hit every town on the ring road before winter closes in."

Sam poured a splash into Warren's mug, not bothering to ask if he wanted it. "Pyron," she said, rolling the word around her mouth. "Sounds like a bad joke."

Warren downed the drink in one go. "Not if you're on the list."

The rest of the evening ran downhill. The parents kept an eye on the windows, twitching at every gust of wind. The children grew quieter, curling up on the benches as if they might turn into mice and vanish between the cracks. Even the regulars left early, muttering about snow and early chores.

Sam locked the doors just after midnight, then sat across from Warren, her hands wrapped around a mug of the bar's cheapest swill.

"Jen's not going to like this," she said.

"She never does."

"Should we warn everyone?"

Warren nodded. "Likely. If it's coming this way, we need to be ready."

"So you think they'll come here?"

He thought about it, weighing possibilities. "If we're lucky, they'll follow the bigger road around the lake. South and west, not to the north, especially this far into autumn. If we're unlucky—" He looked up at the ceiling, where the spiders were scurrying around. "We'll see them soon."

Sam finished her drink and gently set the mug down. "I'm not leaving."

Warren smiled, a bitter twist. "Didn't think you would."

She stood, stretched her bad leg, and leaned on the bar. "You're on watch first," she said. "If anything happens, you wake me."

"Watch?"

"Seems right."

"Yeah." Warren pulled himself up. The stairs to the actual towers were too narrow for him to navigate, but he could keep watch as easily from the bench in front of the tavern.

Sam went up the stairs, limping but unbowed. Warren sat alone in the empty pub, the world's biggest blacksmith, as the wind pushed against the doors and the spiders drummed on the roof.

———

Warren spent the dead hours of night staring at the dark. Inside, the fire in the tavern's stove shrank to embers, painting red eyes on the walls and making everything look a little haunted.

When the world finally lightened, Warren stepped out the front and cut across the dew-damp road to his forge. The air had a bite to it, sharp enough to taste. He was halfway to the smithy when he noticed someone perched on the fence: a woman, all in black, hair so long and dark it looked like it belonged to the shadow itself.

"Couldn't sleep?" Warren called.

Leota turned her head, face pale in the dawn, and gave him a look that said she'd never slept a day in her life. "The spiders are too loud," she said.

He grinned, though it was early and he didn't feel much like grinning. "Can't imagine you afraid of a few bugs."

"I'm not afraid. I'm respectful. There's a difference." She swung her legs over the fence, landing with less grace than usual. "You heard the news?"

He nodded. "Heard it. Felt it." He hesitated, then added: "Does your magic... get jumpy when things are bad?"

Leota snorted. "If magic had a spine, it'd be crawling. The roads are rotten with ghosts, the lake's gone gray, and I saw two crows trying to drown each other in the fountain. Never seen anything like it."

"Is it the cult?"

She shrugged, black sleeves flapping. "Maybe. Or maybe it's just people being people. I'm not a prophet." She eyed him, then looked past his shoulder at the inn. "That one of your swords in the window?"

Warren blinked. "How did you—?"

Leota smiled, sharp as a knife. "Magic," she said, then shook her head. "Actually, I just looked in the window. It's the kind of thing you notice."

He ducked his head, embarrassed. "It keeps trying to turn into something else. Like it wants to be a claw, or a hook. So I finished it as best I could and... well. Trevor's big enough to use it and I think we should all be a litle on guard now."

"It wants to be useful," Leota said. "That's more than you can say for most things. And... I agree. We all need to be on guard."

They stood in silence, watching as the sun tried to burn the frost off the town. Finally, Leota said, "The wards around this place are old. They've been patched, broken, and patched again, but they were never meant to hold back what's coming. It's like... like using a tea strainer to dam a river."

Warren thought of the water, the lake, the black current under the ice. "What happens when the river gets through?"

She pulled a face. "Drown, or swim. I suppose that's always been the choice."

A crow cawed from the rooftops, loud and insistent. Warren tried to picture what would happen if the cult did come—what would be left after the burning, what kind of world his son would inherit.

"We can fight," he said, quietly.

Leota grinned, teeth bright against her skin. "You're an optimist."

"No," Warren said. "I'm just stubborn."

Leota touched his arm, light as a feather, then let her hand fall. "That's good. We'll need it. Just keep in mind..."

"No stone monsters this time."

"No. Just us."

"We'll be enough."

"Good." She turned and walked away, moving slow, careful not to slip on the frost. Warren watched her go, then turned toward the forge, already planning what he'd need to make before the sun went down again.

There were always more nails to hammer, more monsters to hold at bay. He wasn't much for prayers, but he knew one thing: if the world was ending, he'd end it doing his job.

He got to work, and the day began.

twenty

. . .

BY MID-AUTUMN, North Pointe Common Towne no longer felt like a friendly waystation. It felt like a keep under siege, only the besiegers had yet to introduce themselves.

The morning had come in cold and black, with a heavy mist lying so thick on the lake that Warren's forge fires did not show at all, no matter how hot he stoked them. It was only when the sun started to rise—a grudging, pale disk this time of year—that the outline of the far shore came into view, and with it, the new silhouettes that everyone pretended not to notice.

He stood at the smithy's open door, apron already sooty and hands already aching. Wilem was late. Warren imagined the little man sleeping past sunrise, dreaming of wood and pins and fine joinery, blissfully unaware of the world's troubles, but he knew better. No one in North Pointe was getting a good night's sleep these days, not even the spiders.

Warren stepped out of his home and took another bite from his breakfast—three eggs, shell and all, held in his great green palm and crunched together like a breakfast biscuit. He made a face. They tasted like charcoal. The taste of nerves, maybe.

Over the wall that fronted the town square, he caught movement from the roof of the boathouse across the trade road. Something big, with far too many legs for a mammal. The spiders had never ventured up there before. If he didn't know better, he'd say they were getting ideas above their station. He tilted his head slightly as one of them seemed to stare right back at him. *They're keeping watch,* he thought, and then immediately wondered where the idea had come from. Why would spiders post sentries? More likely they were waiting for the humans to leave so they could move in.

He finished the eggs and walked out into the grey blanket that covered the town green. The frost didn't bother him much, but he stomped anyway, more to make noise than to keep warm. He liked the way his boots made the soil and grass thump and and rasp—like the town itself was clearing its throat and preparing to say something rude.

Across the square, the cartwright's little workshop was the only other place awake. Wilem stood in the open doorway, both hands on his hips, staring up at the long wall of the town. Warren did the same.

Most of North Pointe's "wall" was really just the backs of all the stone buildings, with their slate roofs pitched outwards and no windows on the outside face. On the trade road, you could walk from the pub to the gaol without ever losing sight of the gates that guarded the square, which was the whole point of the original design. The people who built it must have imagined a lifetime of sieges and assaults, not seasons of easy trade and festival. But now, the town's defensive purpose felt too relevant for anyone's liking.

Wilem raised a hand in greeting. His beard was as thin as a rat's tail and his hair shorn close.

"Warren," he said. "You brought the bolts?"

Warren grunted, holding up a burlap sack in each hand. Each sack held two dozen massive iron bolts, each longer than Warren's forearm, the points shaped by his own hand to punch through a shield, or a man, or a particularly thick tree.

"They're heavier than last week's," Wilem observed, as Warren set them down beside the half-built ballista at the side of the road.

"You said you wanted them heavier," said Warren.

"I did. Last week's weren't heavy enough. Looked like something for hunting fish."

Warren shrugged. "You want heavier than this, you'll have to mount the ballista to the ground. Wheels won't hold it."

Wilem considered. "Not planning on going anywhere, anyway." He nudged the ballista's carriage with his boot. "Might as well be a cannon."

They worked in silence for a while, hands numb and faces grim. Warren handled the iron parts, driving thick spikes through layers of ash and oak, while Wilem clamped and lashed and muttered at his own joinery. They'd been at this for a sennight, setting up improvised defenses at every point they could. It was not the most dignified work Warren had ever done—he preferred horseshoes, always—but the townsfolk were jumpy, and better a too-strong defense than a too-late regret.

A string of muffled thumps and curses signaled Darby's arrival. The boy was green around the edges lately, literally and otherwise. He came running with an armload of crossbow quarrels, nearly tripping over the ballista's carriage as he dropped them at Warren's feet.

"There's four more barrels in the shed, Da," he announced, breathing hard. "Mom says to come home for lunch."

"Tell her we're nearly done," Warren replied, eyeing the sky.

Darby nodded, then turned and dashed off, his footsteps still too light for someone with Warren's bone structure, but they'd get there.

Wilem watched the boy go, then looked up at Warren. "You notice the spiders?"

"Yeah," Warren said. "They're on the roofs across the road now. Like they're expecting company." He frowned. "I might chase them off the smithy."

Wilem grunted. "If it comes to fighting, I'd rather fight a hundred men than one of those things."

Warren agreed with a grunt. "Men you can understand, at least."

Wilem shot him a sidelong look. "Not sure about that. Men are getting harder to understand by the year." He snorted, then hammered a bracket into place. "You think they'll come through the gate, or go over the wall?"

"If they're clever, both," Warren replied.

"Don't like clever enemies."

Warren was about to reply, but something caught his eye—a flicker of motion down at the lakeside storehouse, where Knodalon sometimes took his tea. Most mornings, you could find the old man perched on the bench outside, hands folded, staring into the mist as if reading the secrets of the world. Today, Knodalon was not in his usual place.

Warren scanned the storehouse windows, but saw only his own warped reflection. The building looked abandoned, but Warren knew better. He'd delivered iron bands there just yesterday, reinforcing the storehouse's great double-doors. Knodalon had thanked him, quietly, and then closed the door behind him, shutting out even the weak autumn sun.

Wilem followed his gaze. "Don't think I've seen him come out all day."

"Neither have I," said Warren.

"You ever wonder about him?" Wilem asked, keeping his voice low, as if the old man might materialize at the mention of his name.

"Every day," Warren said, and that was the truth.

They finished assembling the ballista, dragging it into place so it pointed squarely at the main gate. With the last pin driven home, Wilem clapped his hands together, dusted off the sawdust, and surveyed their work with pride and exhaustion in equal measure.

"Looks like a siege engine," he said.

"It *is* a siege engine," Warren replied.

Wilem grinned. "Let's hope we don't need it."

Warren gave him a hard look, then bent to retrieve the sacks. "Hope isn't a plan."

Wilem grunted. "Neither is dying in your sleep. We do what we can." He squinted up at the sky, then back down the road. "You heading home?"

Warren nodded.

"Keep an eye out for webs," Wilem said, only half-joking.

Warren offered him a tooth-and-tusk smile, then started back toward the smithy, the iron sacks swaying at his sides. As he passed the lakeside storehouse, he paused, staring at the high windows.

He was about to move on when a pale, angular face appeared behind the glass, watching. Knodalon's eyes were unreadable, but they tracked Warren's every step.

Warren raised a hand, but Knodalon did not return the gesture. He just watched, silent as the grave.

Warren shrugged and moved on. He had more ironwork to finish before nightfall, and then—if he was lucky—a hot meal and a warm fire.

As he reached the smithy, he glanced up at the roofline. The spiders were still there, black against the silver sky. Watching, always watching.

He wondered if they knew something the rest of them didn't.

He wondered if they were waiting for the right moment.

He wondered, just for a second, if they were afraid.

———

The next day dawned even colder, the sun a sullen rumor behind the clouds. Instead of their usual clatter, the morning hours brought only the grunts and curses of townsfolk moving crates, barrels, and bushel baskets from every outlying shop and storehouse into the safety of the inner square.

Warren was up early, making his rounds. He'd always prided himself on doing more than was asked of him, but today he barely kept pace with the pace of the town. Galhani, Vamir, Calder and his family, Dardrad and his mate—all had shuttered their shops and were now sweating side by side, hauling goods toward the green at the center of town and from there into the individual homes' cellars.

Even the little herd of goats had been shepherded into a makeshift pen in the middle of the square, where they watched the proceedings with glazed, disappointed eyes.

At first, Warren didn't see Susan or Darby, and that sent a tightness into his chest. He found them eventually at the edge of the green, overseeing a collection of children loading sacks of flour and dried beans onto a cart. Susan wore a wool cap and a scowl, both nearly identical in hue. Darby was perched on the cart itself, furiously scratching notes into a small ledger.

Warren sidled up and reached for the cart handles, lifting it with no effort at all. The children looked up, a little less tense now that the ogre was there.

"Where's this going?" he asked.

Susan wiped her hands on her apron. "Town hall. Or as much as Vamir'll let us put in, anyway. He's already in a foul mood about not having room to teach anymore."

"Anything more for the storehouse? Stuff'll go bad in the town hall."

She shook her head. "These will be fine if we keep them dry, and the hall's roof is tight. If we end up having to fall back to the square, we'll need the provisions here, not across the road." She paused, and then added, "And Knodalon's been acting stranger than usual. We're not sure how much he'll let in."

Warren snorted. "He's been letting anything in lately. Hardly comes out at all, himself."

Darby craned his head around, hair sticking up at odd angles. "Mom says he's scared."=

Warren gave his son a look. "You say that to Knodalon's face?"

Darby considered it. "No, Da."

Warren nodded, approving.

Susan picked up a sack herself, muscles straining but arms steady. "They say things aren't spoiling in the storehouse, even now. That milk they brought in last week—still as fresh as when it came off the cow."

"Always been that way," Dardrad said, stumping over and lifting a bag to his shoulder. "Always. The carrots what go in there come out twice as crisp. We all thought it was one of the town's gifts. But now..."

Warren didn't like this. He never had. He'd seen the inside of the storehouse dozens of times. It was always the same inside: a scentless chill, shadows that clung to the corners, and food that never went bad. Some townsfolk called it the North Pointe Blessing, or the Storekeeper's Trick, or just 'Knodalon's Freezer.' It had never bothered him until the rest of the town's gifts had vanished, but the storehouse remained... still.

"Fine," he said, and started down the road, dragging the cart behind him. "Let's get it over with."

The little town hall was packed, not with people but with boxes and sacks. Warren maneuvered the cart through a narrow space between two heaps of turnips.

The few people there were having a discussion: Vamir, speaking in his usual soft tone; Leota, the witch, in her matter-of-fact mutter; and a few others, all uncharacteristically trying to talk at once. There was fear in their voices, but also a strange bravado—like the time he'd seen two barn cats, both terrified, pretend to ignore a dog by fighting each other instead.

"They'll come by the road, or not at all," Alred said.

"If they do, we can see them coming for miles—"

"Unless they come by the water—"

"Who comes by the water?"

"Calder will see them if they do."

"They could come by the woods."

"And what are we supposed to do about the spiders? Has anyone asked—"

"Ask them yourself," someone else snapped.

There was a hush.

Leota spoke next, her voice low and slow. "Magic helps, but only so much. I can boil a kettle, or freeze a stream, or twist someone's ankle so they fall on their own sword. But I can't make a firestorm, not like the old tales."

"Can you make it so they don't want to come in the first place?" That was Vamir again.

"If that was a spell, don't you think I'd have used it by now? I could make people... disinclined to violence, when the town's gifts were still working. It's harder now. I'm not... I was stronger, in my youth." She shrugged. "Not so much, now."

A soft laugh, but not a happy one.

"Jen says we hold the line at the road gates. If that fails, we fall back to the square."

"If that fails—"

A hard silence.

Leota: "Then we make our peace."

Everyone filed out. Vamir blinked at Warren as he passed the ogre, as if surprised to find him there.

"Ready for another day?" the old elf asked.

"Ready as I'll ever be," Warren replied.

Leota lingered by the door. She wore a bundle of herbs slung over her shoulder and a small bottle tied at her waist. Her hat, for once, was off, revealing a mop of lank, dark hair.

"You ever wonder why the spiders watch us?" she asked Warren, without preamble.

"All the time," he said.

"Do you think they're curious, or do you think they're waiting for us to fail?"

Warren took his time with the answer. "Maybe both. Maybe neither."

Leota nodded. "I'll be by the gates at dusk. If you have anything you want me to bless, leave it in a pile by the old willow."

He grunted acknowledgment.

"Something about the spiders..." she added hesitantly.

Warren raised one thick eyebrow.

"There are tales. Vamir and I have been looking."

The eyebrow rose higher.

"They don't experience time like we do."

The other eyebrow joined the first. "You think they're expecting something."

"Or they *know* something."

"Huh."

Then Leota leaned closer, dropping her voice to a whisper. "And Knodalon. He's holding it together for all of us. I don't know how, or how long he can."

She moved off, her boots thudding softly on the packed earth.

Warren didn't like that, either.

———

At the edge of the lakeshore, Warren found himself alone with his thoughts. The little boats had all been pulled up and flipped over, the dock deserted, and the main fishing boat pulled into the tightly locked stone boathouse. He walked the length of the dock, then turned and looked back at the town. It was a good town, maybe the best in the world. Not perfect, but better than most.

He thought of Knodalon, sitting alone in his storehouse, holding the rot and ruin at bay with nothing more than a willpower so old and cold that it defied decay. He thought of Leota, who couldn't throw a firestorm but who would stand her ground all the same. He thought of his son and wife, loading beans and flour into a storehouse that might outlive them all.

He thought of the spiders, and whether they were a sign of hope or warning.

He thought about the sword waiting in the forge, unfinished and imperfect, its edge uneven but straight enough for the work ahead.

Then he shook off the cold, and went to find Wilem. There was still the matter of the gates, and the iron hinges that needed setting before dusk. The siege, after all, would not wait for him.

———

That night, the Broken Claw overflowed.

The pub had never been large—just the one common room with a few sturdy tables. But nearly everyone in North Pointe had crowded into that common room, even ordinarily dour Prudence. Most of the adults were sober, or trying to be, but there was a stubborn undercurrent of celebration in the air, as if they'd decided to throw a party before the world went to hell.

Warren arrived late, skin still damp with sweat from the forge, and took up his usual post near the bar. Susan was already there, arms folded, one boot tapping a hard rhythm on the floor. Wilem sat beside her, red-faced and laughing, though the laugh didn't make it all the way to his eyes.

Leota sat by the wood stove, hands raised as she led a group of children through a charm of protection, their little voices chiming in harmony. Darby watched from a safe distance, notebook in hand, scribbling down everything that happened.

For a moment, Warren let himself believe that things were normal. That this was just another night in the pub, with good beer and better company, and the only threat was running out of sausages before the night was done.

But then Jen banged her mug on the table and called for order.

"We need sentries," she said, her gravelly voice carrying over the clatter. "Pairs, every two hours, all through the night. Who volunteers?"

Every hand in the place went up save for Leota's. Nobody expected her to volunteer, and they all knew she'd barely sleep anyway as she cast her magic in and around the town.

"Good," Jen said approvingly. "We rotate the youngest with the oldest. No one goes alone. No one leaves the town, not even for a minute. We keep the road open until dawn, then we close it up tight. Anyone got a problem with that?"

No one did.

"Next," said Jen, "fighters to the front. If you've got a weapon, bring it. If you don't, Warren will see to it you have one by morning."

Warren grunted. "If you want something fancy, wait 'til next year. If you want something that works, I'll have it for you in the morning."

A round of nervous laughter.

"Food inside the town gates is good for a week," said Cole, who'd positioned himself right behind the bar for extra security. "Longer, once we're down to the dry goods. And if you count the cheese."

"We'll count the cheese," Warren muttered.

Jen rolled her eyes. "The children are fed first. That's the rule. Last, and I mean this, we stay open. We keep the lanterns lit and the beer flowing and the doors unlocked until the very last minute. If travelers come, we treat them as friends unless they prove otherwise. That's the North Pointe way."

A murmur of assent, but Warren noticed the way a few folk glanced toward the windows, where the darkness pressed hard against the glass.

Leota stepped forward. "I'll be outside making wards and

watching the skies. After that, I'm back to my house. If anyone needs to find me, I'll be there."

The rest of the meeting went quickly: assignments were handed out. Susan signed herself up for the first sentry shift, and Darby for the third, despite Warren's objections.

"I'm not a child, Da," Darby said, with a look that would have cowed most men.

"You're my boy," Warren replied, but it was a losing battle.

At some point, Sam started singing—old songs, the kind that twisted the air and made your skin want to dance off your bones. Most of the townsfolk joined in, even if they didn't know the words.

Warren found himself at the window, looking out. The spiders were still there, maybe a dozen or more now, their bodies dark and motionless against the dark slate of the smithy's roof. They didn't move, but somehow he knew they were paying attention.

He turned away from the window when the front door burst open, nearly coming off its hinges.

A figure staggered in, coat torn and hat missing, blood on one sleeve. Two more followed, dragging the first.

"They're close," one gasped, slumping to the floor. "Half a day, maybe less. They're coming this way."

The room went silent.

Jen moved forward, pulling the man upright. "Who? How many?"

The man shook his head. "A dozen. No more. Men in red. Led by that fire prophet. And they're talking about this town, by name. North Pointe."

Wilem's face drained of color. "How'd they know to come here?"

The traveler looked up, eyes wide and desperate. "Someone's telling them. Someone who knows. They want something from here, and they mean to burn the rest."

"Damn fortune tellers," Cole growled.

Warren felt the cold settle into his bones, deeper than any autumn frost. He looked around the room: at his wife, his son, the friends he'd spent a lifetime building. At the faces turned toward him, waiting for him to say something, anything.

He cleared his throat.

"Then we make ready," he said. "We hold. And we let them know, if they want North Pointe, they'll have to fight for every inch of it."

There was a silence, then a slow, rising rumble of agreement. It wasn't much, but it was enough.

Warren turned back to the window. The spiders hadn't moved, but he could have sworn there were more of them now. He watched as the mist rolled in off the lake, thick and low, curling around the roofs and the walls and the gates he'd built with his own hands.

He waited, with everyone else, for morning.

twenty-one

. . .

BY THE TIME Warren smelled the burning toast, he'd already woken twice: once to the peculiar hush outside the windows, and again to the high, quick squeal of Darby's excitement in the next room. He cracked open one green eyelid, found the hearth dark and the sky outside darker, and groaned. Susan had forbidden him to rise before six bells unless it was an emergency, and he was not keen on getting cuffed for "overzealous smithery." Still, he rolled out of bed—slowly, so as not to shake the house and thus the world—and padded barefoot to the window.

The town green, such as it was, looked normal, except for the spiders.

Warren squinted, then pushed the shutter open. It was not one spider, but nearly a dozen. Webbing stitched every tree, every bit of the rooftops facing the square, and across the trade road it hung so thick it sagged under its own weight.

He reached for his work tunic, but instead grabbed a pair of Darby's woolen pants, realized his mistake only once his thighs threatened to break the seams, and shrugged. Susan would laugh. It was worth it.

"Dad," Darby said breathlessly.

"Yes, I see," Warren said, and fetched his breakfast mug from beside the sink. The spiderwebs outside vibrated with motion. Here and there, fleeting glimpses of carapace—some black legs, some the lacquered red of their bodies—pulsed through the white maze, following lines of tension with single-mindedness.

Darby looked up at him, eyes full of concern. "Are they still good spiders, do you think? There's a ton more."

Warren sipped. "They sure are very industrious spiders."

Darby chewed this over, then pointed with a buttered knife. "Should we tell Jen?"

"She'll see it herself, I expect," Warren said. The constable lived in the rooms above her gaol, with an entrance just off the green. She did not keep late hours, but Warren had observed she was typically the first in town to raise an alarm, or to scold him for a fire hazard, or to notice a disturbance in the chicken population. He imagined she was already cataloging the infestation.

He looked to Susan, who was standing perfectly still behind Darby. Her arms were folded; her hair, which she claimed never needed a comb, had tangled in the night and now looked like an insult to the very idea of grooming. "You're not going out there," she said, before he could speak.

"Darby's going," Warren countered, and Darby's eyes widened with an immediate betrayal.

Susan shook her head. "Not before breakfast, and not without your sword."

That was not the part Warren worried about. He set the mug down, kissed Susan on the forehead—she grunted; this was a ritual—and then grabbed the massive, misshapen sword from its place above the door.

Darby gave it a nervous look. "Why do you need that for spiders?"

Warren grinned, letting his tusks show. "In case the spiders bring friends."

The webbing in the square was mainly limited to the trees and rooftops, Warren saw as he stepped outside and carefully closed the door behind him. The grass itself was clear, save for a few wisps of morning fog.

They'd decided to leave the town gates open to the trade road, and it seemed like that might have been a poor idea.

The gatehouse, like most of North Pointe Common, was stone, built up from the ruins of the old keep that once stood here before the trade road cut a line through the lakeside wilds. On most mornings, the view from the open gate was simply that of the storehouse across the trade road. Today, all that could be seen was web. The entire archway was filled, top to bottom, with gossamer. Strung up in the threads, like flies, were two foxes, a dead crow, and the battered remains of what must have been someone's hat.

Warren ran a hand over his scalp. He could hear the low murmur of voices behind the web curtain, probably from the inn or from travelers who'd spent the night on the far side.

He drove the point of the sword into the lowest part of the web. The blade—a tarnished, uneven thing, ugly as a lie—sank through the silk and came out the other side, trailing an ooze of web juice and bits of spider shell. Warren jerked the sword sideways, opening a ragged mouth in the curtain. A spider skittered by overhead, balancing as on a tightrope. It stopped and angled its body downward, seeming to peer at whatever Warren was doing—but it didn't come closer.

"OGRE EAT SPIDER," he bellowed, because sometimes it was good to keep up appearances.

A chittering sound erupted from overhead. Warren glanced up in time to see a mass of red-bodied spiders—these the size of puppies—descend toward the web-filled gate opening. But, like the first, they stopped short of lowering themselves to Warren's level. Instead, they clung to the webbing, eyeing him with their beady, black, expressionless eyes.

"Watch your head," said a voice from the left. Warren didn't startle, but his eyebrow rose.

Sam stood on the walkway in front of Warren's home. Her hair was pulled back in a makeshift knot, and she wore an apron that had once been white but was now a tapestry of stains. "If you get any spider goo on the path, I'm sending you the cleaning bill."

Warren waved. "Can't get out of town. You're next."

She sniffed. "I'll survive." Her lips twitched at the joke. "Mind if I lend a hand?"

Warren gestured at the sword, as if it had anything to say on the matter. "By all means."

Sam unclipped her sword's hilt from her belt and the blade shimmered into existence at once. She surveyed the mess of webbing, then drove her weapon into the web and twisted. A long, sticky rope of silk peeled away from the mass, parting with a sound like tearing cheese. Sam stepped back.

One of the spiders overhead chittered softly, but none of them moved.

They worked together, Warren with broad, brutal swipes and Sam with her nimble, clever jabs. The spiders merey observed as they slowly cut a narrow, tall opening into the webbing, providing agress from the town. After several minutes, the gate had been cleared to a degree sufficient for a stubborn goat to pass through, which meant it was good enough for Warren. He nodded at Sam, who saluted him with her sword before letting the blade vanish and returning the hilt to its belt-hook. "Thanks," he said.

Sam surveyed the aftermath. "So what now?"

Warren nodded toward the new opening. "Visitors, I think. Hear them?"

Sam's expression tightened, and she followed Warren through the web.

Their eyes widened as they took stock.

The buildings along the trade road had been completely encased in dense webbing. Strands thicker than Sam's forearm stretched overhead, connecting the main town buildings to the boathouse, storehouse, and even the smithy. It created the effect of a long, white tunnel, leading from the eastern road gate all the way to the western. Even the gates' supporting pillars had been covered in the thick strands.

There was movement at the eastern end of the white tunnel. Even through the webbing, shapes could be seen—dark, upright, several in a row. Horses, perhaps, or men walking single file. A sense of anticipation, as cold and sharp as the sword in his hand, traveled up Warren's spine.

The spiders began chittering softly. Insistently.

He looked at Sam. "Should we let them in, or finish our breakfast?"

Sam grinned, the scar at her cheek creasing. "I say we see what they want. Then eat them if they're trouble."

"OGRE HUNGRY," Warren intoned, which made Sam laugh out loud.

As they waited, the chittering of the spiders grew louder. The town, and the web, held its breath.

At first, Warren mistook the sound for an avalanche—a distant, rolling thunder that grew as it advanced, rattling through the silk-draped arches of the trade road and shaking the ground beneath his bare feet. But as the dawn burned away the cloud cover, he recognized the tramp of horses and the scuff of booted legs, muffled by the shrouding web but not erased.

He shifted his grip on his sword and glanced sidelong at Sam. She stood with her arms loosely crossed, as if the arriving party was more nuisance than threat.

"Wasn't expecting cavalry," she said.

"Maybe they're delivering a new plague," Warren offered. "Last one didn't take."

"Easy." They turned their heads to see Jen stepping up behind them, her own sword still in its sheath.

Dardrad pushed his way through the town gate webbing, his battle-axe already unlimbered. His mate, Dalossalda, emerged a moment later, similarly armed. "Thought we'd given up on fighting," she grumbled.

Tyran was the last to push through. "Front door's webbed up tight," he said grimly. He reached back through the webbing and pulled an enormous mace through. "Had to sneak out the back way. Thank you dear!" he called back into the square.

"See you don't damage that weapon," his wife's voice came back. "That's valuable merchandise!"

Then the visitors arrived.

The first of the riders emerged from the web-tunnel, their horses shivering and sidestepping at every new touch of silk. The lead rider wore a long, bright orange surcoat, the color so bold it seemed designed to be seen at a distance. She rode bare-headed, her yellow-white hair streaming behind her like a burning fuse. Her skin was pale and unblemished, save for an odd sheen that caught the light at odd angles; Warren decided it was either magic or vanity, and likely both.

Behind her, a dozen more riders, all similarly dressed in reds and oranges, though the dust of the road had dulled their vibrancy to the color of old brick. Some bore staves, some swords, and all rode with the upright carriage of trained soldiers, though Warren noted that a few were trembling with the effort of keeping their mounts under control.

The leader reined up a few feet from the edge of the green, where the worst of the web had been hacked aside. She surveyed the town with a sneer that bordered on comical, then turned her gaze on Warren.

"You are the ogre?" she said, in a voice meant for stage and spectacle.

Warren bowed, which in his case required only the lowering of his head a half-inch. "Yes'm."

She stared at the sword in his hands, the dull, twisted blade still glistening with spider ooze. "And you are armed," she said, as if this were a personal insult.

Sam snorted. "Last I checked, so are you."

The leader ignored her. "My name is Christa Elledor, Prophet of Pyron. This is my retinue." She gestured with her staff, and the riders fanned out in a semi-circle behind her, blocking off the road, the way to the lake, thereby barricading—by accident or design—all but the western path out of town.

Sam leaned in to Warren. "She rehearsed this."

"I am here," Christa continued, "in peace. I expect to be received in peace. I will remain in peace, and I will depart in peace, so long as the hospitality of your settlement is sufficient to my needs."

Warren, who had once survived the siege of Redstone Tower by feeding rats to the besiegers, had a nose for threats dressed as diplomacy. "We have an inn," he said. "And a pub, if you like the local brew." He grinned, letting a few teeth show. "We may have to cut our way in."

Christa pursed her lips. "Where is your Speaker?"

Warren shrugged. "If you mean the mayor, she's drunk on brandy and makes policy from the bottom of a barrel. If you mean the constable, she's right here." He jerked his chin at Jen, who stepped forward.

Dardrad was snickering at the "mayor" bit.

Christa's left eye twitched. "I speak to the ogre," she said, as if this would deter further interruptions. "I am told you are the blacksmith here."

"Aye."

"Attend closely: My god is with me. Pyron, the Furnace of Dawn, the Flame That Remakes. He demands a gift of you."

At this, Sam looked as if she might laugh. Warren, ever diplomatic, nodded. "What's he want?"

Christa lifted her chin. "A sword. The one the old gods foretold for this place. The one that holds the essence of the Peaks. Pyron desires it. A sword you shall forge. A sword you shall name Rockpiercer."

Dardrad sounded like he was choking on something.

"Er," Warren said.

Christa's face darkened. "You *will* make it. Your town is famous, ogre. The *world* speaks of the forge-fire of North Pointe Common. Deliver the blade, or I will reduce your sanctuary to ash."

She raised her staff in a dramatic sweep. The followers drew back, every one of them prepared for whatever grand miracle she planned next. Warren, uncowed, watched with interest.

Christa uttered a string of syllables that, to Warren's ear, sounded like a drunken squirrel reciting poetry. The tip of her staff flickered, then spat a droplet of fire the size of a pea toward the front of the pub.

It hit the webbing above the door and, rather than ignite, was sucked in like water into a sponge. For a second, the web glowed a clear, cherry red, then returned to its dull gray. The fire was simply gone. There wasn't even a scorch mark.

Sam, deadpan: "Cool."

The Prophet's expression froze, then shifted—fast—as if nothing had happened. "The web is a triviality. Pyron's will is not."

Warren shrugged again, looking up at the dozens of spiders that now clustered along every roof peak. "Might be news to the spiders."

Christa rounded on him. "I will have the sword."

He scratched the side of his head with a knuckle. "Which sword? There's quite a few."

Now it was Christa's turn to lean in. "You know what I seek. I have dreamt of it. I have burned for it."

Sam, emboldened, joined in. "You sure you're not just looking for a date, Prophet?"

Christa regarded her with something approaching pity. "You would be the pub-keeper," she said. "I expect food and drink to be ready within the hour. I expect your people to obey the will of the flame."

Sam gave an exaggerated bow, then caught Warren's eye with a wink.

Warren, for his part, decided to test the fire. He stepped closer to Christa and looked her over, taking in the silver ring at her brow, the finely embroidered gloves, the faint scent of singed sage that clung to her like a badge.

"You want a sword," he said, "I'll make you a sword. But you'll get it as it comes, not as you want it. The forge does what it likes." He patted his own misshapen weapon for emphasis. "And, I should point out, I haven't dreamt of this sword you want. I haven't dreamt of much of anything recently, in fact."

This seemed to infuriate Christa in a way that no threat could. Her nostrils flared; her followers muttered amongst themselves. "You will make the blade for Pyron," she hissed. "You will make it as I say."

Warren's smile did not move. "Ogre don't do custom orders."

This was enough for Christa. She raised both arms, and fire leapt from her staff in an arc. This time, the spray struck the roofs and doors, webbing everywhere, lighting up the square in lines of brilliant orange. But again, the fire was swallowed by the web. For a few seconds, the entire town square glowed with a furious, molten light. Then, as quickly as it started, the fire vanished, leaving the web intact and the buildings untouched.

Except the spiders.

If they'd been agitated before, now they were berserk. The air vibrated with their chittering. They began to descend, not in orderly fashion but in cascades, flooding down walls, ropes, and posts, dropping onto the heads and backs of the Prophet's followers and scattering the horses.

Sam grinned. "That'll show you to mess with locals."

Christa, unfazed, shouted a word of power. A ring of fire leapt from her, driving a moat between her and the attacking spiders. The web caught and sizzled, but each flame only lasted a heartbeat before fading. It was a stalemate: fire that could not stick, spiders that would not burn.

In the chaos, a younger follower dismounted, drew a saber, and slashed wildly at a mass of red spiders trying to reach his boot. He missed, overbalanced, and landed face-first in the muck. Half a second later, a spider the size of a kitten latched onto his ankle. He screamed.

Warren admired the tenacity of both spider and man, but decided the latter was more likely to bleed out. "Dexter."

The chirurgeon was already moving through the opening in the webbing, the torn edges fluttering with the speed of his passage. He held a needle, already threaded, in one hand, and a vial in the other. The spiders retreated at his approach, still chittering angrily as they climbed backwards up the webbing that covered the inn and the pub.

Dexter knelt beside the injured man, ignoring the spasming leg, and emptied the vial directly onto the bite. The man's screams softened to whimpers. Dexter looked up at Warren, shrugged, and swiftly ran two stitches through the man's wound before retreating into the town square as quickly as he'd come.

The Prophet's other followers fared no better. Two were fending off spiders with flaming torches, which proved mostly effective until the torches guttered. Another tried to light the webbing with an oil lamp, only to have the flame snuffed the instant it touched the silk. The horses, desperate, bolted for the eastern gate, dragging their riders like beads on a string. The spiders let them go, rejoining their brethren on the rooftops.

Throughout all this, Christa sat astride her horse, in her self-made fire circle, untouched and unbothered, watching as if this were all perfectly according to plan. She caught Warren's gaze and offered a cold smile.

"I will have the sword, ogre," she said, softly. "By will or by ruin."

Warren considered this. "I'll need a down payment."

She did not deign to answer.

At that moment, a voice rang out above the din. It was not loud, but clear and pitched to carry.

"Is this a bad time?"

The fighting stopped. Even the spiders hesitated, freezing in place.

On the far side of the square, standing just within the main gate, was Aran—the old man who had lived in North Pointe for several fortnights and who, from what Warren could remember, could barely remember his own name some days. He wore a robe of indistinct color and carried a staff as gnarled as his fingers. He peered at the Prophet through the haze of cooling web, then at Warren and Sam.

"I'll just wait," Aran said, with the serene smile of a man entirely at home in chaos.

Christa stared, momentarily undone by the interruption.

Sam seized the moment. "Welcome to breakfast, Aran. You want eggs, or spiders?"

Aran made a thoughtful face. "Eggs, please. The spiders repeat."

A silence followed, as if the entire town had suddenly noticed a new axis of reality and was not sure whether to laugh or duck.

Warren, seeing the Prophet's confusion, grinned all the wider. "How about we put the war on hold until after tea?"

Warren had never seen a crowd—especially one so recently at war with spiders—go as quiet as they did when Aran walked into the square. There wasn't a whisper, not even a hoof stamp from the horses. Even the Prophet's wildest devotee seemed unwilling to make a move.

Aran stopped two paces inside the webbed archway of the western gate, straightened his shabby robe, and inspected the gathering as if it were a market day and he'd been sent out to find the cheapest eggs.

"Morning, then," he said. His staff made a soft click on the paving stones as he moved it from hand to hand. "Hope I'm not interrupting something important."

Christa Elledor was the first to recover. Her smile was immaculate, but her eyes were steel. "Step aside, old man. This is a matter for the gods."

Aran cocked his head, studying her as if she were a tricky stain. "Is it, though? Tricky things, gods."

The Prophet rode forward. She seemed impossibly tall atop her horse, her aura of command more real than ever. "You presume to stand between Pyron and his desire?" She pointed her staff at him—a pose designed to terrify or, failing that, to at least cow the opposition.

Aran blinked. "Never liked fire. Too... hot."

This time, Warren didn't suppress his snicker, and he heard Sam cough once, then again. The spiders, sensing the shift in the air, retreated an inch or two.

Christa advanced another step. "You will move. Or you will burn."

Aran gave her a patient, grandfatherly look. "You're very certain, aren't you?"

"Pyron has chosen me. All of this—" she swept the staff, indicating the web-draped town, the ruined square, the line of battered but defiant townsfolk, "—will be remade in his image. Even the ogre knows the truth: the old magics are lost, and new gods have come."

Aran peered at her as if evaluating the price of onions. "If you say so."

Christa's patience evaporated. "You mock the fire? You mock ME?"

Aran glanced at Warren, as if seeking confirmation that this was, indeed, the best the Prophet and her god could offer. Warren simply shrugged.

The Prophet drew herself up. "If you will not kneel to Pyron, you can join the ogre in the ash heap of history." She raised her staff and spoke three syllables, fast and sharp. Fire danced down the length of the rod and leapt at Aran, a brilliant bolt meant to obliterate.

It hit him and vanished. Not even a smudge on the robe.

Aran looked at his sleeve. "You missed a spot," he said, and brushed away a fleck of warmth. "Try again if you like. I can do this all day."

Sam leaned over to Warren. "Didn't think the old man had it in him."

"Think he's a wizard, then?" Warren asked quietly.

"Something."

Christa was less impressed. "You play games with the will of gods?"

"Not so much games," Aran said, "as... gardening. You see a weed, you pluck it. Sometimes, it grows back. But you keep plucking."

Her horse sidled, sensing the mood. Christa squeezed the reins and barked a word. A ring of fire erupted around her, brighter and meaner than before, and for a moment Warren thought the air might ignite entirely.

Aran stepped through the ring without so much as a sizzle. "Did you want tea, too? Or just the sword?"

Christa, voice trembling: "I will have the blade. Or your ashes."

Aran regarded her with a gentle sadness. "Funny thing about swords," he said. "They're sharpest when you give them away."

For the first time, the Prophet faltered. She looked around at her followers, most of whom were now dusted with webbing, faces pale and unsure. The crowd of townsfolk—still huddled behind Warren, Jen, Tyron, the dwarves, and Sam—were no longer frightened, just curious. Waiting to see what would happen next.

Warren took a step forward, blade at his side but not raised. "He's right, you know. I make the swords, but they don't stay here long. Never have."

Christa fixed him with a glare hot enough to curdle milk. "You mock Pyron."

Warren let his tusks show. "No. But I never took to bullies."

The silence returned. Even the spiders hung motionless, their legs curled in expectation.

Aran tapped the ground with his staff. "Why not take breakfast and think it over?" he suggested to Christa. "Decisions made on an empty stomach rarely end well."

The Prophet, muscles trembling with rage, opened her mouth to speak.

"Now," Aran interrupted, "I should point out that you're not a proper avatar at all, are you?"

She froze, her mouth still open.

"And that little god riding behind your eyes—that's no fire god, is it? Never heard of a 'Pyron.'" Aran narrowed his eyes, peering into Christa's. "That's you in there, isn't it, Grimble?"

Christa's eyes widened.

"Not so much a *little* god," Aran continued, a gleam in his own eyes. "as a *tiny* god. Tiny little trickster pretending to be a fire god? Tsk, tsk." He shook his head in mock disappointment.

Christa managed to gain control over her tongue. "This town—"

"IS MINE!" Aran roared. The townsfolk took a quick step back at the sudden fury and volume, and the 'Prophet' spent a hurried moment quieting her horse. "This town is mine," Aran said, his voice now low and dangerous. "As it always has been."

"Who—" Christa stammered.

"Ask your little passenger."

She blinked a few times, and then managed to pale even further. "Nimarith," she said softly.

"God of the Mistrals," Aran said, nodding slowly. "The Whisper Between Peaks. And I return to my town its gifts."

Warren felt it first as a draft, or maybe a ripple in the stale morning air, crawling across his chest and under his arms and making his scalp prickle. It was like the time he'd pulled a sword from the water trough and touched its edge to his tongue—tasting the iron, feeling it hum in the center of his skull. It pressed at his eardrums; it made the webbing vibrate against his bare feet. For a moment, he was everywhere in North Pointe at once: standing at the forge with his big dumb hands in the coals; hunched in the crawlspace under the back stairs, palming the lump of ore he'd hidden there for a year and a day; looking up from his mug to see the line outside the smithy, travelers and tinkers and the odd thief, all waiting for him to open up and get to work.

He knew, with a certainty that was both cold and a little bit dizzying, that there'd be thirty-three new pairs of boots in town by tomorrow's first bell. He knew the webbing would clear itself by midmorning, rolling up into neat, gluey balls as breakfast was served. He knew the spiders would migrate back into the foothills. He could smell the coming rain, not just as a threat but as a promise. The world had tilted, settled, and every joint in Warren's body was telling him something true.

All around him, the townsfolk let out their breath, as if a fist had unclenched somewhere in the sky. Jen's face had gone a little slack, her usual tightness around the mouth replaced with a bemused, almost drunk-looking calm. Sam was looking at her hands, flexing them in and out, like she couldn't tell if she'd just come in from the cold or the heat.

The spiders had stopped chittering. Instead, every strand and rope of silk across the square had begun to pulse, in and out, a low, even hum that Warren could feel in his ribs. The sound was not unpleasant. It was not even sound, exactly, more like a memory of lullabies, or the way forge-bellows sounded when you struck just the right rhythm and the fire burned sweeter than usual.

The Prophet and her followers must have felt it too. A few of the riders had slumped in their saddles, blinking as if they'd just woken from a particularly nasty headache. One man, the one with the stitched ankle, was quietly weeping, but not like he was in pain—more like he'd remembered his own name after a long absence. Christa, for her part, sagged a little in the saddle, her staff drooping low. The flames that had ringed her were gone, replaced by a faint orange afterglow that flickered and then snuffed.

"You'll dream again tonight, ogre," Aran—Nimarith—said quietly.

"Who are you?" Warren whispered.

"As she said. Nimarith. The man you knew as Aran is my avatar. Something only the *greater* gods can manage," he added sharply. "He's still with me, but he wasn't long for this world when he invited me in. I've paid his price."

"But why?" Sam asked.

Nimarith shrugged. "The gifts? Wasn't sure you needed them. Turns out the world needs... something. Needs it badly."

"Needs what?" Dardrad asked in his low, grumbling tone.

"*Quests,*" the old man said. "Purpose. The impossible journey, the exacting climb, the prize at the end. The shield that defends you from conquerors. The sword that liberates your village." He pointed his staff at Christa. "Quests to keep *this* sort from getting uppity." He lowered his staff and looked hard at the townsfolk. "You had it right, you know. You're not the players in the game. But you're *here* for those that are. And when they come, send them on their quests. Send them to find their prize." He tilted his head a bit. "I was asleep, a long time. I'm awake now. Quests will await."

And with that, he turned and began shambling back toward the eastern gate. Then, just as he stepped through the web-bordered opening, he stopped and turned back. "One more thing."

A wide grin split his face.

"You followers of tiny gods might want to hurry on. My children have been patient, but they're not without their hunger."

He turned and continued walking, but veered toward one side of the trade road. As he did so, the enormous red spiders' thrumming stopped, and they began lowering themselves to the ground on sturdy lines of silk.

"I think you should take his suggestion," Jen said evenly.

The horses managed to outpace the spiders, but Warren strongly suspected the spiders were letting them get away.

epilogue

. . .

"SO OLD ARAN WAS A GOD, EH?" Leota smiled over her steaming mug of tea and shook her head in wonder.

No other travelers had arrived that day, although the sense of the next day's custom was still strong in Warren's mind. The spiders—or some of them at least, it certainly seemed a smaller swarm—had returned and begin dissolving their webs. The townfolk had mainly stayed indoors and out of their way until the buildings along the trade road were clear. Now, at the day's end, they'd gathered again in the Broken Claw.

"You'd think a god would choose a younger avatar," Minnie said.

"No." That from Dexter, delivered in his dry, hollow tone.

"No?" Warren prompted.

"A god in an avatar remains there until the avatar's body dies," Dexter rasped. "Doubtless he chose an older person on purpose."

"How do you know that?" Sam asked.

Dexter merely shrugged and seemed to withdraw from the conversation, his face falling into a shadow that Warren would have sworn hadn't been there a moment before.

"Knodalon was back on his bench," Vamir said.

Everyone nodded at that, but said nothing. It was simply a feeling they all shared—a sense that the town had come back to what they regarded as normal. A sense of *rightness*.

"Decent crowd tomorrow," Galhani ventured.

"Aye," Jen said. "Especially for this late on."

"Don't get a real sense of urgency," Warren murmured, probing his own sense of the next day.

"That'll be a blessing," Minnie said heavily. "I do hope everyone who's wanted out has gotten out. Of the east, I mean."

Calder sighed. "These rosefruit town spats never last long. Likely it's only that woman and her little god—"

"*Tiny* god," Dardrad interjected with a smile.

"—tiny god, of course," Calder grinned. "Likely it was only them keeping things churned up longer. Winter's coming, and folk will settle to laying in stores, not arguing about who's in charge."

"What do you think he—Aran—meant about quests?" Dooley asked. He was cradling a sleeping blue marmot that had slunk into his shop around midday.

"Back in the day," Jen said, "even before my time here, there are all kinds of stories about people questing into the Mistrals. All manner of treasures and magical prizes up there, apparently."

"And all those questers will need a good breakfast to start them off right," Minnie said firmly.

"And a good, cold ale when they return," Sam added.

"And hopefully a new horseshoe or two," Warren said wistfully.

Susan grinned and rubbed his forearm. "I'll allow pots and pans as well."

"And I *could* do with a new teapot," Galhani offered.

The townsfolk laughed and ordered another round.

award-winning fiction

Daniel Scratch: a story of witchkind

- Kirkus Starred Review
- Winner, American Fiction Awards—Best Fantasy (2023)
- Finalist, American legacy Book Awards—Best Fantasy (2024)

———

Clara Thorn, the witch that was found

- Winner, American Fiction Awards—Best Young Adult (2023)
- Runner-Up, American Fiction Awards—Best Fantasy (2023)
- Finalist, American Legacy Book Awards—Best Fantasy (2024)
- Finalist, American Legacy Book Awards—Best Young Adult (2024)

———

Find these books and more at DonJones.com

about the author

Don Jones spent two decades writing tech books before he finally penned his first sci-fi novella, *A History of the Galactic War*. His well-reviewed and award-winning novels span fantasy and science fiction, with a focus on world building and relatable characters.

Connect, get free novels and short stories, and learn about upcoming releases by visiting Don's author website at DonJones.com.